An Echo in the Glen

~~ The Glen Highland Romance ~~

Book 7

Michelle Deerwester-Dalrymple

Cover art/model: Period Images

Virago

This book is a work of fiction. Names, dates, places, and events are products of the author's imagination or used factiously. Any similarity or resemblance to any person living or dead, place, or event is purely coincidental.

Copies of this text can be made for personal use only. No mass distribution of copies of this text is permitted.

If you love this book, be sure to leave a review! Reviews are life blood for authors, and I appreciate every review I receive!

Want more from Michelle? Click below to receive *The Heartbreak of the Glen,* the free Glen Highland Romance short ebook, to read more about Gavin before starting this book! It also offers free ebooks, updates, and more in your inbox!

Get your free copy by signing up here!

An Echo in the Glen

Table of Contents

An Echo in the Glen

Chapter One: Weariness

Late Winter 1307, Lochnora, Western Scottish Highlands

JENNY PUFFED AND blew her light blonde hair away from her face, then pulled the door closed with her foot. Her hands were full, holding a tray of uneaten food and damp cloths. Just as the latch clanked to seal the door, the platter was lifted from her juggling hands.

Her eyes flew to the man towering over her, a sandy-haired giant clad in a tunic stained from the day's work and a pair of loose braies tucked into muddy boots. The man held the tray aloft as Jenny righted herself.

Gavin's eyes sparkled as they alighted on Jenny, and his peek-a-boo dimples cut endearing clefts into his cheeks. The dimples were not the result of a happy smile; rather they appeared whenever Gavin pursed his lips as well, oft making the fierce MacLeod warrior look like an over-sized laddie. And those dimples melted Jenny's heart every time she saw them.

Tonight, his pursed lips were not without merit. Jenny was torn between lifting her hands to cup one dimpled cheek and gripping her middy kirtle in distress. Her hands now empty, she did both, his scratchy cheek warm against her palm.

His hazel brown eyes burned through her, his distress evident on his face. Most likely, he'd just left Ewan's side, trying to keep his best friend and MacLeod Laird busy while his dainty wife convalesced.

"How is she?" Gavin asked in a tight voice.

Lady Meg and Laird Ewan's first babe had been successfully delivered from Meg mere days after Candlemas, and in Elspeth's estimation, the birth had been uneventful, even gone well. Elspeth had cautioned Jenny less than a fortnight before that the birth was an anxious prospect because of Meg's tiny frame and narrow hips. The Lady MacLeod had borne down, drawn from an inner pool of will and strength, and a screaming, black-haired Caitir was born in the early hours of the morn amid the newly blessed incandescent light.

Then Father MacBain had baptized the bairn in the main hall of the keep, and a joyous celebration was had by all. Meg appeared to be in high spirits if a bit pale, even shoving Jenny from the room so she and Ewan might care for the wee bairn alone.

'Twas a memorable night for Jenny, for two reasons. 'Twas the night Gavin formally offered for her hand, convinced, finally, of the joys to be found in the bounds of marriage and children, of the exultation in a meeting of hearts and desire.

Unfortunately, on the heels of such bliss came a harrowing disaster. Meg fell ill.

Jenny knew Gavin had appeared at Meg's door for himself, but also for his Laird. Ewan was certainly hounding Gavin for news about his wife's health.

"She seems to be improving. Elspeth is with her, caring for her now. She does no' believe it to be childbed fever, so that is good news. She has sent me to return these to the kitchens and retire for the night."

Gavin nodded, naturally deferring to Jenny and Meg's mother Elspeth about Meg's health. He knew little of herbals and even less of childbirth.

"Might I carry these downstairs for ye, my Jenny. I would lighten your load as much as I could."

Jenny, weary to the bone, only nodded as she rested her hand on his arm. To have some of her burden lifted, no matter how small, was a welcome reprieve.

***

Gavin escorted a weary Jenny to the empty kitchens. Unlike the space during the day, bustling with women and a welcoming fire at the cavernous kitchen hearth, the room was cold, austere. Jenny placed the tray near the wash basin to wipe them clean while Gavin stood in the doorway, admiring her every move.

Jenny had a grace not seen in any other woman, a calm presence that brought peace to Gavin when his head and chest burned and threatened his behavior. She cooled his hot-headedness, and more than once saved him from reacting in a manner he might later regret.

Her rich blonde hair was braided at the crown and fell into a river of gold down her back. Her slender nose dipped down as she worked, and her light pink lips pursed in a shadow of a pout. As she worked at the basin, he wondered if she realized how beautiful she was, even as she toiled, dressed for the most menial of tasks. Jenny's beauty transcended her work and imbued in everything she did. No wonder he couldn't stop staring at her, regardless of how she was dressed or what she was doing.

His wave of powerful emotions when it came to Jenny oft made him uncomfortable, sending a shaft of nerves through his stomach, and he shifted his muscular frame in the doorway. He'd had women before, loved women even, but no woman engaged every part of him — his mind, his body, his feelings, his spirit. Jenny touched him on every level, and the more he loved her, the more he needed her.

She'd become his life blood. And he struggled to tell Jenny this. He was not a glib man and wore his feelings close to his chest. Of course, he'd told her he loved her, but it seemed so little, not enough to convey the true heft of love, of passion, of desire, of adoration that filled him every time his eyes drifted to her. What Highland warrior was accomplished at the flowery language of love?

Not Gavin, that he knew.

Jenny finished placing the tray on its shelf and was wiping her hands when Gavin moved behind her, wrapping his husky arms around her waist and caressing the milky curve of her neck with his lips. She allowed him this minor liberty and leaned into his stone-wall chest. Dripping water, the lone sound in the kitchen, disturbing the dark quiet, and it seemed to Gavin that in this moment, just the two of them existed. Jenny sighed as Gavin's lips stroked her tender skin.

And after the misery of the past few days, they needed this moment together. Gavin craved it like a starving man craves food, desperate and needy.

His lips moved to her ear. Then his deep, rumbling voice broke the silence, bringing the world crashing back in on their quiet moment.

"How are ye, *mo ghra thu*?" he breathed into her ear, and she shivered in his arms.

Her ear was one of her sensitive spots, Gavin knew. For the first time in days, Gavin's mouth curled — not quite a smile, but close.

Jenny sighed again and placed her hands over Gavin's where they rested on her waist. Threading her slender fingers with his thick calloused ones, she waited several seconds before responding.

"I am well. Tired, of course, and still worried."

Gavin imagined that God's angels must have the same voice as Jenny, light and calm, even amid the most chaotic situations.

"As ye should be," Gavin agreed.

"And I am worried for Meg. Elspeth says she believes Meg has escaped child bed fever, that 'twas something else since it came on a bit late. But until Meg is up and walking, caring for her beloved babe, I will no' be convinced."

Gavin shifted and rested his chin atop her head as she spoke.

"Ewan, too, needs to be convinced as ye," Gavin told her.

Once again, his Laird's circumstances caused Gavin grief, not just for his oldest, dearest friend, but for himself and Jenny. They hoped to have children once they were wed — what if she fell ill to childbed fever and Elspeth couldn't save her?

The mere thought of such a grave event sent a shudder through Gavin, and Jenny patted his hand.

"Ye have done well to keep Ewan from her. If he had seen her . . . Weel, ye know how Ewan is."

"Mmmgh," Gavin mumbled into Jenny's golden tresses.

Aye, Gavin did know how Ewan was. Even more hot-headed than Gavin, if such a thing were possible. And so full of emotion — Gavin had never known a warrior so in tune with his feelings and his willingness to share them with Meg, or even with Gavin.

I could learn a thing or two from him, Gavin had acknowledged more than once.

"No man can suffer watching the woman he loves in pain. A true warrior will fight, claw, do anything in his power to relieve it. And with Meg, there was naught Ewan could do."

"Weel, your time getting him drunk in the study to distract him is at an end, if Elspeth has the right of it."

Gavin grumbled again, and his stomach clenched at the memory.

"*Uisge-beatha* is the finest drink in the Highlands, truly the water of life, but no' if ye are drinking nigh a barrel full every night. My belly will never be the same, and 'twill be a long time before I take a drink of it again."

Jenny giggled at his proclamation, causing Gavin's heart to soar. She hadn't sounded light-hearted in near a sennight. That one slight laugh was enough to lift the yoke that had settled around his shoulders. Gavin hugged Jenny tighter.

"Do I need to walk ye back to Meg's rooms? Or are ye no' staying with her this night?"

Gavin spun her around and she settled into his chest, her head resting perfectly between his muscles. Truthfully, 'twas his favorite position with her, and the prospect of doing this without the barrier of their clothing tingled in his groin.

At Jenny's behest and out of respect for her station as Meg's lady's maid, Gavin had yet to do more than kiss his beloved. She wanted to wait until they were well and truly wed, as a proper lass should, and he was more than willing to oblige. The gift of her virginity on his wedding night was the best gift she could give him.

Still, it made moments like this, where his cock seemed more in command of his body than his brain, difficult to control. What he wanted to do was toss up Jenny's pale-yellow skirts and take her with wild abandon right there on the table.

What he did was take a deep breath and try to enjoy this embrace with Jenny.

"Elspeth dismissed me, demanding I take my own bed and get some sleep."

Only then did Gavin drop his gaze to her face and really, really look at her. When Jenny claimed to be weary, she was speaking lightly.

Fatigue wrapped Jenny in a heavy cloak — her shoulders curved under its weight and purple half-moons discolored the skin under her sunken eyes. She wasn't just weary, she was worn.

"Do ye want me to carry ye?"

He didn't wait for her answer. With a squeal of protest from her rosebud lips, Gavin swept her off her feet. 'Twas the least he could do for her.

"Gavin! What has gotten into ye?"

"Ye have. Your dainty feet have worked too hard this week, as has the rest of ye. Ye weigh less than a bird."

She stopped protesting, draped her arm over his brawny shoulder, and rested her head against his chest again. Sympathy filled Gavin — Jenny *needed* to be carried to her bed. From the looks of her ragged body and how readily she melted into his arms as he lifted her, Jenny's poor legs would never have made it up the stairs to the maid's chambers on the third level of the keep.

By the time he reached her door, Jenny was snoring into his tunic. Her arms and legs were completely limp, trusting him to keep her safe even as she slept. With another swell in his chest with his love for her, Gavin lay her on her low pallet of furs and pulled a plaid blanket up to her chin. His fingers combed through her molten tresses that fell from the bed before he rose and departed on silent toes.

***

Jenny peeked her eyes open in the early morn, rubbing the grit from their corners and grateful for the sleep after so many sleepless nights. No one had come to wake her.

Meg must be faring well. Yet Jenny knew she must soon pry her weary bones from her bedding.

If Meg were recovering, 'twould mean the rest of the keep could resume their daily routines as well. Already, Jenny and Gavin had pushed their wedding, first to wait until Meg was delivered of Caitir, in deference to the laird and lady of the keep, and then again when Meg fell ill. Now a summer wedding on the steps of the village kirk in Lochnora seemed most appealing, and Gavin had been so patient with her. Mayhap he would be patient just a bit longer as Meg recovered and then could help Jenny prepare.

Meg and her mother Elspeth were the only family Jenny really had left. Alyce, her mother, had passed a few years back, and when Meg came to the MacLeod stronghold, she and Jenny had fallen into an easy, familial relationship, the sister Jenny never had. She would not be wed until Meg could be there.

And now that Meg was on the mend — at least Jenny hoped she was on the mend — she could move forward with Gavin and begin her life with this man who was crafted from her very dreams. This man who made her heart race, and when he rested his whiskey-colored eyes on her, 'twas like there was no one else in the room.

Jenny may have stumbled upon Gavin when he was at a low point in his life the year before, but only God could have worked in such a mysterious way to bring Gavin to her when they were both in a place to find solace in each other. When the woman Gavin believed he was to wed had left him to marry the Sheriff of Beauly, he had gone mad — to hear Ewan tell it. The woman had denounced him, insulted him even, when he sought her out, and a solemn Gavin had returned with Laird Ewan to the keep, having become a sad and dejected man.

Jenny's soft presence brought him peace, and over time, the callous woman fell from Gavin's mind, slowly replaced by elements of Jenny and his sense of belonging with the MacLeods. He had walked through the pit of the darkest emotional depths that a man could traverse and survived. He'd come out the other side harder and jaded — Jenny had seen that well enough when Ewan first wed Meg. At the news of Ewan's betrothal, Gavin's behavior had been wary and defensive.

But he had also softened the more he was around Jenny, and Meg and Ewan. The laird had known Gavin since childhood, and his own sense of dedication and responsibility wouldn't let Gavin wallow about in that hard place.

And while Gavin could still be hard, defensive of Jenny and of his clan, he had grown more lighthearted in the past year. His cinnamon eyes danced and sparkled more, his lips rested in easy smiles, and even his tone when he spoke was jovial. To Jenny, he was the fullest of himself, and she loved him for it.

The noise in the keep increased, rising with the inhabitants, and Jenny's sleepy musings came to an end. 'Twas time to rise and see what Elspeth needed for Meg, then hopefully find Gavin and kiss him good day.

Chapter Two: An Echo from the Past

Summer 1307

A LATE, TEMPERATE SPRING ushered in the start of a warm summer — warmer than usual. Meg had finally recouped after several months of weakness and was back to running the manse. Though it had rained the past several days, the wet weather was fortunate for Jenny, as they used the time to sew clothes, mend tunics and kirtles, and finally enjoy time with wee baby Caitir, who was busy growing fat under the care of Meg and her grandmother Elspeth. Though Meg still had her slow days, baby, mother, and grandmother fairly glowed.

Now talk turned to Jenny and her upcoming nuptials. The season of Lent meant she and Gavin had to wait until after Easter, and then the entire clan had been focused on Mayday celebrations as Meg finished recuperating. Now that these events had concluded, and Meg had returned to full health, Jenny and Meg hoped that Jenny's wedding would be celebrated that summer. That was, if the English threat didn't travel this far north, nor did a call to arms come from King Robert the Bruce himself.

The kitchens steamed and sweat dripped from their brows as Fiona and the kitchen maids prepared for a large meal. Most MacLeods labored outside, taking advantage of the sudden bright day, and their appetites would be ravenous come the evening meal.

Gavin toiled near the barn in the bailey, stacking scratchy peat and dried grass for the summer. Women and men scrambled to hang peat on the drying racks whilst the weather was warm, while other men worked to secure the already dry peat against any oncoming damp weather. The stacks would make fine insulation for the beasts and the more they could gather and dry when the clime was agreeable, the more they would have in the fall and winter. On dry days, the MacLeod men worked like men possessed, clambering to amass as much as dried peat bricks as possible before it rained again. And in the northern Highlands, the weather might change in an instant, ruining their hard work.

Though the sun barely peeked from behind the clouds, the day hearkened a blistering summer to come. Like most of the MacLeod men slaving in the yard, Gavin had stripped down to naught but his braies, the weather too warm for even a light woolen plaid. Sweat glistened on his golden chest and dripped down the sculpted muscles of his back.

The view of so many MacLeod warriors bare chested was a welcome sight to the lassies who sauntered across from the keep to their chores, some even going out of their way to enjoy the view of such hardy, well-built men. They giggled and winked and lingered.

And if the men flexed their defined muscles in appreciation, the more the better.

Riders from the east approached as the sun started its afternoon descent, casting purple shadows on the world and bringing with it a gentle breeze and an appreciated nip to the air. The air also brought with it a nervous energy that disrupted the domestic scene. Despite the call for Highland hospitality, strange riders were not always as welcome as one might think.

Gavin noticed several other men had paused in their work, and as the dust and grit settled into his hair, he pulled himself up to his full height to observe the riders as they approached.

They didn't look familiar, not from this distance, but one of the riders — 'twas something uncanny about him.

Then a tendril of hair slipped past the hood in the billowing wind, and Gavin's breathing stopped. He gritted his teeth at the sight, and his blood threatened to explode from his body to paint the yard in swaths of crimson.

The same crimson as that hair blowing in the wind.

An ill wind that blew in an even more foul event.

These weren't just riders. And one of the riders wasn't a man.

Gavin only knew one woman with hair the color of the blood she'd shed, tainting the tears she'd caused, filling the heart she broke. The vile witch that had teased him and strung him along, then crushed his heart to wed into a higher station. The woman who had vowed to never see Gavin again – an echo of his tormented past returning. He cursed under his breath.

Ellen.

***

Jenny strode outside to bring a skin of water to the men hard at work in the barn. And to one man in particular. The sight of Gavin half dressed, his bare chest glistening in the sun, his powerful, muscled legs flexing under the thin fabric of his braies. . . What woman wouldn't want to rest her eyes on that view? Bringing water was merely an excuse to lay her sights on her man.

When Jenny caught Gavin in his labors, resembling an ancient Celtic God on earth, she regretted her vow to remain chaste until they wed. Regretted delaying their wedding until later in the summer. Regretted Gavin's nobility of spirit — she was certain she would have succumbed to his passionate wiles if he were any less of a man.

Reaching the side of the barn, she raised her eyes to see Gavin standing on a pile of grass, his pitchfork slipping from his hand. She sighed like a young lassie at the vision of his dusky, golden hair. His eyes were riveted into the oncoming dusk. Jenny pivoted in the direction he was staring to see what held his rapt attention.

A pair of riders entered the yard, and Gavin didn't even glance at Jenny. The pitchfork had dropped with a subtle plop onto the grass, and Gavin slid off the pile to join Ewan and his brother, Duncan, who stood near the postern gate.

Gavin ambled in a smooth stance next to Ewan, but the tall laird pushed Gavin to the side, almost behind him. Then Ewan leaned to Gavin and spoke into his ear, and Gavin retreated all the more. Finally seeing Jenny near the barn, Gavin reached her in three long strides.

"Come, Jenny. Let us go into the keep. We have no business with these riders."

His face was like stone, with none of the boyish lines that Jenny so adored. In this moment he was a fierce warrior in full, guarding her from the dangers these riders wrought.

What dangers might they be bringing?

Jenny glanced around his wide shoulders, trying to get a better look at these strangers who caused such commotion in her betrothed. They didn't seem overly fearsome, and one mayhap was a woman! What about a woman and her escort frightened Gavin and the laird himself?

"Gavin! What is it? Why are ye so afraid of these two riders?"

"Please, Jenny, just come with me. I dinna want to be here when these riders arrive. Come with me. I will tell ye all."

Gavin clasped her hand in his warm, large fingers, swallowing her pale hand in his grasp. Even under these strange conditions, his touch sent a shiver through her chest. Yet, Gavin's arm was as stiff as the rest of him. She placed her other hand on his arm, pulling him closer.

But he was too late. The riders were near enough for Jenny to see who they were.

Jenny froze, struck by the vision of the woman on the horse who had entered the bailey. She had seen beautiful women before. But this woman, she was something impossible. Like a dream.

She sat atop her palfrey like a queen coming to survey her subjects. Her russet gown reflected the lingering sunlight and matched her wild mass of vermilion curls that defied existence and were pulled back from her face, covered with a whisper of a kerchief. Even her lips were the same hue, striking against her skin which was as clear as fresh goat's milk. The bodice of her kirtle clung to her bust with fine embroidery, flowing over her hips into a train onto the palfrey's haunches. Silver glinted at her neck and on her wrists. And the way she held her head, 'twas as if she owned the yard.

Nay just a queen, Jenny corrected, *an empress.*

Jenny's eyes flicked to her gray-blue skirts, stained with the remains of her day's labors, and to her baggy chemise. She patted her mussed blonde hair, bound back in a ragged, washed-out kerchief, and Jenny felt as washed out as her kerchief. Compared to the brilliant, regal woman peering down her nose at those collected in the yard, she was a dim, weathered shell.

No one announced the woman, no one welcomed her, no one introduced her, but Jenny didn't need an introduction. She knew who this woman was as soon as she laid eyes on her. Once before had Jenny seen this type of haughty beauty, and that harpy lass had been wedded off to the MacCollough clan laird none too soon. This woman, though, had a much stronger connection to Jenny than any other lass. A stronger connection than she wanted.

One woman, and one woman alone, could make Gavin turn and run with such horror.

The same woman who had used him, and once she was done, tossed aside his shattered hulk like offal.

Then Gavin whispered her name, spoken like a curse, the name that had haunted them for years, a ghost from which Gavin had escaped. Gavin said her name aloud just as Jenny's mind formed the words.

"Ellen."

***

What was the spiteful Ellen Fraser doing here at Lochnora? Her father lived southwest of the Fraser lands, a wealthy vassal to Laird Fraser. Those fine gowns? They were a result of his mining silver in the Lowlands, which he then sold to lairds and barons and even, Jenny heard rumored, the king himself.

But rumors also suggested that Ellen's father, Callum Fraser, was so money hungry, he had even sold his own daughter to the Sheriff of Beauly, trying to improve his position even more. The only thing it had done for his position was make loyal Highlanders question the man's allegiances to King Robert the Bruce.

Jenny rose on her toes, trying to peek around the Highland warriors who had arrived in the yard, ready to confront a potential invader. Or get a look at the reputed Ellen, Jenny thought with a sharp, unfamiliar jealousy.

Another man was with Ellen, his steed prancing with impatience. The man's face reflected the impatience of the horse, pinched and nervous. He appeared ready to bolt as soon as his task of delivering Ellen was complete.

The crowd withdrew to the edges of the yard as Laird Ewan stepped near to Ellen, the giant of a laird dwarfing palfrey and the woman riding it. Her pretension slipped, softening at the sight of the Laird.

"Ellen Fraser of Beauly." Ewan's bored tone yet conveyed curiosity which must have simmered under his skin. It certainly simmered under Jenny's. "To what do we owe this honor?"

Jenny bit the inside of her cheek and dropped her face at Ewan's question, filled with sarcasm as it was. *Honor. Ha!* A movement in the corner of her eye caught her attention and Meg was standing next to her. Meg reached out and clasped her hand.

"Is it really the infamous Ellen? What is she doing here? Is the Sheriff with her?"

Jenny shook her head. "I dinna know. Ewan is greeting her."

Then Ellen smiled, and it was as if the entire yard sighed. No wonder Gavin had been smitten. When she smiled, the world lit up, smiling with her. Ellen was, in a word, captivating.

"Ewan," she spoke, her voice full of honey and milk, "I fear I need your keep as a safe haven. My dear husband has been murdered, I have been told, and those who killed him are after me as well. They want to eradicate everything related to him. My father directed me here, as those same vile men would assuredly follow me to my father's if I retreated there. They will no' think to look for me in the MacLeod sanctuary."

She held out a hand, and Ewan waited several heartbeats with one devilishly black eyebrow raised. He flicked his distrustful gaze to Gavin. The dense body in front of Jenny didn't move — Gavin stood as rigid as a stone monolith, and Jenny rested a light hand on his shoulder to soothe him. Ewan returned his attention to Ellen and raised a hand to help her down.

"Ye can send your man away. He looks more than prepared to leave."

Ellen flicked that compelling face to the tense-looking man on the horse and nodded. The man whirled the prancing horse around and galloped from the Bailey as if the demons of hell were behind him. Jenny narrowed her eyes at Ellen. Perchance the man was justified.

Ewan helped Ellen from her horse, directing a stable lad to attend the palfrey, and forced Ellen to face him. Ignoring the mob that couldn't stop watching the dramatics, Ewan leaned in close to her. The harsh lines of his jaw clenched more as he regarded the woman.

"Ye should no' be here, Ellen. And ye well know that. I will welcome ye for a time, but ye will no' stay in the manse. Ye will keep to yourself and ye will no' cause any disturbance, else I will set ye on the road in a thrice. Do ye ken my meaning?"

Jenny would have cowered under Ewan's threatening glare — she oft wondered how wee Meg withstood it — but not Ellen. That proud woman settled a smile on her lips and lifted her chin, seeming to challenge the Laird. Jenny bit back a gasp at the confrontation.

"Why, Laird MacLeod." Her voice poured like honey. "I am here solely to seek safety. I seek naught else." Ellen patted Ewan's hand that held her and shifted so he could escort her to the keep. She appeared to the pinnacle of propriety.

But Jenny didn't miss the flick of Ellen's sky-blue eyes in her direction.

Or rather, in Gavin's direction.

Chapter Three: Unbreakable

"YE ARE COMING with me," Ewan told Ellen. "Gavin, if ye will? Gather Meg and meet me in my study."

Gavin bowed his head and whipped around, finding Meg standing next to a stricken Jenny. He leaned his head close to hers to speak privately into Jenny's ear. His words were for her and her alone.

"Jenny, dinna think on this. Ewan shall resolve it, and the woman will be on her way. I only have eyes for ye."

Then he grasped her upper arms, harder than he should have, but desperation coursed through him like fiery blood. He gazed into her eyes with intent focus, forcing her to fixate on him and nothing else.

"There is only ye, Jenny. Recall what I told ye about what a man will do to salve his woman's pain. I will do everything I can to make sure this woman does no' harm ye or try to ruin our happiness. Now, I need to bring Meg with me to help Ewan deal with this problem. Can ye find Fiona and Davey?"

The last thing Gavin wanted was for Jenny to be alone with her thoughts, imagining the worst about the arrival of Gavin's former lover and his devotion to Jenny. He longed for a way for Jenny to see into his heart, to know that his love and faithfulness to her was pure and unmarked. Unbreakable.

She nodded mutely and turned toward the kitchens, yet allowed her fingertip to drag across his hand, a final, lingering touch before she left. Gavin's chest throbbed at her loving gesture, and he watched her walk away with burning, hooded eyes. He then shifted his attention to Meg, whose face showed every emotion. The lady of the keep had no guile. Shock, curiosity, and caution clouded her face — the same emotions roiling in Gavin. He wasn't the only one concerned about the appearance of his former lover.

"Come, Meg. Please join us. Ewan would have ye at this meeting. Propriety, aye?" He winked at her and her body relaxed, if slightly.

"This is no' a good thing, this woman, is it Gavin?" Meg asked as she took his arm.

They cut through the dispersing crowd toward the open doors of the keep. Gavin shook his head.

"I dinna think so. Nothing good ever seems to follow Ellen."

"Do ye believe what she said about her husband? Is she here for another reason?"

That *other reason* she hinted at was to resume a relationship with him. Gavin paused before speaking, chewing his lip and choosing his words. Too harsh and he might sound like the spurned lover. Too light and he was hoping for a reunion. Neither were on point.

"I believe that she modifies the truth to suit her needs. Aye, her husband might be dead, but her reasoning for coming here? That seems doubtful to me. Perchance we will learn more with this meeting."

"If what ye say is true," Meg said, dropping her voice as they neared the study, "she might just embellish all the more once she is cornered. Either way, she must leave as soon as possible."

Gavin couldn't agree more.

***

The study was stifling, cramped as it was with writing implements and MacLeods. The surprising afternoon heat had settled like a blanket, and none of the early evening air had yet to breach the room. Gavin, though still bare chested, pulled up his plaid to drape over his chest. 'Twas a sight better than being half dressed around Ellen but did nothing to help cool him in that chamber.

Ewan, too, was hot, sweat dampening the neck and underarms of his tunic. He appeared unbothered by it and reclined in the chair by his narrow desk, his fingers tented under his chin in contemplation.

Gavin didn't envy Ewan's predicament. He'd been with Gavin when Ellen harshly rejected him, invited Gavin to remain at the keep as he recovered from the crushing blow to his heart, and then inadvertently introduced him to Jenny — the woman who pulled him back from the brink of darkness and held him in the glory of her light. To have the dark shadow of Ellen taint that glow, invade the sanctity of Lochnora . . . Ewan's turmoil was evident, his top lip pulled up in a nearly imperceptible curl of contempt.

Moving a chair to Ewan, Gavin gestured for Meg to sit next to her husband, and then removed himself to the door. He wanted to be as far from the red she-devil sitting in the middle of the study as possible. He crossed his arms over his brawny chest and waited.

"Ewan, Meg, Gavin," Ellen looked at each of them as she said their names, "I wanted to thank ye again for opening your doors —"

"We haven't quite done that yet," Ewan countered, his voice tight.

"Weel, out of Highland hospitality, I figured ye might. Plus, we've known each other for so long, haven't we, Gavin?"

No amorous suggestibility tainted her voice, no implication, but Gavin heard it all the same. His muscles clenched in response.

"Highland hospitality be damned," Ewan bit out. Meg straightened, her mouth dropping open.

"Ewan! Language in front of a woman! Manners, if ye please!" she protested.

Ewan flicked his deep blue eyes from his wife to Gavin, then sighed heavily.

"Ye can stay for the meantime, until ye find a different place for your sanctuary or return to your father. Gavin and I will repair a small croft off the smithy's. Until then, ye will bed with the maids in the tower. And ye shall stay until we can send ye to your father's."

"Ye canna do that!" Ellen protested, springing from her chair. "The Beauly soldiers will find me and kill me for certain!"

Ewan's eyes hardened like ice. "That is your father's concern, and yours, nay mine. Now, ye must also behave whilst ye are under the Lochnora roof. Ye will work, contribute to the clan —"

"Work?" Ellen screeched again.

Meg dropped her head into her hand at Ellen's response. Evidently, Gavin wasn't the only one who cringed at her voice. How had he ever loved that voice? He once compared it to a nightingale, he mused with disgust. *More like a jackdaw.*

"Aye, work. We work here at Lochnora. Myself, Gavin, even my own wife, the lady of the keep. She will see ye to work straightaway."

"Ye must let me get settled first."

Ewan tipped his head, eyeing her like she was a boar on a spit. Gavin waited — he had seen this expression on his laird more than once. The man could take the measure of a person with alarming acuity.

"Who was the man who brought ye here?" Ewan asked in a low voice.

Ellen sat on the edge of her seat. "The man?" she squeaked.

Ah ha, Gavin thought. *Let's see ye talk your way out of this one.*

"He's a Fraser man. I asked him to escort me here once I heard of my husband's demise."

"And he just happened to be there when ye learned of your husband's death and ran?"

Ellen's jaw dropped. She snapped it shut then lifted her chin, as though the conversation was beneath her.

"My father has unending concern for me. His men are part of my household in Beauly."

The answer was glib and plausible, but her father, the wealthy Callum Fraser, was not one to part with coin, especially if his daughter was now under the purview of a husband.

Yet the answer suited Ewan, at least for the moment, and he flicked his eyes to Gavin and Meg before addressing Ellen again.

"Gavin and I will personally see to your croft. Meg will take ye to the maid's chambers until 'tis done."

Then he dropped his gaze, dismissing her. Gavin stepped to the side of the doorway. She and Meg left the study, and Gavin took Ellen's place, sinking into the chair across from Ewan.

"What do ye think, Gavin?" Ewan asked.

Friends for years, Ewan and Gavin oft consulted before most decisions they made. *Save in our selection of women*, Gavin thought sardonically.

"I dinna ken. I thought I knew the woman, but after she left to wed the Sheriff of Beauly, I questioned if I truly knew her at all. Now, she comes here under a banner of sanctuary. Mayhap there

28

have been difficulties to the east. We are a bit cut off here, so close to the western shores," Gavin answered in full honesty.

Ewan's eyes burned in a blue fire as he stared at Gavin. "We have another problem. Her father is a wealthy man, one who can buy a modicum of power. I've heard he sends resources and coin to the Bruce himself. We canna treat his daughter poorly, or we might find ourselves at the wrong end of his ire. See our predicament?"

Gavin hated giving Ellen any benefit of the doubt, but he tried to keep his head about the situation.

"I shall write a letter to her father," Ewan intoned in a decided manner. "Duncan can take some men and deliver it for me. He can also learn if the Sheriff of Beauly has indeed been slain in a coup. We've heard nothing. 'Twill help us determine the lassie's true intentions and what best to do with her. And then Callum can send for her, bring her home and out of our hair."

Giving Ewan a stern expression, Gavin agreed.

"The sooner the better."

***

It took a bit of time for Jenny to calm the raging storm inside her. Gavin had rushed her to Fiona and departed, leaving Jenny to fume. Instead of going to the kitchens, Jenny burst into her chambers and dropped to her bedding to collect her emotions. *Gavin is a good man,* she told herself, *and Ewan is wise and diplomatic. They will find a solution to this unpleasant development.*

That single thought and several deep breaths helped soothe the tempest surging under her skin. Only then did Jenny descend to the kitchens to help with the evening meal. Fiona labored at the hearth, stirring a giant cauldron of meat and vegetables while Ellen cut freshly baked bread loaves in half. Jenny's eyes widened in surprise at finding Ellen in the kitchens but said nothing. She lifted a knife from the table and joined her. At least Ellen was working. That said something for the woman.

"Jenny, I did no' get to really greet ye when I arrived earlier today. I've heard ye and Gavin are betrothed. I know ye might feel awkward around me, but I dinna want such a thing. I might be here for a little while, and I would like for us to be amicable."

Jenny hesitated and tried to hide her shock at Ellen addressing her directly. Ellen rested the knife on the smooth tabletop and placed a hand over Jenny's. Even the woman's hand was soft and perfect, Jenny couldn't help but notice. Was she telling the truth? And why should she be residing at Lochnora for any length of time? After everything Ellen had put Gavin through, doubt filled Jenny at such a statement, and her overwrought brain struggled to make sense of any of this situation, leaving her ragged.

How could she be friendly with someone who had hurt the man she loved?

"I would like to work toward that," Jenny said in a tentative voice, not truly believing the words as she said them. It would take a saint . . .

Yet, it was a start. God commanded his people to let go of hatred, that vengeance belongs to God alone, and Jenny didn't want to harbor that sin. Perchance this interlude was a step in that direction.

Fiona had stopped her stirring, her profile finding great interest in Jenny and Ellen's conversation.

As for Ellen, her entire being seemed to relax at Jenny's answer. Her regal features softened, making her appear more welcome and engaging. Jenny breathed easier as well.

"I am staying in the maid's chambers for the moment. Are ye there as well?"

Jenny nodded. "Aye."

"Until ye wed Gavin?"

Jenny tensed. Was it her imagination, or did Ellen seem too interested in her relationship with Gavin?

"Aye. We were to wed in late winter, but Lady Meg was ill after the birth of her daughter, so we decided to push our nuptials for a time. Meg and Ewan want to have a large feast for us."

"Ooch, how nice to be so familiar with the laird and his wife."

Jenny's brow furrowed at Ellen's words. *What did she mean by that?* Maybe she was just reading to far into what Ellen said.

"And how kind of ye to bide your time until the lady was well. She must be a good friend to ye."

"Aye, we got along well when she came to the keep."

"I recall my wedding," Ellen said, her face growing wistful, and Jenny had sudden pang of sympathy for the woman she was judging so harshly. "We wed in the spring, when the heather started to bloom, and a bit of rain blessed our marriage vows."

Ellen's voice shifted as she spoke of her wedding — a tender tone. She must have truly enjoyed her wedding vows and her marriage to the Sheriff.

"Happy is the bride the rain falls upon," Jenny commented, and Fiona nodded in agreement from the edge of the room.

"Aye. I was happy with Andrew. I dinna know what I will do now," Ellen's voice grew thick, and she blinked rapidly to halt the tears filled her eyes and tinged her lashes.

Jenny surprised herself by reaching across the expanse of the table and patting Ellen's hand. So, the strong, queenly woman had a weak spot. Jenny hadn't expected deep emotion from Ellen at all, or expected herself to respond to it. The idea of being friendly with this woman, one who had feelings, love for her dead husband, was something Jenny might consider.

"Weel, ye have a fine start here. Ye will find your place soon enough."

Ellen wiped her eyes with the back of her hand and gave Jenny a weak smile. A smile, Jenny noted with a moue of wariness, that didn't quite reach the woman's tearful, stony-blue eyes.

***

"Do ye trust her?" Meg asked as she brushed out Jenny's hair later that night.

'Twas a tradition they had forged shortly after Meg wedded Ewan. They took turns sitting at Meg's narrow dressing table in her private chambers with Ewan, brushing out each other's hair. An indulgence, Jenny knew, but one she didn't deny herself. Or Meg, for that matter.

Even though Ellen had been, well, nice this evening, something about the woman yet rubbed her wrong. Jenny despised herself for such evil thoughts, but it was as though the woman spoke almost-truths. Not full truths.

"Nay," Jenny spoke her heart.

If anyone knew her deepest secrets and kept them close, it was Meg. The lady of the keep locked secrets up in a chest deep inside herself and never opened it again. Jenny could tell Meg anything and everything, and she did.

"She tried to be friendly this evening, opening up to us a wee bit about her marriage to the Sheriff. Yet, something was still strained. I will be as kind to her as I can be. But a true friend?" Jenny shook her blonde tresses. "Nay. I dinna think she knows how to be one."

Meg placed the boars-hair brush on the dressing table.

"Might she learn? Some women, especially those raised in wealthier or noble households, they are oft lacking in that skill. Look at Elayne MacCollough. She had been a hard lass, yet found friendship with the women in her new husband's stronghold."

Jenny pursed her lips at Meg, considering the lady's words. The transformation of Elayne MacNally to Elayne MacCollough had been more than a change in name. 'Twas rumored the woman was a fine lady, warm and welcoming. The complete opposite of the tempestuous woman who had stormed out of Lochnora nigh a year ago.

"Aye, your words are sound. It will just take much for me to trust Ellen truly as a friend. I dinna know what it is. 'Tis something under the surface, I believe."

Meg placed her palms on Jenny's head, smoothing the already smooth tresses in a much-needed motherly gesture.

"I will defer to ye. Until she proves herself, we will tread lightly."

Jenny shifted her chin over her shoulder to Meg. "Ye may want to advise that Hamish and Duncan stay far away from the lass as well. Who knows what other hearts she might want to break whilst she is here?"

Meg nodded at Jenny's recommendation, then dropped her eyes. She hadn't missed Ellen's odd and singular focus on Gavin. It wasn't Hamish or Duncan who needed to worry about attention from the red woman.

She didn't say anything to Jenny, but the only one who needed to guard themselves against Ellen was Gavin.

***

Gavin knew exactly where to find Jenny — in Meg's solar. Out of courtesy to both his bride to be and the lady of the keep, he had taken the time to wash away the sweat and dirt of the day, scrubbing at his skin with abandon. More than trying to wash off the grime, he was trying to scrub away the memory of Ellen.

As he rubbed the cool cloth over every crevice of his body, his mind spun in a dizzy whirl over the day's events. What had happened to have Ellen end up here, at Lochnora? Her excuse for not going to her father, who was more than wealthy enough to pay for her protection, wasn't sound. With enough money, a man can buy any amount of loyalty. Surely Callum Fraser could afford to keep his daughter safe?

At least his body hadn't responded to her at all. If anything, his stomach churned, and bile rose at the back of his throat. Ellen all but disgusted him now. He hadn't really had time to talk to Jenny, to discuss how the messy disaster of his past now landed at their feet. Jenny was an innocent in this awkward situation, and having gifted Gavin the precious responsibility of her heart, she deserved to have her voice heard, to know that none of this changed Gavin's intentions.

Yet, he had a long history with Ellen, and Gavin was compelled to find Jenny and assure her again that anything with Ellen was just that —history.

He reached the door, leaping over the steps two at a time. Urgency drove him to rush up the steps. Gavin found Jenny in Meg's solar, grooming with the lady.

He knocked lightly, and at the sound of Meg's voice inviting him in, he peeked his head around the door. A tiny dimple played peek-a-boo as he studied the women.

"Good eve to ye, Lady Meg. Might I steal Jenny from ye for the rest of the eve?"

Meg scooped up her squealing daughter and smiled at Gavin.

"Your timing is impeccable. I was just going to feed Caitir and ready her for bed. Please, steal the lass away!"

She waved them off, and Jenny exited with Gavin. He led her down the narrow stairwell and out the kitchens to the garden. A sturdy stone bench sat at the edge of the gardens, and Gavin patted the bench for Jenny to join him.

The breezy night air still held traces of warmth from the day, and the skies were shockingly clear. Stars in their multitudes glittered over them, like watchful eyes of the heavens. Croaking natterjack toads and the odd calls of warblers serenaded them as night enveloped the world.

Jenny said nothing, waiting for Gavin to speak. In the dark, he could only see her bright outline, and she resembled a specter, an angel here on earth. His angel who opened his heart in a way he'd not known possible.

"I canna imagine your surprise at seeing Ellen show up here today," he began. *Might as well have it out.*

She had a way of listening that called the words forth from his mouth, as though he couldn't *not* share every inner secret, every desire with her, as though Jenny heard everything he didn't say in between the words he spoke.

Jenny clasped his hand in hers, a sudden and reassuring gesture Gavin didn't know he had been longing for. But his heart soared when she did it. She touched him often when they conversed, trailing her finger across his arm, cupping his face, holding his hand, which only encouraged those words to pour forth.

And each touch was a tether, strengthening their bond, helping them connect with the love they shared.

"Ye might have an idea. I saw the look on your face when she entered the bailey. Ye thought her to remain in Beauly for the rest of her life, I should think."

"Out of sight, out of mind, aye?" Gavin shifted closer, trying to see the shining of her eyes in the nighttime depths. "Once she was gone from my life, she was just, gone. And for all that is holy, I canna imagine what possessed her to come here."

"If she is lying or no," Jenny told him, "she is still a guest. She must have a reason for coming here for sanctuary."

A reason other than me. Gavin shuddered at the thought.

"Since we dinna know why she is here, I would recommend we try to keep our distance. She is supposed to be in mourning, if her husband is well and truly dead, so we can hope that will mitigate any brash behavior of hers. I spoke to Laird Ewan. He is sending his brother on the morrow with missives to Callum Fraser, letting him know what has happened with Ellen. That good man should arrive shortly to retrieve the lass. Until then, Ewan and I shall work to repair that hut to make it livable. Then she will be out of the keep and away from us. I dinna want her near ye."

Jenny stiffened against him at his cautionary words.

"She's just a woman, Gavin. Mayhap a woman who needs a friend. I dinna think —"

"She's devious, Jenny," Gavin countered, his grip on her hand tightening, almost painful. "Conniving. Even her mourning is a guise, if I dinna miss my mark. Dinna trust her at all. Try to avoid her as much as ye can. I would do anything and everything in my power to keep ye safe, even from a seemingly harmless woman."

With his vow, Jenny relaxed into Gavin, and he wrapped his arm around her, pulling her close. His words weren't empty ones. He'd lift his claymore to challenge anyone who threatened his love.

Man or woman.

Chapter Four: A Friend in Need

GAVIN SOUGHT OUT Ewan before they began work on the hut at the smithy's the next day. The laird was busy at work, writing long parchments in the brightly lit study. The tapestry had been tacked back from the narrow window, and daylight spilled right on Ewan, casting the giant of a man in a golden glow. His head bowed low to the desk as his quill scratched against the parchment.

"Ewan, are ye writing to Fraser already?"

Leave it to Ewan to write his letters right away. The man left nothing to chance.

"Aye, him and to the King Robert the Bruce. I have to hope this letter finds Callum Fraser quickly. If the man is at his silver mines, then it might take time for this missive to reach him. But I did hear a rumor that the Sheriff of Beauly is indeed dead, slain by his own men who believed him to be less than loyal to the cause. Evidently, Ellen was truthful about that."

Gavin dropped his wide frame into the chair across from Ewan, which squeaked in protest under his weight.

"And the Bruce? Why are ye writing the king?"

Ewan threw a tattered parchment at him, never lifting his eyes from his cramped writing.

"I received this missive yesterday and put it to the side amid the chaos of Ellen's untimely arrival."

Gavin shook his head at Ewan's choice of words. "Untimely is an understatement. Jenny and I are finally able to wed this month if fortune is on our side, and Ellen appears. 'Tis like the devil himself knew of our plans and threw yet another obstacle our way."

Ewan flicked a smug look at Gavin, trying not to tease him, Gavin surmised. The laird probably had to bite his tongue.

"I do appreciate your patience regarding your nuptials, Gav. Nay, worse timing than that, if ye can believe such a thing. The missive is from Declan MacCollough. He and some of his men are with the Bruce. They have taken Dumfries back from de Valence, and Declan indicates that now the army is planning larger, more aggressive attacks, and shouldn't the MacLeod be there to provide his blade in support?"

Gavin rubbed his face with his hands in aggravation. "Are ye joking with me right now?"

Ewan's good humor had fled, and his lips tightened.

"Ye may want to push up your wedding date and no' wait until later in the summer. Speak to Jenny. I am writing to the Bruce now to see what he wants the MacLeods to do, where we should meet up with him. We may have to depart immediately upon my receipt of that letter."

Clenching his fists open and closed, Gavin rose from the chair with a fury burning from his skin. He was loyal, to a fault even, and if Ewan decided they must ride for the Bruce, for Scotland, then they would ride. But Christ's blood, the timing could not be worse.

"Hurry ye up with your writing. I had a need to take my anger out on the walls of the hut before I entered your study. Now I fear I might tear the hut to shreds. Dinna tally, or I might end up hitting ye."

Ewan finally raised his eyes to Gavin, his lips curving into a weak side smile.

"Ye might try."

***

The work at Lochnora was never ending while fulfilling at the same time. Jenny found peace and joy in most of it. Today, however, scrubbing the main hall after a large supper the night before, she didn't feel much of that serenity.

Some of her irritation had to do with scrubbing the hall. Even with Mairi and Bonnie helping, 'twas a substantial job, and one that required a lot of sweat and muscle. Jenny pushed the sleeves of her drab brown work kirtle past her elbows in a futile attempt to help cool her clammy skin and keep her sleeves from dragging in the dirty water.

The rest of her irritation came from the arrival of the buxom red woman, Gavin's former love. Jenny knew men had lovers before they wed, 'twas expected. But the relationship he'd had with Ellen ... Blonde wisps escaped her kerchief and Jenny blew them off her damp forehead. Gavin had been enamored with Ellen, a true love, at least on his side. She had shattered his heart, and Jenny had done the dedicated work to help him knit those pieces back together. And now she fretted that work might be undone with Ellen's presence here at the keep.

In her head, she knew she should do her best to make Ellen feel welcome, but her heart couldn't let go of the irritation, the general dislike she had for the woman.

And that caused an unfamiliar emotion to well up in Jenny's chest — disdain.

Jenny had disliked Ellen before meeting her for one reason only. She had hurt the man Jenny loved.

Yet, the destruction Ellen had wrought on Gavin's heart had worked in Jenny's favor. Gavin was now Jenny's betrothed. She didn't *hate* the red woman. Nay, she had to thank Ellen for that strange gift of breaking Gavin's heart, and thus giving it to Jenny.

But that didn't make Jenny dislike her any less.

Gavin and Laird Ewan's men spent their day cleaning and repairing a small cottage near the keep for her, but until 'twas ready, Ellen had been given a pallet in a shared chamber not far from where Jenny slept. Under the same roof at the keep as Gavin. Bile stung the back of her throat when she thought about it too much.

She tried to put it from her mind and focus on her upcoming wedding to Gavin as her hands worked the rags absently against the stones. Those happy thoughts made the hall scrubbing an easier task as well. Sweat and dirt and all.

Distracted as she was, Jenny didn't hear footsteps of someone behind her until a pale shadow fell across the wet stones.

"Jenny?"

Jenny glanced up, expecting one of the kitchen maids and adjusted her face quickly to cover her surprise at seeing Ellen standing above her. The woman glowed, radiant in a bronze gown that offset her scarlet tresses so she resembled an exotic jewel.

And in comparison, Jenny suddenly felt more like a sow's ear next to her. Jenny wiped her hands on the cloth hanging from her belt and patted at her hair as she stood. Normally proud of her bright golden hair, her own locks now appeared more like used, dirty straw. Why did this one woman make her doubt herself so much? Trying to gain her composure, Jenny plastered a tight, fake smile on her face.

"Aye, Mistress Fraser," Jenny said as she dipped her head. "What can I help ye with today?"

Ellen did something that Jenny didn't expect — she smiled at Jenny. A warm, earnest, vibrant smile that made Jenny want to give her a real smile in return. Doubt filled Jenny again. Had she judged this lass too harshly? Perchance her beauty was more than skin deep. Mayhap she had her side of the story as to why she left Gavin so heartbroken.

Again, Jenny reminded herself that she benefited from Ellen's missteps, no matter what caused them. She was with Gavin, preparing to wed the fierce Highland warrior, not Ellen. This woman was now a widow, alone in this harsh world. Those thoughts tempered Jenny's ire, and her face softened toward the woman.

"I've been wandering around the keep. With no family or friends to speak of, I'm rather, well, bored. Have ye any chores where I might lend a hand?"

Jenny squinted in a quick reaction before gesturing around the main hall.

"I'm scrubbing here. The maids always welcome assistance in these larger cleaning duties." Always astute, Jenny didn't miss the moue of distaste that pinched Ellen's dramatically beautiful face.

"Or ye can try the kitchens, as ye did yestereve," Jenny offered. "Mistress Fiona oft needs help preparing meals for those in the keep or from the crofts or nearby village who might attend."

Ellen's face relaxed at the prospect of less filthy labor, and her smile widened. Clearing her throat, Jenny wondered if that smile wasn't as earnest as she had originally believed. Mayhap Ellen was accomplished at masking her true emotions. 'Twas what Gavin and Ewan would have her believe.

"Aye. That sounds fine. I cooked a lot with my father and with —" Ellen stopped herself. Intrigue overwhelmed Jenny, and a pale eyebrow rose of its own volition. Ellen did have a story, one that Jenny wanted to hear.

"Ooch, ye dinna have to say it." Jenny forced a tone that was suddenly sweeter than honey as she patted Ellen's milky hand. Ellen wasn't the only one who might disguise her true intentions, if that was what she was doing. And if honey attracted flies, mayhap it might elicit a tale from Ellen as well. Then they might have more information they could use regarding Ellen's presence at Lochnora.

"Fiona would love to have ye in the kitchens. And if ye ever want to talk about anything, I've been told I have a welcome ear."

Ellen's face didn't react, yet her open smile remained.

"Thank ye for that, Jenny." Ellen moved to head toward the kitchens but spun around a few steps away. "Oh, and I meant to tell ye congratulations. About ye and my Gavin?"

My Gavin? Jenny's chest tightened and her brows creased together. Whether intentional or not, she didn't care for Ellen's suggestive words. *Why would she call him my Gavin?* Ellen giggled and waved her hand at Jenny.

"Ooch, or I should say *our* Gavin, aye? Dinna fret lassie. I'm a married woman, ye ken?"

Then Ellen strode off like the lady of the keep, her head held high and her gown dragging on the wet stones. The damp trail she left behind was the royal train of a woman no grander than a garden slug.

Jenny gritted her teeth, conflicted. What a horrible comparison she made about Ellen, but her comment about *my Gavin* rang in Jenny's head louder than any church bell. And the woman *wasn't* married anymore. She was a widow. Ellen's words were at once beguiling and cutting, and Jenny's mind spun at the contrariness of it all.

Her dear mother, Alyce, had taught her to give grace to those who needed it, and oft those who behaved the worst needed that grace the most.

Mayhap all Ellen needed was a bit of grace to put her on the right path. To become a fine addition to the MacLeod clan as long as she was to remain with them.

Which, Jenny hoped, was not long. She knelt on the cloth thickly folded over the stones and resumed scrubbing.

Grace only went so far, after all.

***

Gavin stripped down to his waist, toiling in the surprisingly warm, sun-bathed day. He worked with Ewan to repair the run-down croft just inside Lochnora's palisade wall, adjacent to the blacksmith's house. Gavin found it to be an ideal spot — close enough for Ewan to keep an eye on Ellen, far enough where she was out of the keep and away from Gavin. He'd have to thank Ewan for such a shrewd arrangement.

The woman had said nothing about her arrival, other than the brief information regarding her husband the Sheriff, now deceased. Ellen was sticking to her story that unrest in Beauly and the surrounding lands made her fear for her life, so she ran to the sole place she believed she might hide for the meantime.

Gavin's eyes narrowed to slits as she had spoken to Ewan, and though neither man believed her story in full, as Laird, Ewan was bound to offer her sanctuary. The glare Gavin had shot Ewan could have cut through stone. Then, before finding Jenny yestereve, he'd run from the hall, searching for a wall or stout tree to take out his aggravations on.

Time and effort. It had taken Gavin so much time, so much effort to recover from the mess Ellen had left. With the staunch fidelity of the MacLeod clan and Jenny, who won him over with her calming aspect, intense focus, and fair looks, he had given that fine golden lass his heart and never looked at another. He packed up any emotion that might have remained for Ellen, locked it up and threw the key away.

Gavin's muscles clenched as he pounded his hammer against the beams, his mind focused on his conflicted thoughts, not his work. The red villainess had ridden back into his life. And no matter how sweet Ellen presented herself to the public, Gavin had nothing but the taste of burning bile in his wame whenever he thought of her. She might dupe others, but Gavin knew her true nature. To have the devil herself in his home? Near himself and Jenny? The idea made his insides roil like a tempest in a bottle. How was he to live with this woman here in Lochnora? Seeing her regularly, having to interact with her, extending kindness to her?

How much could a man take?

The iron pin in the wood received the brunt of Gavin's burning frustrations, surely made hotter by the sun beating on his bare back. His arm pumped in a violent frenzy and sweat flew from his hair like a violent rain. So distracted, he jumped when a high-pitched voice called out behind him.

"Gavin?"

He whirled around, his russet-colored kilt flapping around his rugged bare legs. Standing tall against the wall of the hut, he squinted at the buxom lass of his nightmares. She held out a hand, covered with a swath of creamy linen.

"Ellen," he answered in a flat voice. He might have to put up with her, but he wouldn't feign to hide his irritation. "Ye should no' be here. I've my duties to attend to. Ye must leave."

Instead, she beamed at him with her wide, charming smile that misled so many. His heart hardened even more that she might try to ply him with that gesture he knew all too well. He wiped his sweaty hair from his eyes and glared at her.

Ellen's eyes, however, were disquieting, studying him as though Gavin was a venison roast at Christmastide. Even a man as large as he felt exposed, naked under that predatory icy gaze, a mouse under the attention of a cat. She removed the linen to expose a bannock.

"I'm here as a friend, Gavin. I know ye are to wed Jenny. I was baking in the kitchens and thought ye might be hungry. I brought ye some food. 'Tis all."

He stared at her for several seconds. Against his better judgment, he set the hammer to the side and took the bannock she offered. He tried not to notice if her fingers lingered on his, or if her eyes roved over his half-stripped form.

Gavin devoured the proffered treat, thinking it the best way to dismiss Ellen, but she didn't leave. Turning back to his work, hoping she could take the hint, Gavin bided his time. If he ignored her long enough, she would leave.

Yet she remained where she was, even more cat-like than before. From the corner of his eye, he noted her deep crimson hair was loose, flowing like fine wine — the way he had preferred it when he had loved her. If she were laboring in the kitchens, why was her hair not bound in a kerchief like the other women? He clenched his jaw.

Because she pulled it free from its bindings when she came outside. That's why. Or she believed herself above wearing clothing of a kitchen maid. Bitter anger roiled in his stomach like sour milk.

"Ye can leave, Ellen," he said, keeping his back to her. "I am sure ye are yet needed in the kitchens."

"I dinna agree, but I can see ye have work to finish for me here, and I wouldn't want to seem untoward."

Waiting a few more moments before taking her leave, Ellen swirled away and sauntered back to the keep.

Gavin forced himself to stare at the boards before him, pounding harder, faster, determined to finish the hut this day as though his life depended on it.

He had been right – her subtle behavior with him only confirmed what he already knew. Ellen had always been and was still nothing but dangerous, and now that danger had come right to his doorstep.

Chapter Five: The Nature of the Beast

ELLEN'S MOUTH TWISTED in a grimace, an inextinguishable fury burning under her skin. The lone consolation she had was that this croft, this ramshackle excuse for shelter, was hers and hers alone. For now.

Stepping through the refurbished thatched door, Ellen scrutinized her new home. *Temporary home,* she vowed silently as her nose crinkled at the view before her.

The croft — *it couldn't be called that,* Ellen cursed to herself. *It's a hut.* The hut boasted threadbare bedding on a rickety bed pallet, an old table and set of chairs before a hearth, and several shelves next to the hearth that held metal cups, wooden bowls, and a few meager baskets. A low-thatched ceilinged hovel whose only redeeming virtue was its attachment on the east wall to the smithy's, promising her warmth throughout the autumn and winter. *Not that I'll be here in the winter.*

Her mouth curled into a sidelong grin. If she played this right, she'd be in the keep with both her freedom and Gavin, before the year was over.

Befriending Jenny and Meg was merely her way of biding her time, keeping them unaware as she rolled out her plan. She didn't love Gavin, not in the same way he'd loved her years ago, but he still desired her, that she could tell.

And if she couldn't obtain Gavin and gain her liberties, live her life the way she wanted with him by her side and in her bed, then she might have to think of another way to maintain her freedoms here at Lochnora. *There were options.* She grinned as this thought pressed through her mind.

When the Sheriff of Beauly had offered for her hand, the prospect of leaving her father's house to wed a powerful man and have her own house, her own rules, how could she pass up such an opportunity? And to trade power for silver made her father and Andrew eager for the marriage as well.

So, her father had sold her off, and she ended up trading one prison for another. And to make matters worse, the stout old Sheriff wanted her to get with child as soon as possible. That would have tied her to that aged man and limited her independence even more. The best thing that happened in her life was when she learned that Andrew had been killed in a feud with his men before she grew fat with child. He wasn't a grand leader anyway — Ellen was surprised no one had killed him earlier. Not that she hadn't considered it herself.

As a widow with no children? Ahh, the perfect measure of freedom. A widow had the best possible freedom a woman could find. But she needed to hide somewhere, find a place where her father's reach couldn't manifest. And Gavin was the best friend and man-at-arms for a laird who was close to the Bruce. It seemed the perfect place to reside where she might live without the auspices of husband or father.

And to have the opportunity to rekindle a romance with Gavin? Relive that feeling of passionate freedom once more? Why, 'twas the perfect place indeed.

What if he were to wed the pale lass? Ellen didn't require a husband. Men, husbands, took mistresses all the time. Though cheerless now, the hut might make the perfect place to seduce him from his hay-haired paramour.

Ellen giggled to herself. She would make a fine mistress to Gavin indeed.

***

The hall was quiet when Meg found Jenny later that day, readying for more scrubbing.

"Jenny, ye are my lady's maid. That means ye dinna have to clean so much like this. Send in Mairi and Bonnie to do this chore. Come, ye join me in the kitchens, then we will retire to my solar. We still have your wedding gown to finish. The blue damask that we found in the village last market day will suit ye well but will no' stitch itself."

The petite Lady Meg tried to look down her nose at her, which didn't work as she had to raise her face to glare at Jenny. That didn't make Meg's expression any less powerful.

"Meg, I can clean. I dinna have to —"

Meg swiped her arm in a cutting motion. So much ferocity in such a petite creature. And when her ire was high, her whole body blazed like the sun. Jenny grinned at her friend.

"*Haut yer wheest*! I made ye my lady's maid before Caitir was even born! I think ye should be used to it by now!"

She threaded her thin arm through Jenny's and led her from the hall to the kitchens, where a fusion of sweet scents mixed with harsher, more sour odors. Jenny wrinkled her nose at the assaulting aromas. Baskets and pans of all manner of foods crowded the tables. Fiona was there, as always, her round arms coated in flour dust up to her elbows.

"Jenny! Pleased to see ye, lass! We are trying to make oatcakes, jar the honey, and prepare the greens and meat. The early summer harvest came in all at once, it seems."

In addition to the honey and oats, cabbages, kale, haddock, eel, and pheasant were waiting to be either cooked or dried. Jenny reached for the cabbages.

"Fiona, make sure the crofters receive their share of this bounty. With so much food, no MacLeod of Lochnora should go hungry."

Though most of the MacLeods were industrious beyond measure, each croft having a decent sized garden and goats and sheep sufficient for the household, Meg and Ewan held staunch beliefs when it came to sharing the clan's wealth. The laird and lady would never permit a single person to go without.

Jenny made a sudden connection — 'tis why they allowed Ellen to remain at Lochnora. They would not allow her to go without, no matter the cost to themselves. And if that long-lost lass were telling the truth about the politics behind her husband's death, then where else was she to go?

They had just started organizing the wealth of food when said red-headed woman entered the kitchens. All eyes turned her way.

"Good day," she announced, then paused, noting how everyone in the kitchens turned her way. "I've helped here in the kitchens already. I thought I was to keep working here . . ."

Her voice drifted off, and the women shared shrewd expressions. The Fraser woman may be out of the keep, but not out of mind. Meg glanced around the room.

"'Tis enough work for ten of us. Please, Ellen, join us. Ye can place the seals on the honey jars."

Ellen's fair skin brightened, and Jenny wondered if her response was that she felt welcome. Living with the Sheriff of Beauly, far from kin in a strange house, must not have been easy, not even for a callous woman like Ellen. Perchance she felt a camaraderie here, one that might change her for the better.

Jenny moved to the side, creating room for her near the corner of the table. Ellen stood next to her, tossed that abundance of wine-colored hair to her backside, and took an earthenware jar full of golden sweetness. Ellen seemed to be accepting her place and had been nothing but kind to Jenny and the others at the manse thus far. Other than her strange references to Gavin, that was. Perchance Jenny's concerns over Ellen's arrival had been misguided. Jenny relaxed her shoulders, and Ellen must have noticed.

"Thank ye, Jenny. I appreciate that ye dinna despise my presence here. I imagine it canna be easy."

"I try no' to judge people before I know them, Ellen. I would extend that courtesy to ye. I hope ye are settling in well. Ye must have been through much to end up here."

Ellen's fingers toyed with the linen covering of the jar.

"Ye are more right than ye know. My marriage, 'twas no' one of love. I did care for Gavin, please know that," she turned her liquid blue eyes to Jenny, pleading. "My wedding was a political one, an economic one. My dowry was immense, something the Sheriff needed. He had position but no money. And my father anticipated my marriage as a smart political move. Needless to say, I was no' welcome in that household at all. I was a bought bride, aye? And pretentious to boot."

Jenny had to bite back a grin at Ellen's assessment of herself. 'Twas the exact description that many of the MacLeods had given her. Hearing of Ellen's political marriage, however, was fascinating. Such things didn't happen in Jenny's world. To be sold off? It happened with nobles, barons, kings and queens. Even powerful lairds' daughters and sons were paired for political aspirations. To the MacLeods, a small clan in a remote section of the Western Highlands, such things were not as common. Fraser must be extremely wealthy to be able to make such a profound union with Beauly.

"I can imagine how difficult that must be for ye. But to have the Sheriff's men hate ye so? To want to hunt ye down?"

"Well, I have the sense 'twas more than that. Perchance they did no' like that he sold himself to wed me? Or that my father felt he could make demands of Andrew since he had paid a large dowry in silver. Silver! Ooch, many a soldier in Beauly was no' happy with that. I dinna know if 'twas the justiciars or the bailiffs or his knights who were unhappy with Andrew, or all of them. And without issue, a new Sheriff will be installed."

The women leaned in, eagerly absorbing Ellen's dramatic tale. Something in Ellen's words rang in Jenny's head as she pressed on her waxen seal. Politics were not Jenny's purview — she paid little attention when the matter was made public, which was not often. Otherwise, Jenny kept her interest on the inner workings of Lochnora keep and the men and women of the clan. The men and women . . .

"Ellen! Ye say the Sheriff had no issue. Does that mean ye were no' . . .?"

The woman paused her fingers and shifted her stunning, furrowed gaze to Jenny. "What are ye saying?"

"If ye had been delivered of a child, then ye might hold power until the lad came of age to take on the role of Sheriff. 'Tis a hereditary position, aye?"

Ellen nodded slowly. "Many times, 'tis. The king might well replace the Sheriff if need be, but aye, a son of age may take over the role. Or a soldier might hold the position temporarily until the son comes of age."

"And if he is no' of age? 'Twould mean power for ye, or the issue of Andrew Fraser in that seat. Perchance they wanted ye dead because they didn't know if ye were with child."

Ellen's clear skin blanched sickly, and her hand gripped the edge of the table. Fearing Ellen might faint, Jenny clasped her arms, holding her upright. Against her better judgement, her heart went out to the lass, who did seem so stricken and earnest about her present predicament.

"Ellen, are ye well?"

Fiona and Meg joined them, their faces pinched with concern. Ellen waved them off.

"Nay, I'm well," Ellen answered, regaining her control and her coloring. The roses in her cheeks bloomed again. "Ooch, then they would be killing me for naught. I guess I'm safe here. I never quickened with child."

The women fell silent. Ellen sounded shamed, and Jenny moved to reach out to her again, but Fiona's loud chuckle stayed her hand.

"That happens more than ye would believe. Some men just canna cause a woman to quicken. Yet, with another man, she quickens within weeks." Fiona's heavy hand patted Ellen's head, leaving a flour handprint in Ellen's bright locks. "Dinna worry, lass. I am certain your next husband will get ye with child right quick."

Ellen gave each of the women a tight smile and returned to her jars.

Jenny patted Ellen's back below her cape of hair. Ellen had been so forthcoming about her marriage, it cast a shadow of doubt on her terrible reputation. Jenny had a moment of pity for the lass, and she tried to tell herself that had to be a sound reason that, once again, Ellen's smile didn't quite reach her eyes.

***

A knock came at the door of Meg's solar, a bright room with west-facing window slits and a woven rug that warmed the room as much as a fire. When Jenny opened the door, expecting Gavin or perchance Meg's sister Mairi, Ellen stood before her in her red glory.

She must have washed after their day in the kitchens, for her hands and face were milky, not sticky or floured. In her russet gown, which flattered her burnished coloring, Ellen was the image of perfection, a red-gold goddess in human form. How did she manage to make Jenny feel less than the slops in a pig trough?

Jenny plastered a smile on her face, hoping it didn't appear as fake as it felt. Jenny wanted to be earnest in how she treated Ellen. She truly did. Yet every time she tried, it just seemed more and more difficult.

"Good day to ye, Jenny," Ellen greeted her in a cloyingly sweet voice. She peered around Jenny to Meg. "And to ye, Lady Meg."

Jenny caught Meg's cautious gaze, but Meg nodded, nonetheless. After all, they had shared much earlier in the kitchens. Ellen's visit suggested nothing dishonest or improper.

"Will ye join us, Ellen?"

The woman all but glided into the solar and perched on the ornate wooden chair next to Meg, a small sack cupped in her hands.

"I wanted to thank ye for your kindness. To ye, Lady Meg, for welcoming a stranger and putting your kin to repairing a house for me, for listening to my petty problems." Her impossibly blue eyes, more indigo than any blue Jenny had seen, shifted to her. "And ye, Jenny. I know ye are worried about your Gavin, and I appreciate that ye welcomed me as well."

Jenny didn't miss that Ellen hadn't denied any claim on Gavin, and that didn't sit well. Jenny shifted her feet where she stood. Typically, she wasn't a woman prone to such contemptuous thoughts, but Ellen pulled them from her like fish on a line. Yet, she had to give Ellen a chance. She was here offering her appreciation and doubt still filled Jenny. She chastised herself silently.

"I brought these for ye. A thank ye, if ye will?"

Ellen reached into the woven sack she held and extracted two plum-sized silver penannular brooch rings. Not as fine as an engraved brooch, the silver was nevertheless shiny and well-constructed. She held them in her palm and extended them to Meg and Jenny.

"'Tis a wee thank ye. Nothing fancy, but 'tis what I grabbed as I raced from Beauly."

Once again, Meg and Jenny caught each other's gaze. Ellen had them in quite a predicament. If they rejected the gift, they would be seen as rude, even ungracious or insulting. But to accept the gift, take Ellen's few possessions . . .

Jenny didn't move. She'd let Meg take the lead. Meg huffed out a fleeting breath and gave Ellen a slight smile.

"Are ye certain ye dinna need to hold on to these, in case ye might need to trade them for something after ye leave?"

If Ellen took offense to Meg's less-than-subtle suggestion of her temporary status, she didn't show it.

"Nay, I will be in contact with my father soon. I have no fear of my financial status. Here, to thank ye for your hospitality."

Meg shrugged and reached a dainty hand out to Ellen's, filching one circlet out of her palm. Ellen shifted her hand to Jenny, offering the second one to her.

Like Meg, Jenny took it and slipped it into the waist of her skirts.

"I know I have set your household into turmoil, Lady Meg." Ellen's tight smile moved to Jenny. "And the same with your relationship to Gavin. I am just here to let ye know that I will stay until my father retrieves me. I am no' here to cause any strife."

But ye already have. Jenny bit the words back, keeping the abrasive thought to herself.

Ellen rose in a smooth movement and glided to the door.

"Oh and thank ye for your comments about finding a new husband and the hopes that I might one day have a bairn."

Her face flicked one last smile before she exited.

Jenny glanced at the brooch at her waist, then at Meg. They both exhaled heavily.

"I dinna need such finery. It feels wrong to accept it. Shouldn't she save these in case she needs to trade them or needs coin?" Her eyes pleaded with Meg for validation.

Collecting her thoughts, Meg turned toward the cradle where Caitir had dozed. *Better for the bairn to have missed Ellen's visit,* Jenny believed.

"Mayhap she is no' the monster we thought her to be. Perchance, she realizes that she is reliant on our hospitality, especially where she is unwanted. Ye know the saying about gift horses . . ." Meg turned the brooch over in her hand, then dropped the jewelry on the table next to her.

Jenny pursed her lips and followed Meg's gaze to the sweet babe who was presently giving her mother a blessed moment of peace.

"Aye. Only, 'tis no' horse."

Meg giggled at Jenny's joke, and Jenny's cheeks curled into her own smile in spite of her sour thoughts.

"The bairn slept through it all. Ye needed the break, my Lady Meg."

Meg rubbed at her face and shifted back to Jenny. "Aye. Fortunately, the babe sleeps well in the night now."

"What if ye are with child again soon? After being so ill and now run ragged with the babe? Even with the help from your mother, and myself, and your sister and Fiona, 'tis so much on ye."

Meg's eyes dipped then cast a mischievous glance to Jenny.

"Can ye keep a secret?" Her hushed tone compelled Jenny to agree, and she nodded with wide-eyed curiosity. *What dire secret could dear Meg have?* Jenny's heart skipped a beat.

"Aye. What secret?"

"My mother, she knows how hard my labor and birthing was, how hard 'twas for me to care for Caitir and how I fell ill. She recommended I no' birth again for at least two years."

Jenny's face scrunched up in fascination. *How could such a thing happen?*

"But, ye are laying with your husband . . . ?" Jenny's voice was low, shocked at asking such an intimate question.

Meg's sly gaze spread across her entire face.

"Aye. Ewan is far too randy to wait long. Nay, my mother gave me an oil. I soak a wee bit of cheese cloth and insert it —"

Scandalized, Jenny's eyebrows flew to her hairline. "Ye insert it?"

"Ye know what happens between a man and wife, aye Jenny?" Meg's wizened expression became one of concern.

Jenny averted her eyes, suddenly interested in her dun-colored skirts.

"Aye, for the most part. But, how do ye insert it? Before the man —?"

Meg giggled again. "Aye, with your finger."

Jenny cupped her hand over her mouth at the sheer illicitness of it all.

"Does Ewan know about this? Ye are no' lying to him, are ye?"

Meg shrugged a shoulder at Jenny, her green eyes piercing. "I told him my mother gave me an herb to keep me healthy until my body is ready for another child. After all we went through with Caitir, he did no' question it much. He trusts my mother and I, and he waits patiently for when we will make his son."

"Do all women do this?" Jenny asked with awe. She had never heard of such a thing!

"Dinna fret, Jenny," Meg reassured her as she patted Jenny's skirts. "Once ye have had your first bairn with Gavin, I will show ye how to use it so ye dinna get sick and can be hale for your babes."

After having put off their wedding for so long, Jenny despaired at ever marrying Gavin, let alone considered the prospect of having children.

Bright-haired, light-eyed children. Jenny found herself smiling. Sturdy children, with dimples.

***

"Laird! Laird Ewan! Wait for me!"

Ewan lifted his midnight head to the wee laddie calling his name. Davey scrambled over the grasses to join them at the side of the barn, where the collected the dried peat bricks before any more summer rain arrived.

A moue of pride and contentment crossed over Ewan's face at the sight of Davey. The laddie followed Ewan around the yard like his shadow. Gavin couldn't blame the boy — he had done much the same thing when he was Davey's age, chasing Ewan around. Only Ewan had also been Davey's age too, and Gavin often had the upper hand when they hacked at each other with their wooden play swords that their fathers had crafted for them.

"Where have ye been, laddie? Did ye think to have myself and master Gavin here to do all your chores?"

Davey let it slip that he had been bringing in wood and peat for Fiona and had left the keep when the air grew thick as the red-headed woman entered the kitchens.

"Who was in the kitchens with her?" Ewan asked casually as he threw a pile of grass on the lad's dark head. The boy shook it off with a contagious smile.

"Ooch, all the ladies. Milady Meg, my Jenny, and my momma Fi."

A twitch in Ewan's smile was the only evidence of his concerns at having Ellen in the kitchen. Gavin, on the other hand, couldn't stop the grimace that assaulted his face.

"Is Mairi there with them?" Usually, Meg's younger sister helped in the kitchens, *when she wasn't keeping Hamish or Aren from their chores*, Ewan thought sourly.

"Nay yet. Not that I saw."

That was not necessarily good news. Mairi needed to stop playing Aren and Hamish against each other, and Hamish needed to decide if Mairi was the one for him. An out-of-wedlock child between his wife's younger sister and his younger brother would cause more strife than Ewan was prepared to deal with. Give him dealings with the King of Scotland or the English soldiers over those with his wife any day. Ewan decided to change the subject.

"And how did they react to the red woman?" Ewan asked with another flip of peat. Davey threw handfuls of loose grass back.

"Ooch, they seemed fine. Women talk, aye?" Davey answered, obviously uninterested in women's conversations.

Ewan's hard blue gaze beheld Gavin for a brief moment, then Ewan returned his attention to Davey.

"Weel, come along. This peat will not stack itself."

Gavin followed behind them until Ewan paused to grab Gavin's arm. Neither man was overjoyed to learn Ellen was still making herself comfortable at the manse.

"I shall speak to Meg —"

He didn't get the chance to finish.

"I'll converse with Jenny tonight."

Ellen was like the snake in the garden of Eden, alluring with a tongue that dripped of lies. If she were chatting with the other women, she had to have an ulterior motive.

And Gavin would be damned if he'd permit his Jenny to fall for Ellen's ruse.

***

Gavin invited Jenny to his chambers after the evening meal, and she blushed heavily from her brilliant blonde hair to her gown's neckline at his offer. Gavin leaned in, teasing a warm kiss right under the sharp line of her jaw. Her ethereal scent of high summer heather intoxicated him more than the ale or spiced mead, and he found it difficult to calm the raging demand that pulsed through him.

He must wed Jenny soon. His raw, animal desire for her was growing into an uncontrollable crescendo. They had waited for so long, and their wedding was still a few weeks away.

Sometimes he lamented he wouldn't be able to wait. Then when his gaze fell on Jenny, resembling so much an angel on earth, he renewed his vow to keep himself in check until their wedding night.

Oh — how he anticipated that night. Some days it took every ounce of his control not to undress Jenny with his eyes in front of the entire hall.

Tonight, his focus wasn't on satisfying his cock, rather on inquiring as to how Jenny was getting along with that cursed Ellen at the keep. The woman's croft was finished, and she should have removed the rest of her belongings from the maid's quarters. Ewan had informed her before they began their evening meal the day before, and from the flare of ire in Ellen's hooded eyes, she hadn't been pleased to be leaving the keep. Yet, here she was, still in the kitchens – a leech that wouldn't release its grip. After his uncomfortable encounter with Ellen, her departure had happened not a moment too soon, in Gavin's estimation.

Out of courtesy, Gavin didn't close his chamber door behind Jenny, but peeked up and down the dim hallway to ensure that no one might listen in. Ellen yet lingered about the keep.

Jenny had pulled back the tapestry that covered the narrow window slit to let in any manner of cooler air. Late spring and early summer had been temperate, hot even, and wet, so their clothing and hair clung to their skin in a damp sweat without end. Jenny fanned her elegant neck as she leaned toward the open air.

"Jenny, *mo chridhe,*" Gavin began in a low voice, catching her hand gently with his. He guided her to the torch that blazed near the hearth, and something glinted at her waist. His cautionary words regarding Ellen left his mind out of his curiosity for the bauble on Jenny's skirt.

"What do ye have there?" he asked, brushing the silver piece with a fingertip.

"Ooch, the strangest thing happened today. I was with Meg this afternoon, in her solar, and Ellen came to the door."

Gavin tried not to react at hearing the name of the very woman he was going to discuss with Jenny. Why was she bringing up Ellen?

"Oh? What happened in the solar?" His jaw twitched.

"She entered and thanked both Meg and myself for our hospitality and for being, weel, nice to her. She was pitiful, Gavin. Like she needed a friend more than anything in this world. She gave both Meg and I these wee brooches. As thank ye gifts, I believe?"

Pure, raw, uncontrollable fury burst in Gavin, like the bowels of hell erupting from the earth and spilling out in putrid filth.

He grabbed at the bauble, pulling it from her skirts. The ripping sound was as loud as Jenny's protests. Gavin didn't care.

"Gavin! What are ye doing? What has gotten into ye?"

Jenny's attempts to pry off his fingers were fruitless, and a short rend in her skirts was all that remained. The silver brooch was now in Gavin's fierce, white-knuckled grip.

She'd seen Gavin angry before, but as of late, it seemed to be the only way she saw him, and Jenny began to fear him. She despised that the man she loved so dearly was in such a state since Ellen's arrival. His dimples hid when he was angered.

"Jenny, I beg of ye." For all the fury he seemed to emanate, his voice was calm, pleading — that rich voice that sent shivers down her spine. "I know ye have a large heart, too large, and this is one of those times where I would ask ye to guard that heart. Ellen is no friend to anyone but Ellen. 'Tis a ploy, my love, this bauble, her words of thanks to ye. I understand ye dinna know the lass, but I do. Too well. More than I care to admit."

Instead of being furious at his actions, at ripping her gown and cautioning her about Ellen, she behaved as she always did. She cupped his scratchy cheek in her tender palm and tipped her head to listen. Gavin nuzzled her hand, his amber eyes closing at her soft touch.

"Why more than ye care to admit? She is part of your past. We all have a past, Gavin."

Jenny's words were sound and placating, yet they only hinted at the surface of Gavin's reaction to the brooch. He kept his eyes closed. He couldn't look her in the face when he spoke his shame.

"Because I am ashamed, Jenny. I behaved recklessly with Ellen, and she used me hard. And I let myself be used. 'Tis a shameful thing to admit, and my vexation at my foolish behavior I turned into wrath for her, and if Ewan hadn't stayed my hand, I would have done the lowest thing a man can do, and I would have struck her down."

Gavin lifted his gaze to Jenny's compassionate face, which never left his. Her eyes, flickering blue and black in the torchlight, were unwavering. She had no shame for him; only love flowed from this fine woman.

"Ye pulled me from a verra dark place, Jenny, that long time ago. Ye were patient while I overcame my shame. If it hadn't been for ye and Ewan carrying me, I dinna think I would have regained my character as a man. I never want ye to see me that disgraced again, and I dinna want ye to think on that time when I was that low, when I was less than the man I wanted to be. With Ellen here, all that shame rises up. I canna trust her. I will no' trust her. Just promise me ye will be wary of her."

Jenny stepped close to him, her hand slipping from his cheek to his chest, feeling the heat of his body through his thin tunic. Her other hand reached to his head, threading through his buff-colored locks at his neck. He shivered under her light touch, like the feather of an angel's wing.

"I have no shame for ye, Gavin. I see ye as an honorable warrior, a steadfast MacLeod, and a loving man. One woman can no' change who ye are in my eyes. And aye, I promise to be wary."

Then her lips were on his, and he leaned his head down to press into the kiss, to gather her in his arms. Gavin dropped the cursed circlet onto the table by the window and with both hands, lifted her from the ground. His lips sought hers, his tongue venturing forth into the uncharted territory of her mouth, and she moaned at his efforts.

That raging need inside him uncoiled, threatening to take control, and without realizing it, his hands shifted on her body to clench the pliable contours of her backside, thrusting her as close to him as their thin barrier of clothing allowed. Jenny squeaked at the movement. Galvanized, Gavin then dropped her to her feet and stepped back, patting at the folds of his kilt lest the fabric give away just how much he desired her.

Jenny stood near the window, panting just as hard as he, her hand on the delicate swell of her breasts.

"I must wed ye soon, Jenny," Gavin's thick voice cracked as he spoke. "I dinna know how much longer I can wait."

Jenny traced a light finger over the curve of his shoulder, making him shudder. She pressed her face against the rough linen of his tunic, arching her body to his.

"Just over a fortnight. We can wait a couple weeks, aye?" Her voice was a ragged whisper.

Gavin risked touching her again, grasping her hand in his.

"In truth, I would wait for ye forever." Then a comical, leering grin split across his face. "But God save me, I am grateful I dinna have to."

Chapter Six: Misunderstandings

ELLEN STOOD IN the doorway of the keep, eying the work of those in the bailey and just beyond the port gate. Such toil. Ellen had been fortunate — raised as the comely, only bairn of a wealthy man, Ellen had never truly worked a day in her life. The idea of everyday toil perplexed her. Why didn't these commoners try to improve their lot? She shook her head as she waited.

She knew Ewan had sent a missive to her father. Ellen had stood in this very spot and watched the devilishly handsome Duncan depart and had counted the days until he returned. Her father must have been elusive — 'twas nigh a sennight later.

A rider entered the bailey and leapt from his horse. The very man she wanted to see, a slightly shorter version of his brother, Laird Ewan, who had sent him on an important task. Under Ellen's fierce gaze, Duncan shifted his plaid before pulling a folded parchment from his sporran.

Stepping into the shadows of the hall, Ellen lifted her skirts and moved to the rear, near the archway to the stairs. She spun around, feigning surprise, when she heard boot falls on the stone.

"Ooch, Duncan! Ye have returned! I know many a lass who pined for ye whilst ye were gone!" she teased, a coy smile curling her lips.

She sauntered to the lad, plying her womanly wares as she well knew how. Inhaling so the upper curve of her breasts thrust against her neckline, swinging her hips in a way most men found enticing. Charming. Unable to deny.

Ellen had learned early in her life that if a woman could charm a man, everything about him was in her power. 'Twas the lone course for a woman to have any true power.

"Aye. Have ye seen Ewan? Is he about?"

Ellen laid a delicate hand on Duncan's sinewy upper arm. Not quite as muscular as his brother, but getting there. His lips twitched at her touch. *Almost there.*

"I was on my way to ask him a few questions about my time here," she answered in a sultry voice. A *charming* voice. "He's in his study. Do ye need to tell him something? I can escort ye?"

Duncan didn't respond right away, and Ellen slid her hand down his arm and narrowed her gaze. That expression had beguiled more than one man.

And it worked on Duncan.

"I have a letter he was wanting from your father. It probably details your visit here. Would ye like to bring it to him, since ye were going to ask anyway?"

Ellen's coy smile widened in a look of gratitude. At least, Duncan would believe it was gratitude. Making a man think he was a woman's hero had him eating out of the palm of her hand, and Duncan was no different.

"Och, Duncan, ye are so kind to think of that for me! I would love to take this to Ewan, find out when 'tis safe for me to return. And ye must be weary from your journey. This way ye can refresh yourself after your long ride."

She pursed her lips to form a button kiss and placed it on Duncan's cheek. The man's skin burned as red as Ellen's hair.

"I will take it to him straight-away. Thank ye again, Duncan."

She swirled in her skirts and raced for the steps before he could follow her. She mounted the first two, then stopped. Waiting until a count of ten, she peered around the cool stone to see the backside of Duncan exit the hall.

Then she glanced at Ewan's name on the folded parchment in her father's crisp handwriting. She pursed her lips again, this time in anger.

She wouldn't be imprisoned under her father's stern household again. When she had lived in her father's house, her time with Gavin had been the most divine escape, and in truth, she had loved the freedom more than she loved Gavin. Even if he didn't take her as a mistress, Ellen swore she would find a way to remain at Lochnora, away from those who tried to constrain her autonomy.

Wrapping the letter in the folds of her skirt, she made her way back to the kitchens and nodded at the maids working at the tables. They barely acknowledged her.

She scooted past them to the blazing hearth, the heat of the fire causing her skin to burst into an immediate sweat. Under the guise of stirring the pot hanging from the crochan, and without so much as a peek over her shoulder, Ellen tossed the parchment into the fire. The edges browned, then furled under the flames as her father's words went up in smoke.

She hadn't even read what her father wrote.

No one would.

***

Jenny contemplated what to do with the cursed brooch. For Gavin to react so intensely, she didn't want to wear it. Yet, to return it to Ellen would be rude beyond measure. In the end, she left it on her small table near her sleeping platform in the maids' quarters. She would decide on what to do with it later.

The day's weather was fair, with cloudy skies that kept the harsh sunlight at bay, and perfect for digging in the gardens. Tired of cleaning and being cooped up inside the keep, Jenny thoroughly enjoyed having her hands in the dirt. Dark, dank earth, lush greens, and the twittering songs of the birds all relaxed her body and spirit. Bringing things to life, watching the flowers bloom and the vegetables ripen — in a heretical thought, Jenny wondered if this was a bit of what it felt like to be God in the garden of creation.

"So, ye are to wed our Gavin soon, then?" Ellen's cloying voice shocked Jenny from her reverie.

Our Gavin? Jenny wondered at her wording as she spun around on her knees. Why was she still using that phrasing? What was this woman about? She was supposed to be gone from the keep, but managed to find her way back daily.

Since Ellen had been rather amiable in her time at Lochnora, Jenny hesitated. She supposed there was nothing truly amiss about sharing her good news with Ellen. After all, it might reinforce that Gavin and Jenny were together — that Ellen was no longer part of that image.

"Aye. Gavin has decided he can no' wait any longer, so we shall wed in a couple weeks, after all the preparations are complete. Then we might have more kin from around the Highlands to join us. Ewan wants his man-at-arms to have a wedding that might rival any laird's."

"Ooch, 'tis a darling idea. And Gavin, he was willing to wait for ye?"

Ellen lifted her skirts to kneel on the same plaid as Jenny, presumably to help in the gardens. Jenny nodded, again pondering Ellen's strange manner of speaking. *Darling idea?*

"Weel, I am surprised at that." Ellen's lupine eyes cast about the grounds, ensuring they were the only ones in the gardens. She leaned in close to Jenny. "What with how debauched the man can be, aye? 'Twere it no' for his nobility of spirit, the man might be seen as a rake. But ye probably know that already."

Ellen's hands pinched the leeks and tugged lightly at the tops, not dirtying her hands as she gathered her green vegetables. Jenny, however, halted in her efforts completely, her earth-covered hands clenching at her skirts. Ellen had been kind, even charming, the past several days. What was Ellen about now? And why did she speak so freely? 'Twas not proper for a lady to speak so openly about her relations with men.

Jenny's shock must have registered on her face, because Ellen clapped her hand to her mouth in surprised indignation.

"Ooch! My apologies! Ye are a virtuous lassie. And Gavin is to be your husband. 'Tis untoward for me to speak as such." Ellen laid a clean, delicate hand on Jenny's stained knee. "Can ye forgive me, lassie?"

Jenny pursed her lips, cautious about saying anything to this wavering woman who at once spoke both graciously and inappropriately, the very woman for whom Gavin had pined. The woman who broke her love's heart. The woman who spoke so peculiarly. Jenny had the sense she just couldn't trust her. Yet, other than her strange words, Ellen had been nothing but kind to Jenny and had kept her distance from Gavin. She had no reason not to trust the wild-haired, strikingly beautiful woman. Still, something tickled at the back of her neck. *A warning? An omen?* Why was she so conflicted? Jenny's cheeks blazed.

"'Tis naught, Ellen. Truly. Ye ken the man well, and I canna fault ye for that."

Jenny tried to be pleasant to Ellen, tried to be hospitable and a friend, but knowing the past Ellen had with Gavin and her odd manner of speaking was oft too much to bear.

"Oh, that's all well and good. Are we almost done here? The air, 'tis warm, and I dinna want to ruin my gown."

Jenny glanced over at Ellen, who again looked so regal in her finery. Her kirtle was crafted of the finest dusky linen, light for a warm day, and edged in blue and gold shades that offset the stark red hue of her hair. Definitely *not* a gown intended for work. The neckline clung appreciatively low, allowing the generous swells of her bosoms to thrust over the edging as she breathed. Her skin, pale and creamy, contributed to her loveliness.

'Twas no wonder Gavin had been so taken with her years ago. Jenny regarded her kirtle, rough and soiled from gardening, and her skin stained by working with herbs in the kitchen and digging in the garden dirt. Her hair, a comely rich blonde, hung limply as she worked, bound back by a plain kerchief. Jenny's breasts, well-covered by her kirtle, were beautifully formed, but not like the bounty offered by Ellen.

Truly, though she knew where Gavin's heart lay, having Ellen around, like a luscious, tempting fruit, did nothing for her own sense of confidence. She knew what happened when tempting fruit was available — just look at what had transpired in the garden of Eden.

Jenny waved Ellen off, and the woman gave Jenny a grateful smile before leaving to find easier chores in the keep, most likely embroidery or weaving. Exhaling a breath she didn't realize she'd been holding, she returned to her gaze to the dirty plants before her. Jenny had found Ellen setting up her domestic chores in the main hall "for the light" – she claimed her hut was too dim – but in obvious view of the men who paraded in and out of the main hall throughout the day.

Men that included Gavin.

Jenny chided herself for her ill-conceived thoughts and petty jealousies, but that didn't stop them from forming in her mind unbidden. Frustrated, she blew wispy blonde tendrils off her forehead and threw her leeks into the basket. No more solace was to be found in the garden. Her gardening for the day was done.

***

After she scrubbed her hands and adjusted her hair, Jenny joined the kitchen maids to prepare the evening meal. She'd not seen Gavin all day, and her heart ached that she'd let her dire thoughts get the best of her. Tonight, she would join him for their supper, and he would smile at her, that endearing, dimpled smile, and all would be well.

Mairi and Bonnie were already in the kitchens when Jenny arrived, preparing wooden bowls of mutton stew, thick with broth and bright orange carrots. Freshly baked brown bread sat in steaming rounds on platters, ready for dipping. Jenny inhaled deeply, savoring the familiar, robust scents that meant home.

Meg had offered to lighten Jenny's workload since the birth of baby Caitir, hoping to have Jenny assist as a nursemaid. While Jenny was more than willing to rise to the request and help her dear friend, she was not a woman who rested on her laurels. She needed to keep busy, and since Meg was an overly involved mother, never straying far from the wee bairn, 'twould be little for Jenny to do if she played nursemaid for an already well-cared for baby. However, Jenny saw that the offer was more of a ruse.

Meg missed her friend, so instead Meg oft made her way to the kitchens with baby Caitir strapped to her hip in a snug tartan. The fellowship of the wide Lochnora kitchens was unmatched, the abundance of the gardens unparalleled. And it gave Meg the excuse to visit with Jenny.

This night, however, Meg was busy with Caitir who'd been fussing all day. Meg's mother, Elspeth, spent most of her day at the keep, blaming that foul event that plagued all mothers and babies — teething. Mairi, Meg's younger sister, had accompanied her mother and filled Meg's role in preparing the evening meal, something she had been doing more often as of late.

From the roses in Mairi's cheeks, Jenny surmised that the fellowship of women in the kitchens was but one reason for the lassie's presence. The ruddy jawline of the raven-haired Hamish, Laird Ewan's younger brother, was the other.

Noise from the grand hall carried into the kitchen, and Fiona clapped her hands together.

"Come, lassies! Let's feed our kin! No dawdling!"

No one dared disobey a command from Fiona, and the kitchen maids grabbed trenchers, pitchers, and bowls, delivering them to the hungry men and women sitting at the tables. Mairi, of course, made a straight line to Hamish, then to young Aren, her second object of interest.

Jenny first checked for Meg and Ewan. Since Meg had recovered from her lingering illness, she'd been trying her best to join everyone in the hall, to work with the kitchen maids, to toil in the gardens. Jenny, like the other women in the keep, did her best to stop her, claiming the lady of the keep ought not to work so hard. They met somewhere in the middle. And on days where Meg did too much, she ended up in her rooms, resting.

No Meg, only an affable Ewan, whose chiseled face remained open and earnest to his kin while his eyes bore traces of worry and reticence, being absent from his Meg. The bairn must have taken much out of her today.

Jenny returned to the kitchens and prepared a platter of stew and bread to be sent to the lady of the keep and added a small pot of honey and several pieces of summer fruit to the platter. Meg had a penchant for sweets.

***

Gavin's brooding eyes searched the main hall for Jenny as she drifted to and from the kitchens. This behavior had become commonplace, a way to connect with her after his workday was complete. Jenny was as devoted to the clan MacLeod and the laird and lady as Gavin was, and he oft had moments of wonderment that he found a woman as loyal as she. Sometimes the brief moment of a shared gaze was all they had until after the evening meal had ended. And if he were lucky, she'd gift him a smile.

The fact she glided around the keep as captivating as an angel further increased the passion that burned deep inside him, and his eyes followed her every movement in amber fire. Gavin had traveled a long, strange, painful road to have Jenny all but fall into his lap as his lowest point. Whenever his mind dared to think back on those bleak times, he could only marvel at God's amazing foresight.

Jenny exited to retrieve more food for the warriors and families in the hall, having gifted Gavin with a sultry, blue-eyed wink before turning away. He was still reeling with desire over that wink when someone bumped him from behind.

He rose in a smooth movement, ready to knock out the MacLeod warrior who dared to collide with the Laird's man-at-arms. And the hall was not overly crowded — why didn't he watch where he was going?

Gavin's disapproving gaze fell on the wild red ringlets of the last person he wanted to see in the hall. His gaze narrowed as his nostrils flared. *Why was she here? She had her own place to live.* And he asked her that very question.

"Why are ye in the hall, Ellen? Why are ye even near me? Ye have your own place now. Eat there."

His voice was sharp, more angry than he intended, but then, he *was* more angry than he realized. It seemed to be his unconscious reaction to her since she'd arrived at Lochnora.

Instead of recoiling from his ferocious snapping, she swayed and threw out a hip, tossing her hair over her shoulder. A wide smile plastered across her lips.

"Why Gavin. I thought ye'd be proud of me. I'm making friends here, getting to know the MacLeods. Why, I even had an amazing conversation with your Jenny about your upcoming nuptials and have made myself valuable in the kitchens. I thought ye would want that. For me to be amicable."

Her voice dripped with honey, but Gavin knew too well 'twas a poisoned honey made to wound. He had to stop himself from grabbing her arm and dragging her away. How would that look from a man who prided himself on his nobility?

"Nay. 'Tis no' how I wanted ye to be. I dinna want ye to be here at all. Ye used me, dragged my heart through the mud until the only feeling I had for ye was filth. Jenny is the single clean and pure thing in my life. She gives me a chance to feel again, and I will not risk that for anything. Least of all for ye."

Ellen giggled in that annoying way she had and rested her hand on his arm. His skin crawled at her touch.

"Oh, Gavin. 'Tis no' all bad. I'm no' here to cause strife in Jenny's life." Gavin flexed his arm to flick Ellen's hand off. 'Twas like being touched by the devil himself. Ellen didn't even blink at his reaction and relocated her hand to his tunic.

Gavin's chest heaved with anger and frustration, despising her touch on him.

"Or with ye, Gavin. I am as I always was with ye, just wanting ye to be as happy as ye can." Her suggestive inflection on the word *happy* made him shudder. "Ooch, ye've become quite the man, Gavin. I can feel the muscles of your chest under your tunic."

She fanned her fingers as she spoke, and Gavin stumbled backwards, tripping over a bench to get away from her. The bench broke his fall, and he sat hard on the wood. Ellen's hand then cupped his jaw. Gavin flinched his head away in disgust.

"Do no' touch me," he growled at her. Ellen laughed again. *Why that laugh? What is wrong with the lass?*

"Dinna be so sensitive, Gavin." She patted his cheek and spun around, sashaying back the way she came.

Gavin panted with vexation, and a film of sweat coated his skin — dealing with Ellen was one of the most traumatic experiences he ever had, and tonight was no different. Running his fingers through his sweat-damp hair, he searched the hall to see if anyone had witnessed his miserable encounter with Ellen. He didn't believe so, as Ewan or Hamish would have come to his aid. Ewan's eyes were on his daughter, and Hamish was fawning over Mairi before Aren could disrupt his chance with that lass.

In fact, as Gavin scanned the room, only one set of eyes had been watching the exchange between himself and the red devil.

Jenny.

Her fair face was unmasked, every ounce of pain and confusion drawn in stark lines. Gavin's insides crumbled as his stomach dropped to his feet. He rose, meaning to run to Jenny and reassure her that Ellen had severely overstepped. But he didn't have the chance.

Jenny turned and rushed from the hall.

Chapter Seven: Compromising Positions

GAVIN LOATHED WHAT having Ellen at Lochnora was doing to his beloved. He raced up the steps and caught Jenny at the top of the stairs. Shadows danced in the hallway under the dim lighting, but Jenny was a beacon. He grasped her arm, but she slipped away as easily as a kelpie.

"I'm sorry, Gavin. Please, I dinna want ye near me tonight."

The words hammered at his heart. With tears filling her cerulean eyes, Jenny spun in a huff and raced off toward her small chambers at the top of the tower with the other maids.

Gavin could hear her sobbing as she rushed away, using her sleeve to wipe at her eyes. His heart rented apart at her pain, especially because 'twas unnecessary. Jenny had naught to worry about with Ellen — he had buried deep that part of his life, the part where his affections were abused by the woman he'd had designs to marry.

That time had been years ago. He had been younger, naive even, and since then, he'd grown in so many ways. He had learned what it was to have family, to have loyalty, and he had discovered what he wanted out of this life gifted by God.

At the center of all that was Jenny. Through her presence in his life, he had come to understand that she was the fair, foundational nimbus of his life. How could he make her see, have her recognize his true feelings? And here she was, thinking Gavin was the type of man to set a woman like Jenny aside for viper like Ellen.

The mere thought of it set Gavin's stomach rolling. He crossed his arms over his bulging chest as he watched Jenny round the end of the hallway and exit, leaving only the memory of her dark brown kirtle and gleaming blonde hair, tinged by her lingering heathered scent.

More than her abandoning him in the hall was the added insult that Jenny believed he'd rather spend his time with Ellen than with her. That perchance his heart was not as devout as she had believed it to be. That he was unfaithful and lacked character. Of all the somber thoughts that tumbled in his mind, this one was the worst. Why did she suddenly see him that way? And worse – *why would she want to wed a man such as that?*

That was the problem. She couldn't see Gavin's heart under his plaid. If she could, Jenny would have no doubts about where his loyalties, where his heart, lay.

It lay at Jenny's feet. Gavin hated that she didn't seem to know that, and he vowed that he would make his utmost devotion known to her. Other questions plagued his mind. Why was Ellen inserting herself between them? Why now, after she had run off and wed the Sheriff of Beauly? Surely, she had a new life — why did she think to claim Gavin?

No such thing would ever happen, that Gavin knew.

At all costs, he had to convince Jenny that she owned his heart, and no one could set that love aside.

He meant to chase after her again, follow her to the maid's chambers, but Ewan spilled into the darkened hallway, half drunk on summer mead.

"Come," he commanded to Gavin with an impish smile. "Hamish and Aren are having a tiff over Meg's younger sister. Even the lass herself is rooting for Hamish, but Aren swears he is the better man. They are about to have it out with fisticuffs!"

Gavin glanced down the hallway where Jenny had disappeared, desperate to deny his chieftain and chase her down, press his lips on hers, and offer to wed her on the morn. *No more delays*.

Then Ewan was tugging on Gavin's plaid.

"What, ye want me to help ye stop this ridiculous fight?" Gavin gritted his teeth and turned to Ewan, who had already started to march away. Gavin was torn in two.

"Och, nay! I want ye to watch with me! I'd lay a copper penny on Hamish any day!"

Gavin tried to pull back, not wanting to be a party to this event, but Ewan wouldn't let off and practically dragged him past the main hall to the yard.

Woefully, Gavin followed. But Jenny didn't leave his thoughts, and he vowed to go to her chambers as soon as this absurd fight was over.

***

Jenny tried not to cry — she commanded herself to keep the tears from falling, but the broken look on Gavin's handsome face at her rejection was too much to bear. He knew why she was running from him this night, and even if she were overreacting, she was not ready to confront her emotions, her jealousies.

She had wanted to touch that handsomely boyish face, that strong jaw, that dimple that made her knees weak. Instead, she tucked her hand in her skirts and raced away, which was, in truth, the last thing she should have done. Jenny should have been open with her worries. Gavin was the type of man to understand her concerns, even it 'twas nothing more than petty jealousy.

Reaching her chambers that she shared with a few other kitchen maids, she found her pallet and collapsed onto her plaid bedding in uncontrollable tears for a long time.

He'd been so patient with her. Waiting to wed until summer when life had calmed. And waiting to lie with her as a wife until the bonds of marriage were established. There by her side every day, and when one small incident happened, she called his integrity into question. And he was proud of his integrity! Gavin had every right to be angry with her, or at least reprimand her for her behavior. Instead, he stood by, acquiescing to her wishes, and watched her run away.

And in truth, it wasn't his fault, none of this was. It was that red woman's fault. *Ellen.*

Though it was the most unchristian thought to have, in this moment, Jenny detested Ellen. She wished the buxom former lover had never come back to Lochnora.

Everything had seemed so perfect last winter. Then Meg got sick, Ewan grew into a more nervous man — not the same lighthearted man he'd been before, and Gavin's protective traits had grown even more protective, over his laird and his family, over Jenny, over the clan as a whole.

They had to push their wedding back and back again, and Jenny was disappointed but understood. Then that Ellen moved in and became a fixture at the keep.

Why was she still here? Was that Gavin's fault? Was it his fault that Ellen, who had been so nice to everyone, was also nice to Gavin? *Too nice,* that was the problem. Any fool could see Ellen longed for Gavin. Jenny had been duped for too long.

Her fingers brushed against something hard under her plaid blanket. She withdrew her hand and found the cursed brooch gifted from Ellen. With no compunctions, Jenny threw it with all her might across the maid's chambers, where it tinkled against the stones it struck. Let someone else find it and have it. Gavin had been right – Ellen was a leech on Jenny. The brooch had been nothing more than a guise.

Jenny rolled over onto her back, throwing her arm over her eyes. The air in the tight tower chamber was warm, having collected over the course of the day. Her kirtle stuck to her skin, clinging and rendering her even more uncomfortable than she already felt.

Nay, she assured herself, answering her previous questions. Gavin wasn't responsible for Ellen's behavior. She never should have pushed Gavin away or taken her ire with Ellen's flirtatious ways out on him. She should have confronted Ellen. That's what she should have done.

Once she finished flagellating herself, she sat up and wiped her face.

Gavin was her husband-to-be, not Ellen's. He came to her, not Ellen.

Jenny jumped up from her bed. She needed to find Gavin, be open about her concerns, and apologize for her curt behavior.

***

Gavin managed to keep Hamish and Aren from pounding each other into the ground. By the end of the fight, it had taken much of Gavin's brawny strength to wrap his arms around Aren's thinner frame and slam him to the ground, but he did it. Ewan was disappointed, but cheering on his brother helped him recover from his over-imbibing, and the laird was now sober enough to join his wife and baby instead of drinking more with his imprudent brothers.

Hamish and Duncan razzed a dusty Gavin as he departed with Ewan and guided the chieftain to his chambers. Meg's relieved face was the only *thank you* Gavin needed, and he closed the door behind him, leaving the couple to their amusements.

Gavin sent up a silent prayer that his friend might be sober enough by now to enjoy those amusements. While Gavin may not be participating in any amusements at the moment, waiting until he was fully wed to Jenny, that didn't mean he should facilitate Ewan getting too drunk for own wife. They shared a bed under the blessings of the church, but not if he were stumbling down drunk.

His own chambers were a welcome sight. The day had been long, too long, for Gavin — in addition to his chores, his training, and supporting his Laird, he'd fended off Ellen like he would a parasite, and then endured the confrontation with Jenny. He was drained, as though every muscle was falling off his body. He hadn't felt so worn, so frustrated since Meg had been sickly earlier in the year.

When Lady Meg had recovered, all seemed well. He was going to wed his heart's desire and begin a life with the woman he loved. Everything in his life suddenly fell into place.

And then his past showed up to throw it into chaos. Ellen's behavior with everyone, including Jenny, had been seemingly forthright. Yet, with him . . .

He entered the darkened chambers, grabbing the torch from the hallway to light the torch in his sconces. The flickering light brightened the comfortable chambers. 'Twas the same room Ewan had put him in when he left Ellen to her new life marrying the sheriff. These chambers had become a safe haven, a sanctuary, thus he had stayed. Jenny had even agreed to live here instead of moving outside of the keep into their own private cottage. Of course, he knew the true reason for that decision — that virtuous woman was as loyal and committed to the Laird's family as Gavin was.

Pulling the tapestry past the window slit, Gavin inhaled the clean, cool air. 'Twas the perfect weather for a good night's sleep. No moonlight, so the darkness was deep and welcoming. He dropped his kilt to the floor and pulled his dusty tunic over his head. The water bowl still held a bit of warmth from the day, and he relished the feeling of the clean water dripping over his skin, wiping away the grittiness of his exertions.

Gavin snuffed out his torch, which pitched his chambers into blackness, and felt his way to his bed. Not even moonlight

An Echo in the Glen

managed to breach his room. His body protested as he moved, and
he was certain he'd fall asleep before his head rested on the cushion.
He yearned for nothing more than for this day to be over. It couldn't
get any worse.

The covers had just landed on his lower limbs when his
bedroom door creaked open, and before his eyes could register the
shaft of light, it shut in a rush. Gavin sat up under his covers, on
alert and reaching for his sword that he kept unsheathed and resting
against his bed platform. His breathing slowed into a practiced
focus. *Who is invading my personal chambers?*

Then a delicate, light hand pressed against his bare chest,
the fingertips feather-like against his skin. His breath caught in
expectation.

Jenny. She'd come to his chambers! To speak to him? To
make amends? To be close to him after a day of separation?

He didn't care. Gavin grasped her hand, holding it against
his chest. He pulled Jenny close, and her lips slid across his, another
feathery touch in the dark. His cock throbbed with anticipation. She
wouldn't do much more, that Gavin knew, but having her here, in
his chambers, on his lap, was more than he might have asked for on
this miserable day.

Tendrils of her hair brushed against his arms as she lifted
one of his hands, placing it on her breast. Her full swollen breast
pushed against his palm, begging to be fondled. He clenched his
fingers, caressing the cushioned globes. Her hair fell into his face as
they kissed, and her musky scent filled his senses. Something
seemed wrong. Not just her presence in his bed, but her hair and her
perfume. Gavin dismissed it as a result of his heightened passion.
He couldn't think straight.

"Do you want me, Gavin?" Her voice was an aggressive,
husky whisper, that set a warning off in Gavin's head. His cock
throbbed again at her question, his desire for her all-consuming, but
that ardor was tempered by the very question that was supposed to
entice him.

Jenny was an innocent, timid lover. She didn't grab at his chest unbidden. She didn't ask if he wanted her. And she didn't smell of musk. His nose wrinkled at that perfume.

The fresh scents of heather and loch water that typically complemented Jenny were absent.

His mind halted, as did his hands.

This isn't Jenny.

Worse, he knew in an instant who it was. This was not the woman of his dreams. It was the devil from his nightmares.

Gavin grabbed the woman by her upper arms, thrust her off his chest, and leapt from the bed with her locked in his iron grip.

"Ellen? What has possessed ye to come to my chambers? Get ye gone from my bed!"

He dragged her to the door as she giggled. The menacing sound ground into Gavin's ears. He yanked the door open, where dim light from a hall sconce torch caught Ellen in a red, incandescent glow. She wore a thin shift that showed the silhouette of her full, enticing outline. Ignoring his own nakedness, wearing just what God graced him with on the day of his birth, Gavin stepped out of the doorway to shove Ellen into the hall.

"Oh, Gavin," Ellen laughed in that way of hers that grated on Gavin's last nerve. "'Twas just fun. I wanted ye to know that we might still have fun together. Ye are no' wed yet."

She danced a finger up his bare chest, and he pushed her away. She stumbled into the stones on the far side of the hallway but caught herself as her onerous tittering echoed in the hall.

"I said get ye gone," Gavin commanded. He swiveled to return to his chambers when a figure at the end of the hallway caught his attention. His gorge rose and his heart dropped to his stomach. Aye, the day *could* get worse.

Jenny stood stock still in the flickering light, her blonde hair loose against her pale, open-mouthed face that was unable to mask any emotion. The shock on her face was apparent to anyone who might have looked.

Gavin ventured a step toward her. What must she think seeing him thrust Ellen from his darkened chambers? And in his present state of undress? Yet, he already knew the answers to those questions.

"Jenny —" he tried to say, but Ellen's cackling laugh interrupted him.

She was bent over at the wall, covering her mouth as though she was embarrassed at being caught. Gavin knew 'twas a ruse.

Her sky-blue eyes widened as she continued to stare at her nude husband-to-be and the incendiary woman standing with him outside his chambers.

"Jenny, please —" he begged again.

She didn't wait to hear the rest. She swirled in a blur of blonde and brown and ran away.

"Jenny!" Gavin roared, his skin shading in a pink hue as his fury and frustration raged inside him.

Ellen's laughter had quieted but still giggled against the far wall. Gavin's fury reached a fevered pitch, and he slammed his fist into the stone above her head as he gripped her neck to shove her upright. Stone chips and dust rained down on her hair, and she finally stopped laughing.

"We are going to do everything to make this right," Gavin snarled at her, flexing his abraded and aching fist.

Ellen's normally rosy cheeks blanched at his tone. Her haughty visage disappeared under a mask of alarm, and for the first time in Gavin's life, Ellen looked afraid. Gavin's nude body exuded a heat that filled the hall, and his grip was like an iron vise. She *should* be frightened.

"Tomorrow, I will try to speak to her, if she will even listen to me," he told Ellen in a growling whisper. "Ye will apologize for trying to seduce me and make certain she understands ye only *tried*. Ye will emphasize that ye failed, and when she saw us in the hall, I was kicking ye out from my chambers untouched. Ye will tell her the whole truth of this situation, with nary a sidestep around the actual events. Then perchance I might salvage my betrothal."

Gavin leaned in closer, his fiery breath puffing against her face. "If ye do not, I will see to it ye are removed from this keep, from Lochnora and the surrounding village. I would see ye banished from all the Highlands if I could. Now get ye gone for my sights."

He threw his hand from her neck. Ellen grabbed at the length of her shift and scrambled away from Gavin, flicking one last baleful glance over her shoulder before running down the hallway, the same direction Jenny had left.

Chapter Eight: Seeking Much Needed Advice

ONCE THE SEDUCTIVE witch had sashayed her way from the hall, Gavin leaned against the same crumbling stone he'd just punched, cradling his bruised hand. The stone wall and flooring were chilly against his naked back and buttocks, cooling the irritated fire that suppurated under his skin. Sliding down the wall, he rested on the floor and leaned his head against his knees.

Jenny might never believe him. The overwhelming despair at that prospect consumed him. He'd done nothing wrong, rejected Ellen once he'd realized her ruse, but his naked body exiting his chambers with his former lover was just far too damning. Would he believe any denial if the situation were reversed? Gavin wanted to say aye, he would believe her. But some images were far too damming to justify.

Any love, any faith she'd had for him probably left as she fled the stifling hallway. Gavin held his head, which throbbed with the misery of it all. He'd come so far, found everything he wanted, only to have it ripped away in one wretched moment.

Gavin looked down at his nakedness and pressed his uninjured hand against the wall to help him rise. He might not be able to fix the problem with Jenny tonight, but his hand needed more help than he could give it.

He also needed a wee bit of advice. And there was only one person to whom Gavin might go for that advice.

Ewan. Or better yet, Meg. Jenny's dear friend.

Gavin returned to his chambers to wrap his plaid around his hips and shoulders one-handed before seeking his Laird's chambers.

If Ewan had been sober enough to claim his blessings with his wife, Gavin hoped he was finished. His story was not one that lent itself to any further romantic interludes.

***

The knock at the door was unexpected, and when Ewan cracked the door open to see who roused him at the late hour, his state of undress and unruly hair were evidence that Gavin's laird had been abed. He didn't look impassioned or angry, so Gavin exhaled a sigh of relief — he hadn't interrupted any romantic moment.

"Gavin! What brings ye here? I thought ye had found your own bed."

Ewan swung the door wide to permit Gavin's entrance. Meg was wrapping herself in a tartan blanket as she bent over the bairn. Gavin nodded a silent hello, and Meg gave him a weak smile back. Ewan extended his arm toward the seating area off to the side of his chambers, away from the bed and baby. A low fire burned at the hearth, keeping the air inside lit and warm against the encroaching chill of the night air. 'Twas an intimate scene indeed, and guilt flooded Gavin at having to interrupt.

"Thank ye, Ewan. I had a bit of a row tonight." Gavin held his injured hand aloft. Meg approached and surveyed his hand, "tsking" under her breath.

She clasped Gavin's hand in her petite one, turning it over to evaluate the damage. She pursed her lips and clicked her tongue.

His knuckles were torn to shreds from the rough stone, and there was a good chance he'd mangled the middle finger. Not permanently, at least he hoped not, but the appendage would need care, regardless.

"Do ye think ye need Elspeth? That middle finger is quite smashed," Meg asked as she tentatively touched the digit.

Gavin shook his head as he moved the finger. "It yet moves. I dinna think I need her now, anyway. Maybe on the morn I will search her out. Unless ye think . . .?"

"Nay. 'Twill hold. Let me wash the wound and then ye can tell Ewan and I why ye showed up at our chamber door in a state of undress and disarray? And mayhap why ye didn't take this to Jenny?"

Ooch, the wee laird's wife was too astute by half. Little made it past her keen eyes, and Gavin dropped his gaze, a fool to believe otherwise.

But then, wasn't that why he came? To assuage his pained hand and to find conference with Ewan and Meg? Gavin hung his ruddy head, shamed to even speak the words. Yet, he had no other choice, for he was at a loss of what to do.

"There may have been a type of misunderstanding, this eve. Betwixt Jenny and I."

"Oh?" Meg's sunrise-shaded eyebrows rose high on her forehead with interest. "And what manner of misunderstanding would that be?"

Ewan remained sagely quiet. He knew that this was in the realm of women, a realm in which he was still unfamiliar. His presence, though, gave Gavin a sense of support when he needed it most. And Ewan was never one to miss an opportunity for insight when it presented itself.

"It began at the evening meal. Ellen was being her typical, boisterous self, and with a man unbetrothed, 'tis no bother. But for a betrothed man like myself, I rather think it borders on inappropriate, aye?"

"Aye," Ewan readily agreed. Meg flicked him a deliberate glance, then returned to her ministrations with Gavin's hand.

"Aye, rather inappropriate," Meg commented. "And Jenny did no' care for those fawning attentions?"

"Nay, she did no'. She asked me to stay away from her this eve, let her have time to herself. And I agreed. Then, after I brought Ewan back here —" A slight smile crossed Meg's fine features. *Blessings indeed,* Gavin thought, "I found my bed. Before I fell asleep, my door opened, and Jenny came in. At least, I *thought* 'twas Jenny. Mayhap to extend the olive branch? Discuss her concerns?"

"But 'twasn't Jenny?" Meg asked.

"Nay. 'Twas Ellen. She remained quiet and in the dark, and before she spoke, I did not recognize the difference. I presumed 'twas Jenny. Then, there was a smell . . ."

"A smell? Ye mean a scent. Jenny's scent?"

"Only 'twas no' Jenny's scent. Her perfume is that of heather and water from a spring loch. 'Twas when I realized that 'twas no' Jenny in my chambers with me, but Ellen. I pushed Ellen from the room, threw her into the hall."

He raised his head to look Meg in the eye. Gavin swallowed heavily at the mention of his reaction, as he didn't believe in any violence against the fairer sex. His vocation was a protector of the weak. Justified though he might have been, that he handled Ellen with a rough hand cloaked him in shame.

"I am no' proud of my actions, but I had to remove her from my chambers, aye? And when I stepped out into the hallway to force Ellen to leave . . ."

Meg paused her fingers and cupped Gavin's freshly cleaned and treated hand.

"Och, Jenny was no' in the hallway, was she?" Meg's voice held hints of horror and disbelief. *Could Gavin's luck be so poor? Aye. It could.* Gavin nodded.

"Right there. And me in a state of undress, throwing Ellen from my chambers. How badly did that appear to her poor eyes?"

Meg stilled, and she and Ewan exchanged a look before they both dipped their heads, hiding their expressions. A gurgling noise rose from Ewan's vibrating chest. To Gavin's wide-eyed horror, Ewan and Meg burst into a fit of inappropriate laughter. He yanked his hand back as Ewan pounded his bare back with a heavy hand.

"Ooch, Gavin! If ye did no' have ill luck, ye'd have no luck at all! Are ye sure someone did no' place an ill-wish under your pillow?" Ewan bawled between bouts of laughter.

Gavin squinted at the laird and his lady, an irritated glare of offense, and he sat up straight.

"Ye laugh at me! My betrothal with Jenny is at stake and I come here for counsel, and ye mock me?"

He started to rise, but Ewan shoved him back into his seat. Meg bit at her lips, trying to control her smiles.

"My apologies, Gavin. We aren't laughing at ye. In fact, this is harrowing. We are laughing at the sheer implausibility of it all. If ye weren't telling the story, I would nigh think it a fairy story. But Jenny has a good sense about her," Meg assured him. "If ye sit with her and tell her just as ye told us, I am sure she will understand just as we have. She must ken how steadfast ye are, and the manner of woman Ellen is."

"Aye, but Ellen has been kind to Jenny, deceiving her. And even the most steadfast of men can be led astray. Or at least appear to be."

"Only if they want to, Gavin," Ewan countered, keeping Gavin locked in a fierce gaze. "Many a man claims to have that integrity, to be steadfast and loyal to his vows, but few prove it. And ye, my old friend, are naught if no' steadfast. More importantly, Jenny knows this deep in her heart. Just speak to the lass."

Gratefulness swelled inside Gavin at his friend's words. Gavin prided himself on his constancy, and to have his laird see that trait in him gave Gavin hope. Perchance, they were right. Perchance, once Jenny calmed, she would see the truth of Gavin's unfortunate situation.

Chapter Nine: Finally, A Wedding

WHEN GAVIN ENTERED the kitchens, Fiona and Mairi gave him short bows and left. Jenny didn't have to say anything to them – she wore her sadness like a veil. 'Twas more than obvious that Gavin and Jenny needed to speak privately.

"*Mo ghràdh,*" he broke the silence. "I am going to beg that ye listen to me afore ye do or say anything."

She didn't move from her spot, her head hanging low as she hid behind her curtain of golden hair. Her hands were rooted to their spot on the table in front of her. He placed his fingertips near hers, but not touching. He needed to wait until she was ready and to let her touch him. When she remained silent, he started his story, telling it just as he had the night before. She said not a word as he detailed everything.

"Ye see, Jenny?" he asked when he was done. "'Twas a mistake. A horrible prank, if ye will. I've done naught inappropriate with that lass. Nor do I want to. I want her to be as far from me as she can get and I want to wed ye, be with ye, share my life with ye. Can ye find it in your heart to believe me?"

Gavin sat across the kitchen worktable, his gilded eyes pleading with desperate affection. His entire face was shrouded in hopelessness. So fretful, so broken – could Jenny's heart go out to him and the horrible predicament Ellen had put him in? He held his breath.

One slender finger extended out to rest atop Gavin's in the most gentle touch, tracing the scrapes on his skin. His whole body deflated, and he thought he might sob at her contact.

"I know ye, Gavin," she started slowly. "I have known ye for years, seen ye here at the keep, and ye have been nothing but virtuous and resolute. In my heart, I knew 'twas a good reason for what I saw in the hallway. It was just so, so . . ."

"So unbelievable? That your naked betrothed was parading in the hall with a known round-heel? I can see how the obvious reason had to be the worst imaginable."

Gavin clasped her hand to his tunic, desperate to feel as close to her as possible. Touching her. Tethering that connection with her that formed his foundation. She was his sanctuary in the tempest of his life, the one single calm moment in the chaos. With his position as Ewan's man-at-arms, the conflict with the English, and now the return of the disturbance that was Ellen, Gavin needed Jenny and her calming force.

"I just fret that until we wed, she will be like this, trying to cajole ye, force herself upon ye," Jenny admitted. "I know ye to be the noblest of men, but even rock wears down against the water of the sea. I dinna know if I can stand by and watch that happen until then."

Jenny dropped her eyes, and that one gesture tore Gavin's pulsating heart from his chest. Had he been the one who was selfish? He had convinced himself that he was waiting for her, thinking he was accommodating her wedding desires, her schedule, her time.

But 'twas a lie. She had postponed their nuptials over and over, when Meg was ill, when Meg struggled to recover, when life in the clan overwhelmed her. So many in the keep took demands on her time, and Jenny gave over to all of them, to her own detriment. She sacrificed herself time and time again. Had he been *too* eager to delay their wedding?

Another much more dreadful thought came to Gavin on the heels of that one. Had her protestations and delays been a sign of something else? Had her heart turned against him? Did she still want to marry Gavin?

Placing a tender finger under her chin, he lifted her face to his. Her eyes, while speaking of a deep sadness that reached her core, were yet dry. Gavin took the lack of tears as a good sign, but he had to know for certain.

"Jenny, lassie, *mo ghràdh,* do ye still want to wed me? Or has your heart changed after all that has happened?"

Her bright eyebrows flew upward to her hairline. Lifting his hand that was still clasping hers, she moved it to her lips and kissed his fingertips.

"Gavin, nay! I'm not a vapid woman whose emotions are as fickle as the weather in the fall! I'm steadfast and true, just as I know ye to be. I love ye, *mo leannan,* more than I did the day I met ye. More than the day I sat with ye after your falling out with Ellen. More than I did the day ye declared your love. More than I did yesterday. And I look forward to each new day, knowing that I will love ye more on the morrow. The day I wed ye will be the happiest day of my life, until the day after, as I will love ye even more."

Rising in a flash of plaid, Gavin moved to Jenny's side of the table, clutching her against his chest. He pressed his lips against her surprised ones, his kiss both gentle and eager. As always, when he touched her, his good sense flew from his head, and he lost himself in her depths. Jenny was everything, and he couldn't get enough of her, never enough of her.

He thrust her away, otherwise he feared he'd take the kiss too far. His eyes blazed as he regarded her.

"Then wed me today, now. We've waited so long. *Too* long. Let us not waste any more time. 'Tis only ye and me. And I want ye for my wife. I will wait no longer."

The intensity behind his voice was forceful and shocking, even to himself. He expected Jenny to shy away, question him and his motives. Instead, she moved closer, her body thrust tight against his, clinging to him as though her life was already joined to his.

And truthfully, it was. Their lives had been entwined since the day he'd returned from his wasted trip to find out why Ellen had left him heartbroken, and not a day passed when his first and last thoughts weren't of Jenny.

"Today?" Her eyes were as wide as the sky. "Ye want to wed today?"

"I shall retrieve Father MacBain. The skies are clear, the mists thin, and the steps of the kirk are just as ready for a wedding as they will be any day."

The slow smile that brightened Jenny's face was worth every moment of that miserable night. She placed his hand on her heart.

"But what of the food for a wedding feast? Or visitors? Or —"

"All I need is ye and the priest under the sight of God. Food and visitors be damned."

Jenny paused for two breaths before jumping at Gavin's broad chest, wrapping her slender arms around his neck. He caught her lithe form in a giddy embrace.

"Let me find Meg," she told him. "She must be there. Ye gather Ewan and the priest, and I will meet you on those steps."

"Midday, when the sun is at its brightest. 'Twill have to be, for even the mighty sun pales when ye are by my side."

She tipped her head at Gavin's wooing words, her long locks cascading over her shoulder.

"Ye must vow to keep up such sweet speech after we are wed."

"Always. Every day. Until my last breath."

Jenny giggled as she spun away, holding onto Gavin's hand until the last moment before racing out of the kitchens.

Taking a deep breath, Gavin followed.

'Twas time to get married.

***

Jenny was oft surprised when Gavin's emotions spilled forth. He was not the sort to wear such emotion on his sleeve where everyone could see it. He was a rough man, a man who rarely smiled, who stood by his laird's side amid the best and worst that life had to offer. The rigid lines of his face were usually tight and frightening. And while he might joke or laugh with the men, or Jenny on occasion, his hard edge was his usual expression.

That is what made his dimples so special to Jenny — he showed them to no one. She alone was the recipient of his joy, and thus his dimples.

She walked to the narrow stairwell, then when she was out of Gavin's sights, she lifted her brown woolen skirts and ran as fast as her worn leather shoes would take her.

When Jenny reached the second level of the keep, she raced for the wide wooden door at the end of the hallway.

"Meg! Meggie! I'm sorry if I wake the bairn, but I have news!" Jenny pounded her fist against the door and stumbled inside when Meg yanked the door open.

"Jenny! What is it? Is something amiss?"

She swept tiny Meg in her arms and danced her around the room. Truly, 'twas the lightest, the happiest Jenny had felt in a long, long time. Meg's hard birthing, her illness, Ellen's untimely arrival, all of it weighed on Jenny's slender shoulders in a heavy yoke.

Today, though, she threw off that mantle of responsibility and unease, and her pure, buoyant joy was infectious. Meg's jubilant smile matched her friend's.

"Today I wed! Gavin and I shall wed! He is finding the priest as we speak!"

Meg's mouth fell open. "What? Gavin found ye and explained what happened? Such joy! And 'tis about time, if I have my say in it. Let me grab the babe and I'll start Fiona and the kitchen maids to work. Ye must have a feast, and I'm sure Fiona will have a solution."

Meg stepped back from the brilliantly happy Jenny, ignoring the squeaks of the disrupted babe in her cradle by the bed. Her discerning eye roved over Jenny — her loose hair, her everyday kirtle — and "tsked" her tongue.

"Ye knew?" Jenny asked as Meg looked her over with a keen eye.

"Aye. He came to our chambers yestereve distraught and with a scraped-up hand. Ewan and I told him to find ye right away."

Meg clicked her tongue and pursed her lips.

"Ye need a gown. At the verra least. The blue damask is no' finished and ye canna be wed in your kitchen gown! Alyce, your good mother, God rest her soul, would never forgive me."

Blushing at Meg's observation, Jenny spun around.

"I dinna have any finery. And my mother had none either. Where might I find a gown on such short notice?"

"Well, ye can no' wear one of mine. 'Twould be too short by half. Fiona might know where to find a gown. We must call on her resourcefulness now."

Meg lifted the fussy bairn from the cradle and, wrapping her in a linen against her breast, she settled wee Caitir. Hands free and spirit soaring, Meg grasped Jenny's arm and led her to the stairwell to search for Fiona.

***

Davey, Fiona's adopted son, sat at the center table Jenny had recently vacated. He was growing into a strapping young lad, probably as a result of his voracious appetite. Even now, the lad was eating a sour summer apple as he waited to break his fast.

"Davey, have ye seen your mam?" Meg queried as she swept into the kitchens with Jenny and the babe in tow. Davey pointed to the hearth.

"I'm here!" a voice called from the opposite side of the kitchens.

Fiona stood, her stout frame rising above the table that had blocked her from their view. Her gray-streaked auburn hair was pulled back in a loose, two-pronged plait that joined one larger queue hanging down her back. She brushed a tendril from her face and smiled at the women.

"What has ye so excited this day?" Fiona's smile joined those of Meg and Jenny's.

"Jenny is to be wed today!" Meg cheered, and Fiona clapped her hands with delight.

"Huzzah, Jenny! I'm so glad ye and Gavin spoke this morn! 'Tis time ye stand before the priest. Father MacBain will rejoice. He's been afeared of your moral standing for a while now, aye?" Fiona winked at Jenny, whose skin pinked like a rose from her hairline to her chest.

"We need your aid, Fi. We must make a feast, and fast, with whatever we have."

"Och, 'tis simple enough. The larder is well stocked from the start of the summer gardens. I'll set the kitchen maids to work." The kitchens were efficiently run under Fiona's capable hands.

"Call on Bonnie. And Mairi, too. The lass will be more than willing to assist at the keep."

"Och, I'm sure of that," Jenny commented.

Poor Mairi and her quest of Hamish, 'twas no secret. The women giggled.

"But we need ye for something more, Fi," Meg continued. "Gather the lasses to work in the kitchens, but we need a gown for

Jenny as well. We hadn't finished hers, and it lies in pieces in my solar. None of mine will work, as she is taller than I. Do ye know who might have a gown the lass can wear? We can't have her wed in her work kirtle!"

Fiona wrinkled her nose at Jenny's present state of dress. The middy shift under a plain, tree-bark colored kirtle were perfectly serviceable, but not fashionable at all. Especially not for a wedding. And if the MacLeod women believed one thing, 'twas that no lass should be wed in her stained, everyday work clothes.

"Can ye give me a wee bit o'time? I have an idea. Meet me in your chambers in a quarter of an hour?"

Meg nodded and grabbed Jenny's hand again, dragging her back up the stairs as Fiona called out directions to the kitchen maids.

'Twas nothing like a long overdue wedding to make Meg and her household giddy.

***

Once they were in Meg's quarters, Meg commanded Jenny to wash at the water table while she fed the now-squealing Caitir. The babe had been content most of the morning while they had rushed around, and the wee bairn's meal was well deserved.

Undressed to her shift, Jenny used the cloth to wash her dried tears from the night before from her face, and the rest of yesterday's work from her body. Meg's water had rose petals floating in it, so the lingering scent on Jenny's fresh skin added to her sense of cleanliness, and made the day seem even more special. 'Twasn't her typical scents of heather, and the rich aroma fit the tone of her wedding day. She inhaled the heady scent with a deep breath to calm her jumping stomach.

My wedding day! Those words kept repeating in her head in a distracting chant, and Jenny had to force herself to focus. And her grin never left her face during her entire bath, but on the heels of that, a worrisome thought struck her mind — there was no rain for her wedding day. Rain was considered good luck, rather 'twas warm and bright. Would she and Gavin yet be happy?

After Caitir was satiated, Meg set her on a fur by their feet so the babe could gurgle and grab her fat toes as Meg set to work. Meg's cat, the black tabby she called Fate, curled up on the fur just out of reach of the babe's grabbing hands.

Then Meg turned to Jenny with a gleam in her green eyes. She was a woman with a singular focus — to give Jenny the best wedding possible.

On a stool near the barren hearth, Jenny sat patiently as Meg brushed out her lustrous blonde locks. Her deft fingers threaded through the tendrils and plaited several braids before wrapping the largest plait around the crown of Jenny's head. Then she wrapped the braids at the back of her head, until Jenny's hair was an intricate golden coronet.

And because Meg couldn't resist, she wove ribbons into the fair locks as she braided, until Jenny's hair rivaled the jeweled crown of any monarch.

Fiona burst through the door, breathless. She held a deep green gown aloft, with a saffron yellow plaid thrown over her shoulder, and her hand clutched against her breast.

"I had luck, lassie! I had Edith help me, and with her, I found ye a gown, a fresh plaid, and look!"

She held out the hand she had clutched against her breast to reveal a golden pendant necklace, set with Scots freshwater pearls. Jenny reached out a tentative hand to the divine-looking piece.

"Who gifted this to me to wear this day? 'Tis too fine, I fear. What if I break it, or lose it?" Jenny's slender fingertip traced the pearls set into the dangling pendant.

"Och, lassie. Many women before ye wore this. 'Tis passed down with some of the MacLeod women. I dinna know who had it when our Meggie here was wed, but Elspeth had told me she'd seen it with young Mary, and I retrieved it from her months ago. 'Tis been sitting in a box in my chambers since!"

"Oh, Fiona. Surely 'tis too fine for me," Jenny protested. Fiona patted her shaking hand.

"Shush, lassie. As long as ye return it so I can gift it to the next MacLeod bride, then I am overjoyed to share this with ye."

A dizzying flush of warmth filled Jenny, who was unable to draw her gaze from the generous gifts of her clan, all to ensure her wedding to Gavin was as perfect as any wedding day should be. Fiona The stout woman glowed as much as Meg and Jenny. She handed the wedding finery to Meg and rushed toward the door.

"The wedding cakes will no' bake themselves. The poor lassies in the kitchens are racing to make as much as they can. I will be present for your nuptials, my Jenny, but then I must race back to the kitchens if we are to make ye a feast."

"Wait!" Jenny called out. "Have ye seen Gavin? Is he almost ready?"

"Ooch. I'm sure he is. When ye are finished dressing, have Meg come to the kitchens and one of us will see if Gavin is at the kirk." Fiona's exuberant face softened into a gentle smile. "Dinna fret lassie. Gavin will be on the steps with the priest soon enough."

Then she was gone from the room. Meg spun to Jenny, giving her shift a once over.

"Your shift will suffice. Let's get this gown on ye. I canna wait to see ye in it. Ye will rival any queen of Scotland!"

They swept the rich gown over Jenny's head, keeping the neckline wide so as not to disrupt her coiffure, then they tugged and adjusted so the fitted bodice and draping skirt showed off her shape perfectly. The sleeves, tight at the arm, flared at her wrists, and her old leather shoes barely peeped from beneath the hem. If Jenny didn't look like a princess, she certainly felt like one.

Meg's cool fingers slipped around Jenny's neck, fastening the pearl pendant so the heavy piece hung with the bottom of the jewel brushing her décolletage. Then Meg swept the plaid from the bed and draped it over Jenny's shoulder, fastening it with a brooch of her own. The subtle yellow and black contrasted against the dark green, and flattered Jenny's coloring as though the costume had been created just for her. Meg gasped at the picture Jenny presented.

"Gavin will no' be able to control himself. Never has there been a more beautiful bride."

Jenny wanted to contradict her, tell Meg that *she* had been the most beautiful bride, but Jenny's words fled her. Standing in Meg's chambers, wearing her borrowed wedding finery, she was astounded that the moment was real, that she was a bride waiting to wed her handsome groom.

"I'm off to tell Fiona 'tis time. Wait here until one of us retrieves ye."

Meg gathered up baby Caitir, re-wrapped the babe against her breast and swung to the door, then paused, glancing back at Jenny.

"Your mother would be so proud to see ye right now. I'm sure she's up in Heaven, smiling down on ye."

Jenny glowed at those words. Then, like Fiona, she was gone in a flash.

And Jenny was alone.

For the last time.

Chapter Ten: Then Two Become One

"ARE YE SURE, EWAN? Does this look right? I've no' been marrit before!"

Ewan couldn't help but smile at his oldest friend's discomfiture. 'Twas the highlight of Ewan's day, especially after Gavin had been so rough on Ewan when he had wed Meggie the year before. Turnabout was fair play, at least in Ewan's estimation. He grinned at his man-at-arms.

"Aye, man! Ye are getting married, no' jumping off a cliff!"

"'Tis no' the same thing?" Gavin squawked in his irrational tone, tugging at his tunic again. His hands shook as he moved. *Why was the neck so tight on this tunic?*

"Ye have wedding jitters, 'tis all. After all this time, and now 'tis here. Ye are hopeless."

Ewan reached over and adjusted the shoulders of the freshly laundered tunic so it lay across Gavin's width neatly, and stopped choking the nervous groom. Gavin may have been brawnier than Ewan, his neck and shoulders thicker, but the laird had a few inches on him, and he used it now to grab Gavin's arm and stare into his tight, panicked face.

"Ye could be naked, standing before the priest in naught but what God gave when you were born, and be painted in blue woad, and Jenny would still stand next to ye and wed ye. Christ alone knows why. I've never seen two people more enthralled, more focused on each other than ye two are. She loves ye, Gav! No' the clothes ye wear."

Gavin dipped his head as he blushed, his tawny hair falling into his eyes. Had any man ever been as fortunate in a friend as he had with Ewan? The son of the chieftain and the son of a poor crofter . . . A friendship that never should have blossomed, yet here they were, a little over a score of years in age, standing with each other at their respective weddings.

Gavin wrapped his thick arms around his friend and laird, crushing him in a bear-like embrace. Ewan slung his arm around Gavin's head. But for their opposing looks, one might assume them to be brothers.

"Come, ye softie," Ewan told him. "Brush back your hair and let's get ye to the kirk steps. Ye dinna want to be late for your own wedding. Meggie would have my head on a plate."

Ewan opened the door to Gavin's chambers and led the bridegroom from the keep, across the yard to the church that sat between the bailey and the village.

Gavin squinted as he walked, a nervous smile tugging at his cheek. Warmer weather, pale sunlight, dry ground — 'twas as if the earth welcomed their wedding day. Nature dressed in her most brilliant greens, yellows, and purples to celebrate.

Several clansmen and women had started to gather outside the church, including his elderly parents and his brothers. His mother and father had struggled to bear children, with Gavin as the oldest coming late in their lives, then two more boys spaced out by years. Those years had worn his parents down, and they were aging more quickly than Gavin was prepared for. Another twinge of gratefulness pulsed through him as he was thankful his parents lived long enough to see him wed. He flicked his eyes to his younger brothers as he greeted them — they might not be as fortunate on their wedding days. Amid his wedding plans and nerves, Gavin made a mental note to discuss his brothers' future with Ewan.

Then he was rushed past his family by Ewan and the priest and escorted up the steps. Father MacBain beamed as he whisked Gavin to the church door, nearly tripping over his robes.

"Ooch, Gavin lad. God smiles on ye this day, he does! We've been waiting for this day, that ye might save your everlasting soul and wed the lassie before ye committed a grave sin!"

Ewan leaned across Gavin as they were walked. "Ooch, a bit late for that, Father. If no' with Jenny, but I can give ye a list of his less grievous sins!"

Gavin punched Ewan, who cackled with the priest at Gavin's expense. It was his wedding day — he was anxious enough! He didn't need the added mockery of his laird and priest on top of it all.

They settled him on the top step, and from this vantage he could see all the way to the keep. The joyful faces of his kin below shone in the sunlight. Meg appeared, the baby wrapped against her, and she gave Ewan a light wave. Only Fiona was missing, probably readying Jenny for their walk to the church. For a sudden wedding, the number of those gathered in attendance was staggering to Gavin. They formed a welcome line from the keep to the church. How had they found out so quickly? Come in from their chores?

He didn't need an answer. The smug look on Ewan's face told him all. The laird and his wife could work miracles when necessary.

And they waited. The sun's heat pounded on Gavin's head and neck, and the crown of his combed back hair became warm and dampened into deep waves. Was it just the sun? Nerves as well? His hands yet trembled even as he tucked them into the folds of his brown and yellow kilt. Drops of sweat tickled his back as he stood on the stone steps. And they waited longer. Fiona had told them Jenny was ready and for Gavin to mount the steps, so where were they?

Meg must have noticed as well, for she pushed her way back through the line of well-wishers.

Where was Jenny?

***

Jenny glided down the narrow steps to the main hall. The fluttering in her chest spread to her whole body, so even her toes shook as she walked toward the main door. She'd expected someone to meet her here — Meg, or Fiona? Mairi or Bonnie? Shouldn't she have an escort to the church? She had waited, but when no one arrived, she made up her mind to go on her own.

A shadow appeared in the main doorway, and Jenny shivered with excitement. *'Twas time!* She was prepared to walk the short distance and join Gavin at the steps of the church.

The figure entered the hall and cleared the shadows of the door, and Jenny's heart lurched. 'Twasn't Meg or Fiona.

Instead, Ellen stood before her. Jenny flicked her eyes around the chamber to see if anyone else was nearby. She hadn't spoken to Ellen since she'd seen the woman with Gavin the night before and had hoped not to see her until she was soundly wed to Gavin. *Why was Ellen here now? Was she going to watch the wedding?*

"Ooch, don't ye look fine on your special day." Ellen's words were sweet, syrupy sweet. And coupled with the vexed look in her eyes, rang false in Jenny's ears.

"Thank ye, Ellen. I'm on my way now to go to the kirk, so I must —" Jenny tried to walk past Ellen, but the woman stepped to the side, blocking her exit and brushing Jenny with her breasts. She was so close, and Jenny's breath stuck in her throat. Despite her words, Ellen didn't appear happy for Jenny. Her tone, her pinched mouth — she wasn't congratulating Jenny. Nay, she was angry with the bride. Mocking her. Jenny stepped back, trying to slip around Ellen's other side.

The redhead only countered the movement.

"Ye think if ye wed the man, he's yours? What a fool ye be, lassie."

Ellen's tone bit fiercely enough to draw blood. Jenny's heart pounded in her chest. *Where was everyone?* "Men may wed, but they dinna resign themselves to one woman. Gavin's been mine since he gained his manhood. Who do ye think was his first? Who do ye think taught him what it was to lay with a woman? To love a woman? Ye should be thanking me." She paused, reaching a hand out to Jenny as she giggled.

"Please, Ellen. He's moved past ye. Ye left him to wed another. Let him just have his happiness. Let us have our happiness," Jenny pleaded with her.

"Och, ye are naught but a consolation, lassie. A frail lass whose innocence is more of an encumbrance than an enticement. He might wed ye, because he vowed to, but once he grows tired of your boring attempts, he will search me out. I am his prize, no matter what finery ye wear to convince anyone otherwise."

Ellen's reaching hand abruptly twisted, grabbing the beautiful pearl pendant, and yanked. Jenny flung forward at the painful thrust against her neck, and she screeched as the pendant snapped off the chain.

"What are ye doing? 'Tis no' mine! 'Tis borrowed for my wedding!" Jenny cried, clutching at Ellen's hand to retrieve the pendant.

"Is there naught ye don't take from others? That gown, surely ye don't own anything so fine. This pendant? Even Gavin? Ye have a habit of taking what does no' belong to ye."

"Jenny? Is that ye? I was getting flowers for ye!" Fiona's voice echoed from the kitchen doorway.

Ellen glared at Jenny, then threw the pendant on the stone floor and stormed out the way she had come. The tempest was gone, but the destruction was left behind.

Jenny stooped to retrieve the pendant as Fiona entered, arranging a cluster of summer heather and grasses. She raced to where Jenny crouched with tears streaming down her cheeks and her stomach clenched in a tight, painful ball. The jewelry was ruined.

"Jenny, lass! What happened?"

"I'm so sorry, Fiona. 'Twas no' my fault, but I will have it repaired, I vow." She held up the pendant as she spoke in her wavering voice. The pendant's thin chain still dangled around her neck.

Fiona's face tightened, then in a flash, her soft features returned. She cupped Jenny's cheek in a plump hand, wiping at her tears with her thumb.

"Nay, lassie. 'Tis naught. Ye think this jewel has no' been repaired in the past? Ooch! The smith is well acquainted with me! Come now."

Fiona grasped her elbow to help Jenny rise. Using her sleeve, Fiona wiped at Jenny's face, trying to erase any trace of her tears. Jenny wanted to feel grateful, but all she felt was guilt-ridden in the broken heirloom. She clutched it with desperation, as though she might lose the pearled pendant itself.

"'Tis your wedding day. No tears. Only joy, aye? And we can fix this, I think." Fiona's eyes scanned Jenny, then lit with inspiration. "Aha!" She thrust the poesy of flowers into Jenny's open hand.

With delicate fingers, Fiona grasped one ribbon from Jenny's hair and tugged gently, extracting it from her woven plait. Then she threaded the green length of fabric through the pendant's link. She pulled the broken chain from Jenny's neck, and noting the mark left behind, rubbed it tenderly with her hand. Shivers coursed over Jenny's spine at the light touch.

"What happened here, lassie? The chain didn't break on its own?" Fiona tied the ribbon behind Jenny's neck, and it hung just as beautifully at the swell of her breasts. Toying with the newly replaced necklace, Jenny marveled at Fiona's quick thinking.

"'Tis like it never happened. Now, how did ye get that mark on your neck, lass?"

Jenny's fretful blue eyes studied Fiona. How much should she tell? Would she look jealous or spiteful if she pointed her finger at Ellen? Was it a bigger sin to lie, or to be a gossip-monger? Jenny pursed her lips. She now knew Ellen's true intentions, and they were not friendly. 'Twould be easy to point a finger. And being a gossip-monger was not a sin, merely a character flaw.

"I came here looking for Meg or ye, to walk to the kirk," Jenny started, her voice trembling more than she cared for. "And then Ellen entered."

"Och, for the sake of Mary and Joseph!" Fiona erupted. A dark glare shadowed her warm, open face. "We welcomed her here, ye befriended her, and she does this to ye?"

Jenny nodded, picking at the pale flowers she held. "I fear she is still smitten with Gavin. She said . . . She said . . ."

Tears threatened to fall again at the memory of Ellen's hateful speech. Fiona patted her hand, trying to soothe her.

"Dinna think on it, lass. 'Tis ended, and women like Ellen will get their comeuppance. Ye wait and see. Ye are the one who is to wed our fair Gavin. Now, I believe yon handsome man awaits ye before the priest?"

Jenny inhaled deeply, cleansing her congested chest and clearing her mind. Fiona's words were sound. 'Twas her wedding day. *She* was the one marrying Gavin and spending the rest of her life with him. The idea of Gavin as her husband-to-be — that was what was essential to focus on. The thought of Gavin worked its charm and did what it always did. A smile appeared on Jenny's refined features, wiping away her sadness even amid the chaos.

Fiona grasped Jenny's arm again and escorted the stricken lass from the hall and toward her future with Gavin.

***

Meg stood at the other side of the double door, as brilliant as the sunrise, smiling at Jenny. Her clan and kin formed a set of two lines, with a dirt corridor down the middle that led directly to the step of the church. As Meg and Fiona followed her, the crowd chanted "huzzah" as she walked past.

'Twas like a dream, an impossible fevered dream, and she beamed. Only nobility, princesses, and in fairy stories she'd been told at her mother's knee did lasses have a wedding such as this.

And at the end of that line of cheering MacLeods and their kin and allies was Gavin, standing as steady as an oak in his golden kilt. Her attention was so intent on the man perched on the church steps, she almost missed nodding to Gavin's parents and siblings who stood near the base of the church. They smiled widely in return, and Jenny raised her face to the top of the stairs.

The man who was destined become her husband reached a sturdy hand to her, and she lifted her skirts with her other hand as she grasped his. Gavin practically hauled her to top where she stood with him and Father MacBain, their faces shining in the misty sunlight.

She took one last glimpse around at the shocking number of people in the church yard, at the beaming faces of Meg and Ewan standing a few steps below, and finally landed her eyes on the MacLeod warrior who held her hand.

Everything about Gavin was golden and beautiful and perfect. His nervous smile matched hers, and his dimples played peek-a-boo in his twitching cheeks.

He inhaled deeply as his eyes studied her in that intense way he had about him.

"Are ye ready, lass?" he asked in a whisper. Jenny nodded lightly.

"Aye. More than ready."

Gavin's grin grew steady at her answer, and he turned with her to face the priest. Father MacBain took a solemn moment, then raised his face to the sky to begin their wedding ceremony.

The priest's words were a blur to Jenny. Did she answer appropriately? Did she say *I do*? All she could see was Gavin's boyishly handsome face, which was as tight and nervous as she felt. The moment passed as if a dream — they had waited so long for this wedding, now that the event was upon them, it didn't seem real.

Until the priest slid the dirk across her palm, scoring her skin and pressing her palm to Gavin's in a burning clasp of hands. Father MacBain offered up the blessings to God as he knotted their hands in a strip of MacLeod plaid. Then Gavin knelt on one knee, swearing the blood of his blood and bone of his bone. Words Jenny knew meant more to him than they might the common man. Gavin was a man who honored his vows seriously.

Gavin rose in a rush, and Father MacBain declared them man and wife. Before Jenny could blink, Gavin was crushing her against him, his lips capturing hers as ardently as he dared in front of the entire clan, their kin, his family. Without thinking, Jenny kissed him back.

The entire time, her brain wrestled with the idea that 'twas complete, official. She was Gavin's wife, *Gavin's wife*, and no man could put that asunder.

Nor any woman.

Then Gavin pulled back, his dimples creasing his face with pure joy.

Man and wife.

The witnesses below cheered and cheered, and Jenny blinked back tears.

Here in this moment, in a borrowed dress and her hand bound to the man who had bound his life to hers, everything was perfect.

***

Ewan joked throughout the early evening, sending up yet another cheer to Gavin and Jenny, encouraging Gavin to wait, to tell Jenny to eat more and celebrate longer. Anything he could to halt Gavin from leaving with Jenny and finally, *finally* consummating their marriage — a duty Gavin had been anticipating for far too long.

At first, Gavin participated in Ewan's joviality — leaving too soon would be rude, of course. Fiona and the kitchen maids had pulled off a veritable miracle with the spread of meats and fruit and cakes. But by the time Ewan gave his fifth or sixth reason to stay behind, Gavin caught on. Always the jester, Ewan was.

With a broad grin and a piercing need that overpowered everything else, including his dedication to his laird, Gavin grasped Jenny's hand and lifted her in his arms.

He didn't even say goodbye. With a wink to Meg and Ewan, Gavin plastered kisses over Jenny's cheeks and forehead as he raced to the stairwell. Her giggles mixed with the laughter and bawdy comments of the hall as they departed.

Gavin carried her into the chambers then set her on his bedding and stepped away. They both still laughed like children and required a moment to collect themselves. Jenny flopped back on the bed, panting.

"I have to apologize on behalf of Ewan," Gavin said as he caught his breath. "He's always been like that with me. Now, it appears, he is like that with ye."

Jenny sat back up, inhaling a deep breath to calm her laughter. Gavin's eyes dropped to the swells of her breasts that heaved against the neckline of her deep green gown. So enticing . . . Gavin's laughter fell away as a wave of heady lust flared in his groin and washed over him. Sitting there in her gown, gold and green and bright, Jenny was everything fetching and ravishing all at once. Gavin feared he might lack the power to control himself.

They had waited so long, and that alone was enough to drive his need to impossible heights.

And to have the object of his desire right there, on his bed.

And to have that object of desire be his wife . . . It was almost too much.

Though his body vibrated with a longing to toss up her skirts and take her with wild abandon, Gavin reminded himself that she was yet a maid, untested. While they had gone far as they huddled in the shadows, their passionate kisses leading to depraved touching and caressing, she was still a maid.

Gavin drew in a deep breath, trying to cool his ardor. No wild abandon this night. *That shall wait until next time*, he vowed as he fought to curb that raging animal. Tonight, he would be as tender and as gentle as she needed him to be.

He slipped his plaid off his shoulder and let it fall where it gathered around his waist. His tunic held the heat of the day and of his body when he knelt before Jenny, taking her hands. His large, warm hands swallowed up her slender fingers, and he bowed his head to her breast, as if in prayer.

"I will do my best to treat ye as ye should be treated, to honor ye and your body, this night and every night for the rest of my life. I will respect and love ye in every way, with my words, with my deeds, to the depth of my heart. All I am lives for ye and ye alone."

Jenny untangled her hands from Gavin's, cupped his chin, and placed a gentle kiss lighter than a butterfly's wing on his smooth brow.

"Ye have honored me since ye have met me, Gavin. I trust ye to no' stop now," she whispered into his hair.

His arms snaked around her waist, and she spread her legs under her skirts so he might wiggle closer, enveloping Jenny with his heat.

His face came right to her décolletage, where the rich scent of her heather perfume exuded from her gown, from her skin, from between her breasts. That scent, one he had come to know so intimately from that first night he returned to Lochnora years ago, whirled around in his head, surrounding him in a veil of heady temptation. That raging animal inside him surged, commanded to life by her scent, and he tamped it down as best he could.

His cock, however, would not be tamed so easily and throbbed under his kilt.

Jenny, sensing the frenzied need inside him, reached her hands to his back, tugging his tunic from the plaid and over his head in one swift move. Gavin stilled as Jenny continued to stroke her hands, first over the muscled, broad planes of his back, then tickling around to his chest, and his skin dimpled under her touch. The palm of her hand cupped the defined planes of his chest, threading through the light sprawl of chest hair that matched the rich tresses on his head — downy, golden brown. He shivered under the riveting touch of her fingertips, and hot blood hammered in his temples.

Jenny explored more, going farther than they'd had in any shadowy corner of the hall, her boldness making a furious ache exploded in his skull and in his groin. Her caress was a command he could not deny. Her fingertips dipped below his belted waistline, and he groaned — a deep growl that drew a side smile from Jenny.

"Like this?" she questioned as one bright eyebrow arched at him.

Gavin couldn't speak. Instead, he growled and gripped the neckline of her gown until his knuckles whitened. With his other hand, he pulled one ribbon-like lace to untie the bow and loosen her gown. Then he yanked with a light hand. Pressing his mouth to her shoulder, he kissed, licked, and sucked at her skin, and she gasped at his brazen touch.

Withdrawing her hand from his kilt, she twined her fingers in the laces, undoing them, then rolled her shoulders so the gown fell to her waist. Just her thin, nearly translucent kirtle separated them, and Gavin didn't hesitate. He wrenched the kirtle so the garment joined her gown in a pool around her hips.

"Just like this," he groaned in appreciation before shifting his lips to her breast, encircling her pale pinkish nipple in a gentle grip.

She gasped again at the intimacy of his lips on her skin. He lifted his head, his throat tight. Was he moving too fast?

Jenny's hand gripped the back of his head and pressed it to her breast.

"Dinna stop," she told him.

Gavin obeyed with a rush of heated desire alighting him like a lightning storm, and his lips moved from one nipple to her other.

He pressed her back onto the bedding, then rose to his feet, standing bare-chested before her. She must become comfortable with his body, he knew, and though she'd explored much of his skin from the waist up, he'd never been fully naked before her. His hope was she would welcome his body as much as she'd embraced him thus far.

Without another thought, he unwrapped the plaid from his narrowed, chiseled waist where it landed in a woolen pile at his feet, and he stepped on his boot heels to remove those as well. Jenny propped herself up on her elbows and tilted her head to one side as her eyes roved over his body. From his head, over his chest, to his turgid manhood that thrust forward with urgency — a sword searching for its sheath. Jenny's sheath.

She reached for his throbbing cock, not with fear or trepidation, but with curious wide eyes. She stroked the taut, smooth skin up and over, and he shuddered.

"I will be gentle with ye, lass. This a vow."

"Oh, I hope so," Jenny answered with a nuance of coyness in her tone. "At least to start. But after that, I want ye to love me with everything ye have. Ye vowed all of ye, Gavin, and I would have that."

His cock nearly erupted at her words, and he stared as she lifted her hips to remove her gown and kirtle, kicking them to the floor to join his plaid. She lay on the bedding in her full golden glory, an impossible creature put on this earth for him and him alone.

Aye, he would be gentle, but how long could he master that? And what happened if he completely lost his mind, his control, once he was inside her? God save him, being gentle was going to be one of the hardest tasks he'd ever faced.

***

Jenny's heart fluttered in a mix of panic and excitement as she eyed Gavin, from his rich locks to his hard-ridged muscles to his thrusting manhood that she had felt trying to probe her from under his kilt but had never seen until this day.

Drinking in the full sight of him as her husband was a thrilling sensation, if a bit fearsome. Her life changed today, and now, in Gavin's bed, the culmination of that change was here. She'd shivered and removed her gown, shoving it and her kirtle down her body and off her legs.

Now she was laid bare, just as Gavin was, skin calling to skin.

Gavin moved with a slight shift of his arm, trailing his finger over her breast, over her belly and to her woman's mound that was strangely buzzing and throbbing. Then his finger found a spot between her legs, and she mewled as the buzzing and throbbing coursed over her body in waves, tingling all the way to her fingers and toes. She wiggled, and the sensation burrowed deeper.

His lips replaced his fingers, licking and kissing a burning trail back up to her neck. Gavin joined her on the bed, supporting his weight with his elbows and settling his legs between hers in the most intimate touch she'd ever had. Unable to land on any one thought, her mind swirled — at his touch, at the excitement he elicited from her, at the sheer newness of it all.

Gavin's forehead pressed to hers, and his breath, like his body, was hot on her face. He cupped her cheek gently with one hand.

"I need ye, Jenny," he whispered, his voice but a wisp on the air. "More than the air I breathe. I canna live without ye. Are ye ready for me?"

She nodded, unsure of what exactly to be ready for. Her body seemed to have a mind of its own.

"And ye can tell me to stop at any time. I vow to ye, I will do what ye ask."

The urgent strain in his voice told her that she would be asking for the impossible if she did such a thing. And he was her husband — she loved him, craved his touch, wanted to belong to him in every way. So she repeated herself.

"Dinna stop," she commanded again.

And Gavin obeyed once more, driving forward until his cock entered her, and she stiffened in shock, pain, and a nuance of fervent pleasure. Jenny gasped sharply at the sensation of being one with Gavin, of being filled by him, and he paused. His concerned eyes flashed.

"Jenny?" he rasped.

She didn't answer but twined her arms around his back to draw him closer, and he continued his movements, thrusting in and out of her in a steady cadence that wore away the dull ache and heightened that sense of intimate bliss until she was panting as loudly as he. The world rolled beneath them, as though the universe was water and they battled the waves, riding higher and higher together. Her back arched as she rose to meet his movements. The more they rode with each other, the harder and faster the waves crashed upon them.

Gavin squinted at her, his eyes narrow and intense as the pace of his body changed. He kissed her, slashing at her tongue with his own as his thrusts grew frenzied. Then he lifted his head and with a furious roar, like a beast unleashed, he stiffened between her thighs, holding himself tight before every muscle in his body slackened and he dropped to her breasts in a hot, sweaty mess. The waves calmed, and their union became still, like a placid loch of the early morn.

Jenny wiped her stringy hair from her face and focused on the heaving man lying bonelessly atop her. They were united, man and wife, one body and one flesh. *This is what 'twas to be one with a husband,* she thought. No wonder 'twas a sacrament of marriage — the power shared between them rivaled the power of God.

The priest had been right. What she shared with Gavin, no one could put asunder.

They were one in every way.

***

After a time, Gavin grumbled into Jenny's chest, enjoying the tingling of Jenny's fingertips playing in his hair. He must rise, pull his hulk to the side, and ensure Jenny was well. Yet, in this moment with her body beneath him, the bewitching feel of her fingertips on his scalp, and the steady thumping of her heartbeat in his ear, it would take a miracle to get him to move.

She wiggled beneath him, and Gavin rolled to his side. Jenny had held his weight for far too long. His hands remained on her skin, wrapping her in his strong embrace. The warm night air did nothing to cool his skin, and they were sticky with their remnants of their loving.

"Ye are well?" Gavin asked in a hesitant voice. "It did no' hurt ye overmuch?"

She shook her head against his arm.

"Nay, no' overmuch. Ye were as gentle as ye needed to be."

Gavin nuzzled his face into her hair, inhaling her scent now tempered with perspiration and the lingering scent of their coupling.

"We waited so long, I feared I might have rushed ye. My control left much to be desired."

Her back vibrated against him. *Was she laughing?*

"Ooch, my love," she told him. "Ye are oft the paragon of control. 'Tis good for ye to lose it every once in a while. And even better to lose it in passion with me."

"Weel, ye didn't help me with that control, urging me on with your full breasts, enticing scent, and your words 'Dinna stop.' What man could have any control?"

"Then ye fared well," Jenny assured him in a breathless tone, patting his arm. She paused for several heartbeats before speaking again. "My full breasts? They urged ye on?"

Gavin chuckled with her. "Aye, that and your scent. They work together, ye know?"

Jenny giggled with her husband as they slipped into the nether of the night.

***

They had slept entwined with each other, and when she awoke, her hair was wrapped around Gavin's arms, as if even her tresses feared being separated from him. She blinked into the dim sunlight that peeked into the room, bathing them in a gold light that made the two of them shine.

His face was even more boyish in the early morn, with his eyes closed and his face slack. No dimples, but this relaxed, with no worries nor hard edges, he could be a lad sleeping in a trundle bed. Jenny traced the lines of his face, his soft cheeks, his long nose, the golden-brown edge of his hairline.

"Ye make it hard for a man to sleep in, wife," Gavin's scratchy morning voice announced. His eyes, though, remained closed against the daylight.

"Ye dinna want to sleep the day away, do ye, husband?"

He moved suddenly, kissing her lips and plopping back onto the bedding. "So long as ye are here, I will remain in bed all the day."

"Ooch, then the rumors will fly that I turned ye into a layabout."

"Or that I turned ye into one. Ye are up with the birds, *mo leannan*."

"Someone needs to prepare the meal to break your fast."

Gavin peeled open his eyes. "Aye, and I am glad 'tis ye and no' me. I am no' the sort of man who likes to rise early."

Jenny bit at her bottom lip with a grin and slipped her fine-boned hand over Gavin's body under the coverlet.

"Your body would disagree."

Gavin growled at her and placed another kiss on her nose.

"Weel, 'tis good we are up. I am famished, and before I break my fast with ye, I have a bit o' news ye should be aware of."

Jenny withdrew her hand to her neck, and her sultry smile disappeared from her lips. *Och,* he worded that badly.

"Nay, my love. Nothing too dire, I assure ye."

Gavin grasped her hand from her neck and kissed her fingertips.

"Ewan's received a missive from our good King Robert the Bruce." Jenny's face tightened all the more. "The king has made strong inroads against the English this spring, surprisingly so. While several MacLeods are with him as we speak, 'tis a poor reckoning that the laird of the MacLeods and his right-hand man are no' there. Ewan is waiting on a response from the king as to when and where we should meet him."

The words clouded in a thick fog that clogged the air in the room, choking them into silence. Jenny didn't speak for several moments. Her teary eyes shifted to the ceiling beams.

"When?" Her voice was lost in that oppressive fog.

"I dinna know. We have to wait for a response from the king, then plan our journey, so we do have time. A bit of time. Ye are no' rid of me yet, wife."

A despondent smile tugged at his mouth, and his deep dimple danced in and out of his cheek. Jenny's entire visage calmed with her insides. She wasn't losing him yet. That was agreeable news. She cut him a sidelong look and dropped the coverlet from her breasts.

"Then let's break your fast and make better use of the time we have, aye?"

Gavin all but tackled her back into the blankets.

Chapter Eleven: All Manner of Suffering

"MAIRI! PSST! MAIRI!"

Mairi tucked a rogue lock of sunset-hued hair behind her ear and peeked around the edge of the keep near the gardens. Hamish stood in the shadows cast by the setting sun, fidgeting in a nervous habit. Mairi frowned at him.

"Truly? Psst? What is wrong with ye, laddie?"

"Dinna call me *laddie*, please, Mairi. I just needed your attention, without Aren lingering about." A shadow not cast by the dusk crossed Hamish's face, giving his tender features a harsh edge, and made him look so much more like his oldest brother, Ewan.

Mairi relaxed her pursed lips at his confession. The poor lad had competed for her attention so fiercely the past few months, and at every turn, the blond Aren had foiled his attempts. In stark contrast, Hamish's devilishly black locks and ice-chipped eyes more gray than blue reminded her of a villain in folklore. Yet here he was, trying to find a quiet moment of privacy with her, and he appeared more a fae creature than a devil as he dug the toe of his boot into the dirt.

"Weel, here I am, and Aren is no' about. What do ye fancy from me?"

A flare of intense heat flushed Hamish's bare cheeks, and Mairi twisted her lips at the suggestive implication of her question. She shifted her bucket to her other arm and flattened her gaze at Hamish.

"Ooch, please. Let me take that," Hamish offered.

He reached for the bucket, easily plucking it from her grasp, and 'twas only then she realized how brawny he was. As the youngest brother, he had long seemed smaller and leaner than his brothers. The little brother amongst dark giants.

Now that he was entering full manhood, his girth had increased, and while he might not be as tall as Ewan (*truly, who could be?* Mairi thought), he could very well be just as broad, just as muscular as his brother. His skin brushed against hers as he pulled the bucket back to his chest, and an unexpected shiver rippled over her skin like water in a loch. *What was that about?*

"Thank ye," she told him in a soft voice, nervous and awkward around this fine specimen of a man she had dismissed as nothing more than a young admirer.

But Hamish was no lad, as he had pointed out. He was a man, a powerful and fine-looking one at that.

"Ye are verra welcome. I would assist ye whenever ye permit."

Mairi dipped her face so Hamish didn't see it flame with a deep blush. He was still standing so close to her, closer than 'twas appropriate for a young man and a lass. Still, she didn't step back.

"Ye had a desire to speak with me?" Mairi reminded him.

Hamish stood taller, tugged on his plaid, and cleared his throat. "Aye. I know that ye are mayhap in a difficult place, a lass in the keep, sister-by-law to the laird, and with many eager men competing for your affections."

Mairi flicked her veiled gaze to Hamish as she kept her head bowed. What courage it took to speak one's heart so plainly. And Aren had spoken to her in front of others, coarsely and of his own prowess, where he might appear the winner in a game of which she was the prize. To have a man speak with no hope of showing off before others? It made plain the truth of his genuine interest in her.

Was this how a man behaved when he had an honorable interest in a woman? Mairi didn't know — she was too inexperienced to understand the inner workings of men.

What she did know was his presence, his words, the way his gaze never drifted from her face, that had to be some indication of his earnest intentions.

"I would ask that ye consider me in those attentions. And know I am here for ye. If ye need assistance at the well?" He lifted the bucket as his case in point. "Ye can ask me. In truth, I shall make it my life's endeavor to know what ye need when ye need it."

This statement, though he wanted it to sound true-hearted and resolute, struck her as funny, and she chewed at the inside of her lip to hide the burgeoning smile that threatened to escape. She shouldn't laugh at how he lay open his heart. But she couldn't pass up a tease.

"What of the chamber pots? Will ye help me clean those?"

A slight grimace passed over Hamish's mouth. Though he recovered quickly, Mairi yet noticed it, and this time the bubble of giggles burst past her lips.

Hamish squared his shoulders at her laugh and raised one bushy eyebrow. Ahh, he recognized the tease.

"Aye. I will help ye in an instant. But I must warn ye, I can be awfully clumsy. I would hate to trip and spill any offal on ye. . ."

His lips split into a wry smile, and Mairi couldn't hold her laughter in any longer. She wheezed with giggles.

"And if I need to scrub grime from the kitchen hearth?" she ventured again.

Hamish leaned in impossibly closer. Mairi's chest fluttered. How did his presence manage to touch her with fire when a breath of space separated them?

"Och, I will race from the stables straight away, covered in manure, ready to assist ye. I will most likely track it into the kitchens . . ."

"Och, ew!" Mairi laughed at his taunt. "Fiona would have both our heads for certain!"

"If she promised to mount our heads together, then I would willingly expose my neck to her."

Hamish may have meant to keep the tone light, but the force of his words made her heart jump in her chest. She lost her smile as his eyes devoured her as a wolf consumes its prey, and before she could gather her thoughts, Hamish crossed the barrier of narrow space that separated them and captured her lips in a soft kiss that did little to hold back the urgent longing behind it. Hamish managed to control his urgency, keeping his lips light on hers, and despite her better judgment, Mairi found herself kissing him back.

Before she lost herself too much, Hamish snapped his head back. His icy eyes were glazed over, and his panting matched hers.

"My apologies, Mairi." His voice was gruff, contrite. "I overstepped."

Mairi gulped and acknowledged her complicity in the rogue kiss.

"I would have stopped ye if I hadn't wanted ye to kiss me," she told him.

His eyebrows flew to his hairline like black-winged birds. Mairi clipped the bucket from his loose, stupefied grip and sashayed off.

"Next time, dinna wait so long," she threw over her shoulder as she returned to the keep.

'Twas a tease, but the kiss from Hamish revealed deep emotion and was more earnest than Aren's pathetic attempt to kiss her, and in the hall no less. She might revel in the affections of the young men, but to force a public display of that affection, right in front of her older sister and the laird himself? That young man was a fool, without a doubt.

Mairi was a clever lass. She enjoyed the affections of men, but she would never lose her heart to a fool.

She touched her lips, the lingering sensation of Hamish's tender kiss still warm. The earnest younger brother of the laird, however . . .

That was a different story altogether.

A light smile toyed with Mairi's face as she replaced the bucket and returned to her duties in the kitchens.

***

Ever astute, Fiona squinted an eye at the blissful expression on Mairi's face, and while Fiona appreciated the look of young love, Mairi was the sister of her lady. If a young man was inappropriate with her, that information needed to be reported directly to Lady Meg.

Fiona set a tray with vittles, and with the excuse of bringing it to the lady's solar in case she missed the evening meal, brought it to Meg.

Jenny and Meg were both in the room, catering to Caitir and cleaning the babe's clothing and bedding.

"Fiona! How nice to find ye here. Why do ye bring a tray? Is the eve tide meal to be delayed?"

Fiona set the tray on Meg's small table by the hearth, then took up a tiny plaid and began folding the baby blanket. She was so grateful for the new babes in the clan. She had lost her own young son years ago, and then her husband soon after.

The arrival of wee Davey had helped fill an unimaginable void in her life, and the birth of Caitir less than a year later completed filling that void. The more babes in the clan, the more distracted Fiona found herself in the world of bairns that had been so untimely ripped from her. She saw these babes as a second chance, and new mothers were more than happy for her support.

She folded the plaid with deft hands and seized a second.

"I've come from the kitchens. Mairi is still there."

"Ooch, good. I'm glad she's found a place where she is of use. Unlike my mother, Mairi has no interest in midwifery. My mother and I are relieved she's assimilated well."

"Aye. Too well, mayhap. What with the interest of the young men, and the fisticuffs that occurred between Hamish and Aren."

Meg huffed and rolled her eyes. "Ewan's brother can be too much like Ewan was at that age, hot-headed and ready with his fists. He can hold his own, which is fortunate, for I've heard Aren can fight quiet well. And Ewan and Gavin put an end to the fight before it could get out o' hand."

Fiona nodded, setting the tiny red plaid aside.

"Aren is a brash, outlandish lad. I dinna think any clever lass worth her salt will fall for him until he learns to control those behaviors. Like any young lassie, Mairi likes the attention. The laird's brother, however, can be as roguish and endearing as the laird. And that's why I'm here. I dinna know for certain, but I'm a woman who's seen a thing or two. I think that lad holds a special place in her heart. When Mairi took the bucket to the gardens to dump it, she was gone longer than usual, and she had that smile on her face when she returned. Ye know what smile I speak of."

Meg and Jenny shared a knowing look. Of course, they knew *what smile*. They had each worn that smile as their love for their men blossomed.

And Meg had been prepared for it, seeing how the lads vied for Mairi's affections and resorted to fighting like stags in heat.

Yet, if she were kissing the lads in the garden shadows, that was something more. That merited a conference with Ewan, most likely followed by a conversation with poor Hamish. Meg and Jenny didn't envy Hamish in that conference with Ewan.

It also meant Meg and Elspeth must speak with Mairi and learn of her intentions. She was of age for a suitor, of age to wed, preferably before she found herself in a compromised position.

"Thank ye, Fiona, for this. Aye, if she is kissing lads in the corners of the keep, 'tis time to speak to them of their intentions and see if yet another wedding is in our future."

Fiona curtsied to Meg before leaving the solar. Jenny plucked a dried fruit from the platter and popped it into her mouth. The levity of this news, the sheer normalcy of it all, was welcome to the women.

"Mairi is a stunning young lassie, Meg. I warned ye she'd be trouble for the MacLeod lads!"

Meg joined her in laughing at Mairi's, and perchance Hamish's, youthful antics.

***

Ewan called for Gavin and Duncan to join him in the study. Expectation leapt like trout in the water at Ewan's demand. It could only mean that Ellen's father had responded with instructions to send her home.

That expectation shattered harder than church glass when Gavin entered and sat across from Ewan, who hung his head in his hands. Duncan was already seated when Gavin arrived, and from the sweaty, pasty expression on Duncan's face, something dire had transpired.

Ewan didn't raise his head when Gavin sat, and keeping the heels of his hands pressed against his eyes, he spoke to Duncan.

"Tell him," Ewan commanded in a tone that bit. "Tell him what ye've told me."

Gavin's skin bristled at Ewan's voice. *What now?*

Duncan kept his eyes on his hands, unable to look at Gavin as his tale haltingly rolled off his tongue.

"My brother, the laird, had been wondering what was keeping the letter from Callum Fraser. I had returned yet didn't bring the letter to Ewan. I explained that Fraser's daughter intercepted me in the hall. She said she was going to speak with Ewan and would bring the letter straight away. I thought ye had the letter." Duncan's desperate eyes flicked to Ewan.

Gavin ground his jaw as his heart dropped to the pit of his stomach, ill at the prospect of Ellen's intervention.

"And ye never received said letter?" Gavin asked Ewan in a measured tone.

He had to work very hard not to take his fury out on poor Duncan, who had most likely been trifled with by Ellen. He was a young and trusting man. And Ellen was a master manipulator. Why *wouldn't* he give the lass the letter to deliver?

Duncan shook his head. Ewan finally raised his eyes, and they shared a hard look with each other.

"Do ye know what happened to the letter?" Ewan asked.

Duncan's dark head shook again. "Nay. I presumed she brought it to ye, left if on your desk."

Ewan swept his hand over his mussed desk with an exaggerated movement. He, unlike Gavin, was not trying to hide his ire at his brother's naïveté.

"I dinna have such a letter, Duncan. Did ye at least read it so ye might tell me what her father wrote?"

Another shake of that somber head. Gavin's chest clenched in pain for the lad. Ewan was not going to take it easy on him — Duncan would be working off this misdeed for days.

"Well, then I will write another letter. Only this time, ye will deliver it to the man yourself, and ye will ride back with either the man's letter or the man himself and bring either one to me. No one else. If ye fail in this, ye will regret it. Do ye understand my words?"

Duncan nodded heartily, eager to correct his horrible misstep. Ewan waved his hand at his brother.

"Be off. Prepare for a longer trip, and I shall write another soon and send ye off within the next few days."

Scrambling out of the chair like a chastised child, Duncan then raced for the door. He'd gotten off light —the three men knew that. Duncan wouldn't fail again.

All three men knew *that* as well.

Gavin watched the poor lad escape, then turned to Ewan.

"Are ye going to speak to Ellen? She should face retribution for interfering with your letter."

Ewan rubbed at his face, and Gavin grasped his laird's predicament – he couldn't make an accusation with evidence, especially not against the daughter of Callum Fraser.

"Ye realize I can no' do that. For all we know, she did leave the letter on my desk and I lost it, or someone else removed it."

The shock of Gavin's fist hitting the desk made Ewan jump.

"Ye've got to be making a jest. Ye know verra well she didn't bring ye that letter!"

"I know that," Ewan's voice was low in warning. "But I have no proof either way. Until we have word directly from Callum, we are to tread lightly with Ellen."

Gavin's glare might have killed a lesser man.

"What of my Jenny? Why must we tread lightly for a woman who means nothing to this clan, yet my poor, loyal Jenny must suffer the woman?"

Ewan didn't harden himself or react at all. He well knew the font of despair within Gavin.

"Jenny knows she is loved, has a place here. Ellen has nothing, as far as we know, and I'll no' have the MacLeod clan earn a reputation for displacing a helpless woman. She is a guest, as unfortunate as that may be, and until we can find her a place with her father, she must be treated as such."

Gavin audibly snorted at Ewan's use of the word *helpless*, and one tawny eyebrow rose on Gavin's face. "Helpless? Ellen is anything but helpless."

"Be that as it may, we will suffer the lass for a few days more."

Suffer was a more apt word than Ewan knew.

***

Ewan entered their chambers, sweaty and with his tunic in his hands instead of on his back. The dark swirls of his chest hair gleamed in the torchlight of the room. His tall form, like a demon in the shadows, surprised Meg as she placed a sleeping Caitir in her cradle just outside their bed curtains.

The babe had started sleeping more throughout the night, a trait that Meg esteemed more than any other the babe had. Even with help from her mother, Fiona, and Jenny, Meg was still weary to her bones when she woke in the morn.

Ewan, for certain, was happy at the change in Caitir's sleeping habits, and once the babe was nestled into her bedding, Ewan grabbed Meg in a sweaty embrace and threw the both of them through the bed curtains onto their plaid coverlet.

A squeal tried to squeak from between Meg's lips, and she clapped her hand over her mouth to halt it. The last thing she wanted to do was wake that sleeping babe.

Meg sat atop Ewan and giggled at his boyish antics. Even after a day of back-breaking work, he came to her like a fresh, newlywed husband. His eyes glittered in the dim light shut out by the flax curtains.

"I take it ye had a good day," she threaded her fingers through his chest hair so her palms cupped the thick muscles nestled beneath.

"No' good enough yet. I must have one more thing to give today that title."

Then he growled like a beast, and with his teeth, pulled her kirtle off her shoulders. He began at her breasts, kissing and sucking. Once she was panting as ferociously as he, Ewan reached between them with one hand to untie the laces of his braies and shimmied them down to expose his swollen staff. Meg moved just as swiftly but with a bit more grace, impaling her eager sheath with

An Echo in the Glen

his cock. Their shared moan resonated within the confines of their bed.

They moved in unison, a dance that their bodies knew well and practiced often, building in a rush of sweat and groaning and hands and lips until Meg threw her head back and shook, her sunset tresses sweeping against the hair on his thighs. With the sharp curve of her back and her eyes closed, she reminded Ewan of a sultry cat. He could almost hear her purr.

That vision of Meg finding her release was all Ewan needed to find his. His hips bucked uncontrollably until he poured himself into her, clenching his jaw against the power of their joining.

Then they both crumpled into one another, catching their breaths in each other's embrace.

Meg spoke first.

"I have something that might make this less of a good day."

"Ooch lassie, ye tell me now?" Ewan shifted his eyes to his side to find Meg boldly watching him.

"I certainly wasn't going to tell ye *before*. I figure ye are more relaxed right now and might take the news with a better perspective."

Ewan closed his eyes. This meant another petty concern he'd have to deal with.

"Don't keep me in suspense. What is it?"

"My sister and your brother. And Aren."

He pressed the heels of his palms into his eyes, as though he might hide from the world and this news in it.

"I believe I'd rather fight the English in the rain and mud than deal with these concerns of women. First the spectacle of Ellen's arrival, and now histrionics of Mairi and Aren and Hamish. Uh, Hamish, my own brother!" Ewan dropped his hand to the bed. "Ye would think he'd at least give me a break!"

Meg giggled at his exasperated cry of mock contempt and patted his shoulder.

"There, there. Fiona thinks Mairi is just enjoying their rival affections but has a soft spot for Hamish. What if ye have a

130

conversation with Hamish and I with Mairi, and we can see if we must start planning a betrothal."

Ewan's jaw dropped as his eyes popped open.

"For my baby brother? Ooch, that happened far too quickly. Even Duncan does no' have a woman in mind yet."

Meg waggled her eyebrows at Ewan. "No' that ye know," she teased.

Ewan pressed his hands back into his eyes. God save him from these petty concerns.

***

The warm, hefty weight of Gavin's arm had encircled Jenny as she slept, and she awoke snuggled into his chest. Their bed chamber was silent in the gray light of early morn, and in this moment the rest of the world fell away, and there were just the two of them. And the world was perfect.

Though her responsibilities of the day called to her — the kitchens, helping Meg with the bairn, sewing and mending — Jenny shrugged them off, choosing instead to remain where she was. In the safety of Gavin's sleeping embrace.

Long blonde tendrils slipped onto her face and with a stealthy hand, she flipped them back over her head. A puffing sensation blew across her skin, carrying with it more loose tendrils.

"Your hair tickles, so light as it is. 'Tis like I am being attacked by an angel's wing."

Jenny took the compliment for what it was, even if it meant her rogue locks made it impossible for her man to sleep in. Her chest shook in a silent laugh.

"Be wary. They might start another attack. They can be aggressive, aye?"

"Ooch, don't I know it," Gavin agreed, and his arm flexed and shifted under her, rolling Jenny onto her back so she was gazing up into Gavin's golden boyish face made more youthful with sleepy eyes and wild hair. She reached up and laced her fingers through those golden-brown locks. His lips weren't sleepy, however, and his kiss was both soft and demanding, as if questioning for more.

Jenny responded in kind, her hand caressing his face and cupping his cheek as the kiss drew out. Gavin moaned low in his throat and moved so his thighs were between her willing legs. She smiled into the kiss and sucked on Gavin's tongue when he thrust it between her lips.

When he entered her, he contained the beast that roared from his chest, moving slowly as though they were riding the gentle waves of a loch. He was patient in his movements, his kisses and fingertips working in tandem to bring Jenny higher and higher, until she stepped off the precipice and plunged in a wild swirl.

Gavin soon joined her, panting her name into her ear, hot and breathy, and he finally groaned mightily and dropped his head next to hers, spent.

He was a giant beast, with a giant heart to match, and he was hers. And he made sure she knew it every day, every minute of her life.

A hard pounding resounded at the chamber door, and Gavin raised his head in a groggy response.

"Aye! Who's there?"

"Gavin? Are ye in there? Have ye risen yet?" Ewan's teasing voice reverberated on the opposite side of the door, and Gavin hung his head with an abashed smile. "Or have ye already risen? Has your wife taken care of that for ye?"

There it was. Jenny slapped her hand over her mouth in shock at Ewan's bawdy tease and to hold back a barking laugh. Gavin's flashing eyes caught hers with a wry look on his face, and he rose from the bed.

"Aye, I'm awake ye annoying lout!" Gavin called back to his laird. Ewan's laughter vibrated against the door almost as much as his pounding had.

"Turnabout is fair play, Gav! I've been waiting for this moment to taunt ye since I wed Meg! Now get ye dressed and get out here. These fields won't till themselves."

Gavin wrapped his plaid around his waist and, flipping the tartan over his shoulder, flashed one final, enticing smile at Jenny before leaving the chambers.

"That was fast, Gav," Jenny heard Ewan before the door closed fully. "Ye could have at least let the lass finish . . . Ow!"

Jenny giggled to herself again at the sound of Gavin punching his jesting friend and threw herself back into the bed. Then she too got up to dress, search out Meg, and begin her day.

***

Once their post-nuptial time ended, Gavin and Jenny resumed their daily duties and made sure to join each other at supper each evening. Jenny helped serve those in the hall, then took her seat next to Gavin. Their deviously euphoric faces shone brighter than the warm summer sun, and they fed each other morsels from their trenchers in a sickeningly sweet manner.

Ellen wanted to vomit. She'd left the wedding the day before, not waiting to watch the event. Her hope that she might sway Gavin away from Jenny or discourage the blonde woman from marrying her Gavin — *her* Gavin — had failed horrendously.

All she had wanted was a second chance. She was never going to wed Gavin, not for a first marriage at least. Her father had higher aspirations and the money to guarantee it. The Sheriff of Beauly was a political and economic match. And when the man was killed? Well, that was just fortune on her side, wasn't it? It also meant her father could sell her off *again*.

Ellen had made her way to the MacLeod's, figuring now that her husband was dead, and her father had achieved whatever machinations he'd worked out with the Sheriff (she'd ignored most of it — politics and economic deviousness were not her strong suits), she came to the conclusion that she was free to wed who she wanted, regardless of her father's demands.

And by God, she wanted Gavin.

Her shapely figure and captivating russet hair had sent Gavin spinning for nearly a year. Surely, he'd fall for her feminine wiles again, especially since she was a woman in distress.

The entire time she'd been married to the Sheriff, Ellen was forced to overlook his rotund belly and mouth that reeked of stale mead and suffer under him as he huffed away without fruition. She hadn't been surprised she didn't quicken. Not only was Andrew a poor lover, but Ellen had also learned a trick from the village midwife when she first started laying with Gavin. An oil extract soaked into a bit of cloth prevented his seed from taking root. 'Twas far too easy to do the same with Andrew. She craved the man's power and money, not his babe.

Then when she had shown up at Lochnora and saw Gavin standing there — he looked exactly the same as when she'd seen him last, at the Inn north of Beauly. His light brown hair the color of a young oak sapling, his skin with a touch of summer sun, and those eyes — deep set and intense, and as compelling as his broad chest and chiseled muscles that were even more enticing after a year with the portly, unkempt Sheriff. Ellen had dreamed of him, pictured his face and body when the sheriff finally managed to roll on top of her, and then he'd been there when she had ridden into the Lochnora bailey. 'Twas just as she had imagined.

Then she saw the mousy blonde shrinking into him. Too slender, no shape, sallow skin . . . Jenny MacLeod.

And he wanted to marry *that* woman? He shunned Ellen for *her*? A pasty commoner?

Ellen had assumed 'twould be easy to seduce Gavin back, wed the man and live the life she had dreamed when she was married off to Andrew. And if not that, at least become his mistress and preferred lover. 'Twouldn't be a shabby life, that.

But something about the blonde stuck to Gavin like a leech. Ellen couldn't see it. Who wanted a skinny, weak woman like Jenny? And Gavin chose Jenny over her! Somehow that woman had her hooks in Gavin, and no matter what Ellen did, she couldn't shake Jenny loose. Gavin's lone interest was the sallow blonde.

Biting at the inside of her lip, Ellen focused her frustrated gaze on Gavin. She didn't even see Jenny, pretending the lass wasn't there. Ellen only had eyes for her brawny, blond man.

And now she needed to take dire action since he'd wed the blonde shrew. Something that would drive Jenny from him forever.

Chapter Twelve: Willing and Unwilling

MAIRI JUGGLED THE HEFTY bucket in one hand as she tried to wipe wisps of her hair from her eyes. Stinking heat — it made her fair locks stick to her face and get in her eyes . . . *Why won't my kerchief stay knotted?*

"Mairi. Ye are here. Are ye seeking me out?"

She peered through her limp hair at the young blond man standing near the field. Aren. *What nonsense did he speak? Seeking him out?* 'Twas obvious to even the most foolish of the clan that she was trying to complete her chores.

Aren could speak such tender words when he wanted, but the rest of the time, she worried for his mind. She squinted at him.

"Nay, Aren. As ye can see, I've just scrubbed the kitchens, and I'm dumping the dirty water. If ye dinna wished to be splashed with it, ye should step away."

Her voice was gruff when she spoke, but he did as she advised and moved as she tossed the filthy water onto the vegetables in the garden. Muck splashed up onto her skirts, and she sighed heavily. That was more laundry on her already long list of chores for the day.

The pail dangled limply as she held it to her side, ready to return to the kitchens. Aren grabbed her arm before she could take another step.

"Dinna leave too fast, lassie. I might like some affection from ye, meeting ye here and all."

Mairi's face twisted at Aren's words. *Why was he suggesting such a thing?* "I told ye was I no' here to meet with ye. I must return."

Before she could brush past, he thrust himself close and grabbed her other arm. Mairi tried to lift the bucket to put it between them as a piercing spear of fear shot through her chest. In her panic, she had an unexpected realization about the difference between Hamish and Aren, and that realization also forced her to make up her mind between the two. One's tender interest held her heart, the other would force it.

When Hamish had met up with her in the gardens, he'd kept a respectful distance until Mairi welcomed something more. He'd taken the bucket to relieve her burden and spoke to her in light tones.

Aren. He watched her work and did nothing, and now he overstepped. This was more than flirtatious smiles or friendly banter. And Mairi didn't want a man who didn't know his boundaries, a man who didn't listen to her, a man who would try to force her love.

"Aren," she said in a shaky voice, "ye have been a good friend, and I apologize if I have led ye wrong. But I have realized that ye canna force someone to love ye, otherwise 'tis as useless as a lame mule, and I dinna love ye. Now let me be."

Aren stared at her with furious eyes for several heartbeats. "Nay."

Then he reached over the bucket between them to slam his rough lips on hers.

***

Laboring in the yard with Orion, an older MacLeod man well versed in farming techniques, Gavin overheard two voices. One was Mairi's, Gavin was sure of it. He dropped his spade and waved at Orion to join him around the edge of the keep.

Sure enough, Mairi stood before one of the young men who'd fought over her, Aren. While at first the lass might have relished the attentions of two men, presently she didn't look pleased with his intentions. Her face was tight, and she strained away from the lad. Gavin's body hardened, but he didn't move right away as he watched the scene unfold before he stepped in.

"I have realized that ye canna force someone to love ye, otherwise 'tis as useless as a lame mule, and I dinna love ye. Now let me be."

There 'twas — the lad's touch was not desired by the lass. Gavin strode with Orion toward the couple.

Until the young blond man said *nay* and thrust his lips upon hers. Ravishing Meg's younger sister! The lad truly overstepped and rage exploded like vitriol within Gavin. His muscled legs brought him to Mairi's side at a pace Orion couldn't keep up with, and his hammer-like fist landed on Aren's face before the lad even knew Gavin was there. Aren's injured cry rang with shock and pain. Gavin didn't doubt the man would have a colorful bruise as a reminder of his rude, overreaching manners.

"Mairi, are ye well?" Gavin asked, taking the bucket from the lass.

Her eyes were wide with surprise, either from having Aren's hands on her inappropriately or at the sudden manner by which Aren was hauled away. She wrapped her arms around herself, as if to ward off any further offense, and nodded slowly.

Orion placed a consoling arm around Mairi, and accepting the bucket from Gavin, walked the shaking lassie back to the keep. Gavin turned his wrath on Aren.

"Ye understand I have every right to slay ye for putting your hands on the sister-by-law of the laird, a lass under his protection, aye?"

Aren paled, washing out any golden details of his hair. "But she seemed to want me. She talked with me, smiled at me. She wanted me!" His whining grated on Gavin's ears.

Gavin reached out and smacked the lad on the side of his pasty head.

"Nay. And she told ye so. A true man, a Highland warrior, never oversteps with a woman. Never tries to take what he's been told is no' his. 'Tis a lesson I had to learn myself, and I learned it hard. But learn it I did." Gavin shifted closer to Aren, his nose nearly touching Aren's face so he wouldn't miss Gavin's words. "And she spoke to ye, man. She told ye nay, that ye canna force it. Now, will ye accept her choice, even if 'tis no' ye? Even if she chooses another?"

The lad didn't disappoint. He lifted one shoulder in an cavalier shrug. "I guess ye are right. I will have to find another lass for company."

Gavin clenched Aren's bony shoulder in a bruising grip. Aren grimaced and shrank to his side, trying to escape Gavin's fingers.

"A willing lass, do ye understand?" Gavin demanded.

Aren nodded, his eyes wild. "Aye! I understand!"

Gavin released his grip. "And dinna plague the lass, try to chase after her, or anything like that."

His words reflected his own present, painful experience. If he could prevent the same from happening to Mairi and whichever lad held her interest — Gavin guessed it was Hamish — then he would do whatever was required of him.

Aren rubbed at his shoulder, his doleful face pouting.

"Aye, I hear ye."

He sounded earnest enough for Gavin to believe him, and he waved the lad to be on his way and returned to his own work in the fields.

At least the minor heartache of the MacLeod youth gave Gavin something to distract his thoughts. Picking up his spade, he exhaled a deep breath. He recalled being that young, when life seemed like it would end if the one he loved didn't love him back. These thoughts also reminded him to speak to Ewan on this matter, as yet another bout of fisticuffs had erupted regarding Mairi. She was a ripe fruit too many men wanted to pluck, and if her heart lay elsewhere, Ewan might want to act on that before any further discord was sowed in the clan.

God knew there was more than enough discord to go around.

***

By the end of the day, sweat tickled as it dripped down the curve of Gavin's back, rolling in large rivulets to his waistband and pooling at the top of his buttocks. *What was this heat?* The Highlands were renowned for its cooler weather, the beauty of its snow. These past several days of the sun beating upon them with a vengeance was a strange occurrence indeed. Gavin glanced at the cloudy sky – *a good amount of rain must be on the horizon.*

The heft of scratchy peat he held upon his broad shoulder didn't help cool him at all. If he were any sweatier, he'd be afraid that he might dampen the peat too much to be useful.

He'd left Orion to the farming and assisted in the stables with the never-ending peat. He dumped his bricks just inside the door of the barn, where the stable lads would place them in storage against the north wall, then turned to make another trip.

And bumped into Ellen, of all people. Gavin's groan was loud and full of disgust.

Maybe 'tis so hot because I'm in hell, Gavin thought. That reasoning seemed sound.

Because the red devil herself stood before him.

"Ooch, Gavin! Watch yourself! One might think ye were bumping into me for another reason!"

A sickening shudder coursed through Gavin, whether from her screeching voice or the insidious intent behind her words, he didn't know.

What he did know was he needed to leave the grassy area next to the barn. *Now.*

"Trust me, Ellen. I was no' bumping into ye for any reason. God save me, I dinna want to bump into ye at all. Please leave here."

"I'm just walking back to my hut, that tiny, pathetic croft ye set up for me. Tsk tsk," she added. "Ye would think that ye might extend more hospitality to me, set me up in the keep, which is more in accordance to my station."

Gavin grimaced at her suggestion, her pretentiousness. The haughtiness in her eyes, peering down her nose at him though he stood nigh a foot taller than she, none of her behavior surprised him. Ellen had always believed nothing was too good for her. Spoiled Ellen.

"Ye are a guest and are receiving naught more or less than any guest at the keep. Given how ye have behaved the past month, in front of my wife, no less, *my wife,* ye are fortunate Ewan didn't set ye out on your heels. He is still waiting on word from your father on what to do with ye, and as soon as he has that letter, or a guard sent by your father, ye shall be on your way."

Instead of recoiling from his harsh words, she pressed close, almost melting into him, not caring if his sweaty chest stained her fine linen gown. He sucked in his chest, trying to pull away, and her hand followed her body, resting in the sweat that coated him like a second skin.

He slapped her hand away. "Dinna touch me, Ellen. I am a married man."

A hard bubble of laughter escaped her sickening, pouty lips. "Ooch, Gavin. Ye and I both know that she canna please ye as I did. I know ye still want me. Who else can make your body respond with such desire?"

The movement of her hand followed the suggestive tone of her words, dropped to his braies, and curled around his manhood. She tightened her cupped hand against him, and his cock flexed in return. He jumped backward like a startled colt, hating himself for how his body responded without thought.

More, he hated her, abhorred her. Gavin prided himself on his integrity, of being as fair as possible, but nothing was reasonable when it came to Ellen. Just as she threw his body out of balance, she also made his mind burn with a hatred unknown in this mortal world.

Why, why did she leech onto him so? What was wrong with her to make her behave this way?

Gavin pressed his back to the barn wall, putting as much distance between Ellen and his body as he could find. 'Twasn't enough. She could sail to the holy land, and 'twouldn't be far enough.

He flicked his eyes around the side of the barn to the yard, praying no one saw them in a position that could easily be mistaken for *in flagrante*. Jenny was hurting enough over Ellen's gratuitous behavior toward Gavin before they were wed. What would a scene like this do to her?

That prospect made the hatred in Gavin boil all the more, and he clenched his fists as he glared at her. A righteous man didn't strike a woman, but *Christ's blood,* she was pushing him to his limit.

And for Jenny, to protect her, he would strike down anything or anyone. Man or woman.

"Leave me, Ellen. I am no longer yours. Find another."

Her face never shifted, that cloyingly sweet and irritating hint of a smile hanging on her lips.

"Ooch, Gavin, I think ye are mistaken."

Then she rose on her toes in a sudden move and forced her lips to his. She stepped back before he could even overcome his shock and lift his arms to push her away. She sauntered off, throwing a scheming azure glance over her shoulder before turning toward her croft.

As he watched her leave, a short, shadowy figure appeared around the edge of the barn. Squinting against the sunlight, Gavin flinched as he recognized who it was. Davey. And Gavin knew that Davey's next stop would be the kitchens, and Fiona, where he would share what he saw.

Gavin slapped the back of his head against the barn wall and swallowed several times to stop the vomit that threatened to gush from his wame. He broke into a thicker sweat, his tawny hair stained a dark brown with it.

Aye. The Devil walked the yard of Lochnora. He truly was in hell.

***

Gavin's head hung low, his chin on his chest, as he trudged in the same direction as Davey toward the kitchens. Better to nip this problem in the bud than let Davey share what his youthful eyes might have seen and misconstrued. Once he did, Fiona would storm the keep to find Meg and report what Davey had told her. Then Meg, as Jenny's dear friend, would be obligated to inform Jenny, and Ewan, of what had transpired.

Which was nothing, in truth. All Gavin wanted to do was wash his mouth to rid it of the lingering taste of Ellen, and instead he had to speak to Davey, or at least Fiona.

How had everything been turned upside down in so short a time? He ran his fingers through his damp hair as he reached the kitchen door, just as Davey stepped across the threshold.

When he entered, Davey stood wide-eyed next to Fiona, hiding under her skirts. Mairi froze in her space near the pantry, her moss-green eyes as round as Davey's. Had the lad said anything yet? From the looks on their faces, the lad may have had a start.

Gavin leaned his burly shoulders against the door frame, collecting his wits. The realization of what he needed to do flooded him in a rush. 'Twas time to employ the women of the manse to aid him in his quest to keep as far from Ellen as possible. No more secrets. Everything must be out in the open.

"Davey, laddie. Can I ask what ye've told your mam here?" Keeping his voice level and controlled, he prayed his imploring tone worked on Davey and his mother.

Fiona's eyes narrowed, cutting into Gavin like black daggers. She placed her hand on Davey's shoulder, reassuring the lad as he peeked around her skirt.

"The lad's told me something concerning, Gavin." She tried to hide the curtness in her voice, but Gavin heard it all the same.

"Aye, that the laddie saw me with Ellen, in what looked to be a wee bit of a compromising position."

If Mairi's eyes could pop out of her head, they would have. She froze in a gawking stare at Gavin.

"Can ye explain it?" Fiona's tight voice rose a notch, along with her chin.

Gavin dipped his head lower, hating how he had to defend his good name over and over. These were his kin — he'd known this woman for years. Fiona knew what a devoutly loyal man he was, that his word was his bond, and he did everything under a banner of integrity, nothing less. Why did everyone think the worst of him? Was that all it took? One lie of a scorned lover? Hiding his face did nothing but make him appear more guilty, so he raised his eyes to stare earnestly at Fiona.

"The lass came to me. She cornered me. Davey can attest to the fact he saw me back up as far as I could go against the barn wall." He tipped his head at Davey, who nodded meekly from his hiding place. "See? And I told her to leave, over and over, and just when I thought she was going, she pressed forward and put her foul lips on mine. Did I touch the lass, Davey?"

Desperation tinged Gavin's voice, he knew, but then, he *was* desperate. Fortunately, Davey shook his head. Gavin hadn't touched Ellen at all.

"She has once again pursued me. I am on my way to tell Ewan that she has threatened me, my Jenny, and the peace and contentment of this clan for the final time. She must be sent away."

He stood in the doorway, his chest heaving as he panted out his pleading explanation. Fiona pinched her lips together with contempt, whether at Gavin or Ellen or the whole situation he didn't know, but she swept to the side, clearing the way so that Gavin might seek out Ewan in his study.

Gavin bowed his thanks, fearing his voice might tremble if he tried to speak, and strode past Fiona and Davey to the stairwell.

Ewan wouldn't be pleased with this change of events, Jenny less so, and 'twas vital Gavin speak to them both right away, before any rumors of a supposed interlude with Ellen reached them, or God forbid, they encountered Ellen herself.

Ewan and Jenny must hear him and agree on that of which Gavin was already convinced. *They must!* The laird was as faithful to his men as Gavin was to him. Ewan would believe Gavin straight away.

Yet, as he mounted the steps, he sent a prayer up to God that Jenny, who had already been burdened by so much with this red devil in their midst, would believe him as well.

He was less certain of that.

***

Gavin had requested both Ewan and Jenny in the laird's study. They had believed Gavin's account, and relief washed over Gavin. He dropped his weary head into his hands. His honor remained untainted.

In the tight quarters of Ewan's study, each of their faces wore matching masks of tight bewilderment.

"What is it with this lass?" Ewan's voice held a nuance of disbelief. "What is the root of her bitterness? She seemed so pleased to be marrying the Sheriff when we encountered her in Beauly those years ago. Has the man's death driven her to madness?"

Gavin's forehead rested in the palm of his hand. He had no answer for any of Ellen's actions.

"Ewan, we dinna know what happens in another's marriage," Jenny said. "Mayhap the marriage she believed would grant her the life she desired ended in disaster. Mayhap the Sheriff had a heavy hand. We know she did no' quicken with child, which may be telling. But we dinna know what kind of husband or wife they were to each other."

She flicked her eyes to Gavin, then lowered her contrite gaze again.

Chagrined, Gavin raised his tired eyes and marveled at his wife. Jenny had been the recipient of some of the worst Ellen had to offer, and here she was, trying to explain the woman's irrational behaviors. Mayhap her explanation would provide insight into how to deal with Ellen until her father arrived.

"Even if that were true," Ewan responded, "'Tis no' *carte blanche* to behave so violently to the kin that has housed her. Or especially to my man-at-arms and his wife. An affront on ye is an affront on the laird and the clan itself, and it must be dealt with."

Ewan's eyes brightened, and he stood suddenly. "Duncan hasn't left yet. Come, we'll deal with this now."

For Ewan, Ellen's most recent conduct was the final straw. He tore through the hall where she like to hover though she'd been banned from it, with Gavin and Jenny close behind. Once he found her, he cornered her and made his demands.

"Ellen, 'tis time for ye to depart Lochnora. The disharmony ye have sowed is beyond measure. I will have my men escort ye back to your father's house, whether he be there or no'."

An Echo in the Glen

Ewan had been called a black devil before, and right now, watching the confrontation between Ewan and Ellen, Jenny had no doubt to the nickname. Jenny gripped Gavin's hand, her fingers quaking against Gavin's, and he held hers in his strong, reassuring grasp. Jenny might be a shivering bag of bones, but Gavin's whole being was as resolute and stoic as ever.

As for Jenny, she was certain her emotions were plastered on her face. While she did feel a bit of shame at her selfish feelings, just having offered possible insight into Ellen, her joy at this change in events was immeasurable. In Jenny's opinion, Ellen couldn't leave the Lochnora keep soon enough.

Ewan waved to his brother Duncan, and his other man, John, to come forward. Their own dark expressions mirrored Ewan's — they'd drag Ellen away from the Lochnora kicking and screaming if necessary.

Ellen's comely face blanched a stark white at Ewan's demands. Her arm snaked around her waist protectively, and she lifted her other hand in protest. That arm circling her waist gave Jenny a niggling sensation at the base of her neck. She'd seen that type of gesture before...

"Wait! Ye canna remove me!" Ellen screeched at Ewan.

Ewan's blazing eyes rolled to the rafters before he dropped them back to the complaining woman.

"I can and I will remove ye. Gavin is as close to me as a brother, and your behaviors against him, against his wife, who is like a sister to Lady Meg, border on criminal. I will no' have such discord in my home, in my lands. Lochnora is a place of calm, and I will eject anyone who disrupts that calm."

Ellen's arm clenched against her stomach again, and a flare of pain shocked Jenny's head. Women only held their bellies in such a way for one reason . . . The stones upon which she stood seemed to lurch beneath her feet, and she swayed against Gavin's side.

"Ye canna eject me, Laird Ewan," her voice was overly sweet. Sickly sweet. The pounding in Jenny's head grew, throbbing in her ears as Ellen continued in that voice. "Ye wouldn't send a mother-to-be out into the cold, now would ye?"

Her words sucked all the air from the main hall, and Jenny's whole body palpitated as she crumpled into Gavin's side. He held her aloft — and thank goodness, because her legs were too weak to hold her upright.

"Ye are no' with child," Ewan breathed in a harsh whisper, pulling back as though Ellen thrust a serpent at him instead of her dainty hand. "Unless 'tis the Sheriff's. Who could ye . . ."

Everything in the room froze, and Jenny believed her chest was going to explode as Ellen's insolent eyes shifted in Gavin's direction, followed by her finger. Jenny was certain she might faint away as Ellen pointed her pudgy, accusatory finger at Gavin.

At Jenny's Gavin. At her husband. At the man who swore his love and devotion. Ellen's finger was a spear, striking into the very heart of Jenny.

"Nay," Gavin gasped as the color drained from his skin. He appeared as though he might swoon.

Jenny's brain burned. Gavin was a good man, a loyal man. He'd never break his wedding vows so recently pledged — *would he?* Trying to control her erratic breathing and pounding heart and blood that hammered in her temples, Jenny twisted away from Gavin to stare at his pale, shocked face.

Chapter Thirteen: Loyalty and Fealty

HIS BREATH CAUGHT, and he was choking. Oh Lord above, he was dying. He was a warrior, yet this woman's finger was going to kill him as assuredly as 'twere a blade cleaving his chest in two.

And the pain! The devouring, shuddering agony — had he ever known such a pain? His mind scrambled, trying to understand what in the Lord's world was going on.

But she wasn't done.

By God, she wasn't done killing him.

"'Tis Gavin's."

The words fell like a giant, splintering oak in the woods. And Gavin couldn't deny her accusations because words wouldn't form on his lips. But his head shook from side to side unconsciously against her impossibly foul words.

What could he say? Though he had rejected the woman at every turn, any denial would resonate with guilt. Anger would sound like a confession.

Jenny's hand was no longer on his. She faltered away from him – her deep blue eyes fettered with her own suffering. His wasn't the only heart wounded by Ellen's cutting accusation and infernal finger.

Ewan was the only one of those gathered in the hall to regain his voice, shaky though it was.

"Surely ye are mistaken, Ellen. Ye must have been with child before ye came here — Andrew's child. 'Tis too soon to know."

Ellen angled her head, her pinched face never leaving Gavin's.

"Nay. A woman knows. I would know because of the changes that have come with this first child of mine. Our first child." Ellen studied Gavin as she rubbed her belly protectively, as though the bairn might feel her movements through her skin. "Gavin and I lay together the first night I arrived here. He is smitten with me, Ewan. Ye know that. Ye were with him when I was sold off like cattle to Beauly. How could he not seek me out the moment I returned?"

Ewan was snorting, a boar ready to attack, and the more Ellen spoke, the louder his snorting became. Gavin ripped his eyes from Ellen and circled the already spinning room. Ewan's devilish anger, Meg's stricken face, the bleak looks of Duncan and John who wanted to be anywhere else but in this hall, and finally landing on Jenny's beautifully distraught face. Even in her horror, she was perfection.

Unsure of what to do for her, Gavin extended his hand — an olive branch, an alliance against this evil, anything she needed. Jenny blanched more.

Then her eyes shifted upward in a strange movement, and she collapsed to the ground.

"Jenny!"

The knife of pain in his chest at Ellen's accusations became inconceivably larger and more agonizing. *What's wrong with Jenny?* He crouched next to her and lifted her head onto his lap, panic emanating from him in a heat. Sweat burst out onto his brow.

Meg rushed to his side and pressed her palms to Jenny's pale face. She whipped her hair to the side and listened to Jenny's chest before her face and shoulders relaxed under the steady rise and fall.

"A faint. Gavin, take your wife to your chambers."

Gavin slipped his arm under Jenny's limp head. He'd found his voice.

"Dinna speak to that bitch again 'till I return," Gavin commanded of Ewan as he kept his gaze on the face of the woman he loved more than his very life. "I would have the opportunity to defend myself."

He then slid his other arm under Jenny's knees and lifted her in a swift move. His normally vivacious bride was so still, so tiny in his arms.

Meg brushed wisps of Gavin's hair from his forehead.

"'Tis naught to defend. I know the man ye are. Ewan knows ye better than anyone, and he would never take to a man who'd break his vow. A man, a laird, must have men he can trust, and there are none more dependable, more loyal, than ye. Take your wife. We will remove this conversation to Ewan's study. 'Tis no' fit for all ears."

Sweeping her nervous gaze around the hall, Meg patted Gavin's arm and sent him off.

***

Jenny had awoken as Gavin lay her in their bed. Her pale blue eyes, so full of anguish and bewilderment, caught his gaze for a scant second. Then she stiffened her jaw and rolled to her side, presenting her back to Gavin. Jenny said nothing. She didn't have to. Gavin understood her meaning with that one gesture. He told her he would send in Meg as soon as she was free, then stormed off to the study. His temper flared in a white heat with each step.

John had been dismissed from the study with stern directions to say nothing under penalty of punishment.

Ewan was a man of his word — John would keep this secret until his death if need be.

The laird grabbed Duncan's tunic before he exited. Duncan's fury matched his older brother's.

"Ye leave on the morrow for Fraser, Duncan. I'll finish penning the letter this eve. Fraser must be appraised of this development and brought to the keep as soon as ye can find him. Bring the man here. Do ye hear me?"

Duncan nodded once and marched off, his lips sealed as well. Ewan settled into his chair behind his worn desk, with Ellen seated across from him.

When Gavin entered the study, his stomach roiled at the sight of Ellen seated in that chair, her posture much the same as that fateful day she'd first rode into Lochnora, a queen surveying her subjects. *Had this vicious plan been formed in her head when she arrived?*

Gavin clenched his teeth and moved to Ellen. To what end? To throttle her? Strike her? He'd never struck a woman in his life, yet for the second time, she'd driven him to that point. And once again, Ewan saved him from a horrendous sin. He lifted a stiff, immense hand to Gavin, halting him in his tracks.

Meg sat in the corner near Ewan, her hands covering her mouth, as though she didn't trust any words she might speak.

"Ellen. Once again, I am going to tell ye that ye must be mistaken. Gavin is devoted to Jenny. His heart is hardened against

ye. That I know well. And ye have been here little more than a
month. Ye must be mistaken. So ye are to be congratulated for
carrying the progeny of the Sheriff of Beauly."

His icy blue gaze shot daggers at Ellen, trying to convince
her to agree. Instead, she lifted her chin at Ewan, challenging him.
The same gloating gaze she shot at Ewan on that fateful day she'd
ridden to Lochnora. *Who challenged their laird in such a scornful
way?* Gavin's chair scraped against the floor when he flinched,
meaning to charge at her, and Ewan's commanding hand halted him
again.

"Ye see, Ewan? Gavin canna control himself around me. I
was no' with child when I left Beauly. That I can confirm." Ellen
leveled a knowing glare at Meg, who hung her head. The ways of
women were lost on Ewan and Gavin, but Meg recognized exactly
what Ellen was intimating — their private conversation in the
kitchens shortly after Ellen had arrived.

"Gavin and I lay together several times when I first arrived
until the day he wed. He didn't break any vows, Ewan. He is a good
man, and ye know that well. Before he wed the fair lass, however
..." her voice drifted off, and she rubbed her flat belly again.

Gavin's blood pummeled against his temples as his
attention followed her hands. *Could she be carrying the bairn of
another man? If she were with a bairn, shouldn't her belly be
swollen? How can such a flat, empty body hold the fullness of life?*
He shook his head and wondered if he would ever stop. The world
had turned on its head, spinning out of control, and Gavin spun
helplessly with it. All he could do was shake his head nay, over and
over, at the awfulness of her words.

He moved his pleading face to Ewan's, who himself was
unable to control the throbbing vein in his forehead at this series of
events. And how might Gavin prove he was not the father? Men
didn't have the assurances of women. 'Twas her word against his,
and no matter how many times he denied it, given her recent
behavior around him at the keep, her story sounded easy to believe.
How could he prove Ellen a liar?

The sole hope he held onto like a lifeline was that she'd be proven a liar in nine months, when she was not delivered of a babe. Yet, Gavin didn't put it past Ellen to have lain with another man, quicken with his child, and claim it as Gavin's. Would this red devil go that far to destroy him? Destroy his love with Jenny? Such a dire, singular focus seemed too much, even for the likes of Ellen.

Ewan rubbed his head roughly, not hiding his frustration that Gavin felt like a deathly pain in his bones. Then the laird lifted his dark, angry head.

"Here is what we shall do. Ye shall have to remain here until the bairn is born. That timeline might give us a certainty of whether ye are lying or no'. That will tell us if ye were with child before ye came to Lochnora."

Ewan glanced at Meg, hoping he was correct in his understanding of pregnancy. Meg nodded her head in agreement. It was the only real option they had to prove Gavin's innocence.

Gavin gaped at this news. *She would remain here?*

"A measure of certainty," Meg added in a hollow tone.

"The MacLeod clan will care for ye in your confinement. Until that time, ye are no' to enter the stronghold without invitation. Ye are to stay away from both Jenny and Gavin. If ye need anything, ye are to contact my Lady Meg, her mother the midwife, her sister Mairi, or Fiona from the kitchens. If I see ye in the keep otherwise, or near Jenny or Gavin, I will set ye on your way, babe or no'."

Ewan lifted his powerful body from his chair, and placing his palms flat on his desk, he leaned so far over the surface that his plaid pooled on the tabletop and his twisted face was less than an inch from Ellen's. Still, she didn't move. She faced him as fearlessly as any valiant warrior.

"Dinna doubt my commands, Ellen. Ye have heard that I imprisoned my wife's own father for betrayal. I would do that and more to ye."

Gavin expected her to flee. They all did.

Rather, she reclined into the chair and crossed her hand over her knee. An unkind smile spread over her face.

"I should live in the keep. 'Tis fitting that I live near my babe's father. And I would need the amenities of the keep whilst I am with child. 'Tis what I am accustomed to, aye?"

Ewan's skin transformed from his angry red to a violent purple, and Gavin feared someone might have to move to protect Ellen from Ewan's fury, as much as he would have despised the effort.

In truth, Gavin had never seen his laird so infuriated in his life. Gavin was on edge, waiting to hear Ewan's response.

Ewan's hand twitched on the desk. Tamping down his desire to strike out at the lass, a measure of control that impressed Gavin to no end, Ewan leaned even closer to Ellen. He was a giant, formidable laird, and a red devil of a woman wasn't going to challenge him and succeed.

"Ye must be hard of hearing. Ye are to leave the keep now and go to your croft. If I see ye in here, I will strike ye myself."

Hatred flew from his skin like small daggers aiming for Ellen. Even Gavin would not have wanted to meet Ewan on the battlefield when he looked like this. Blood wouldn't be enough for this man.

Ellen must have realized the same, for this time she eased off the chair and sauntered to the door. Her hand brushed against Gavin as she moved past him, and he recoiled as though her touched burned him like a hot iron. Unperturbed, Ellen gave him a coquettish curl of her lips and finally exited.

The heavy and despairing air of the study left with her. Meg breathed out an audible sigh and rested against the stone wall with her eyes closed.

Meg had an idea of Jenny's misery. Her own husband had been accused by Elayne MacNally of having an illicit affair with that harpy of a woman. But that lie had been revealed, and Elayne had never claimed to be with child. What must poor Jenny be feeling at this moment?

Meg would soon find out.

"Lady Meg?" Gavin's voice was hesitant, like a lost lad, it could make anyone's heart weep. "Would ye see to my Jenny? She is distraught beyond measure."

Meg nodded and rose from her stool. She, too, patted Gavin as she departed, and this time, he leaned into the affectionate gesture. He needed all the support and reassurance she might give.

Once she departed, Gavin slumped into the chair Ellen had left. Ewan pressed his palms into his eyes as if trying to wipe the vision of the day from his mind. Then he dropped his hands.

"Gavin, my brother, ye have got yourself into quite a quandary this time."

If he weren't so devastated, Gavin might have laughed.

Ewan's face tightened and became serious.

"I will only ask ye once. And I will believe the answer ye give. Ye are my closest man, closer than even a brother. I ask ye for the absolute truth no matter how damning it might be."

Ewan leaned on to the desk, staring into Gavin's face.

"Did ye ever, *ever*, lay with the lass once she arrived at this keep? Can this supposed babe be yours in any way?"

Gavin sucked in his breath. *Ewan believed the lying harridan?*

Ewan read him as only a brother, one's dearest friend, can.

"Nay, Gavin. I dinna believe her. But ye have pledged your fealty and loyalty to me, and I know ye to be a man more honest than most. I have to ask. Did ye?"

Gavin's stare back to Ewan was harsh, icy, a look he'd never shot at Ewan before. He both understood what Ewan was doing and hated his chieftain for it. But then, that is what friends did — they were brutally hard, honest, even when one hated it the most.

"Nay, Ewan. Ye know me to be faithful, honest, a man of his word to ye. I am, if at all possible, more so with Jenny. Ye must know this. I have never touched that woman, other than the fiasco before my wedding day, never laid with her since her arrival, and I actively try to avoid her. She is a leech on my side, sucking away everything that is good in my life. I'd sooner find my death at the tip of Davey's dull wooden sword than be near that woman a moment more. If she does have a babe, 'tis impossible that 'tis mine."

Ewan's gaze never wavered. With a sudden move, he lifted his hand and slapped Gavin's shoulder so hard that even burly Gavin shifted in his seat. Then a wicked smile broke Ewan's stony face.

"As we must apprise Callum Fraser of these events, Duncan is leaving to retrieve him. I will have Duncan update him on this mess. He must know of his daughter's possible current state. I told ye from the verra beginning that lass was a dangerous fruit. Mayhap now ye will have learned to trust my sage advice?"

Ewan collapsed back into his chair, and for the first time, his face bore signs of fatigue, a weariness with life.

"Now, Meg and I will do everything we can to convince Jenny that ye are a man of your word. Go find your wife and see if she trusts your word as I do."

Gavin waited several heartbeats before rising from his chair. His shoulders slumped as he walked to the door.

'Twas as if he were marching to his doom.

***

Jenny sobbed on her bed, painful gut-wrenching sobs that shook her to her bones.

A light knock sounded at the door, but Jenny didn't answer. She didn't want to take the risk that it would be Gavin. She wasn't ready to see him, to ask him for his truth, to learn that her husband could have been less than faithful. That Gavin, her honorable, stalwart Gavin, could be a liar.

Such a thing seemed ridiculous this morning. Gavin was nothing if not irreproachable.

Now? Jenny couldn't say the same, and it killed her heart to have these dire thoughts.

The knock came again with a squeak of Gavin's chamber door opening (*Gavin's! Nay mine! Nay ours!* she cried silently).

"Jenny?" Meg's voice barely broke above a whisper. "Jenny, may I enter?"

Jenny remained silent. She wanted to hide from everyone. How could she face the world when the embarrassment of Ellen's accusation overwhelmed her to the point that breath didn't fill her chest? She choked as she cried.

Meg swept into the room without an invitation and rushed to Jenny's head and sat on the bedding next to her. Her dainty but surprisingly strong hand wiggled under Jenny's lush blonde hair and shifted her head to Meg's lap.

Jenny didn't fight her. She lacked the strength. Would she ever be strong again?

Meg must have read her mind.

"Aye, Jenny. Cry for all ye are worth. Wear yourself out. Ewan is speaking to Gavin now, and he will figure this out."

Meg's fingers brushed at Jenny's hair, exposing a bit of her smooth forehead that yet held a touch of color from the sun. She cooed at Jenny as though Jenny was her bairn, not her grown friend.

Yet, Jenny needed it — she craved such a motherly touch. Right now, she longed for her mother to coddle her in her lowest moment. Meg noticed this need and stepped in to serve in that role. What broken-hearted lass didn't need motherly coddling?

Even if that lass was but one month wed to her love.

Was Gavin still her love? Was the ferocity of Ellen's words strong enough to break their love?

Crying on the bed until her chest ached, Jenny thought *yes*.

"Jenny, please dinna fret so much until we know that truth," Meg pleaded as her fingers worked their soothing magic through Jenny's hair.

Jenny wiped at her tears, just to have them replaced by more. How did she still manage to have tears to cry?

"The truth?" she mumbled into Meg's lap. "What purpose would it serve for Ellen to lie? She would be discovered in a few months! And to what end? Gavin is married! She is naught more than a strumpet, but he now owes her an obligation due to her condition."

Her sobbing increased to a nearly uncontrollable weeping while Meg patted her back.

"Women lie for all sorts of reasons. I've known Gavin for years. My husband, our good Laird Ewan, he has known Gavin since they were wee laddies. Gavin is not a man to lie with a woman while betrothed or wed. *He's not.*"

Meg added the emphasis, but it fell on deaf ears. Jenny could only focus on Ellen's words, and her finger, that cruel, accusing finger that pointed and pointed and pointed. Meg leaned to Jenny, covering Jenny's shivering body with her own.

"If she is lying, we will know within a few months. Ewan is also writing a letter for Master Fraser to come and confront his wayward daughter. Either way, the woman will be out of our care soon enough."

Jenny didn't answer, but another thought plagued her mind.

She might have to be out of the MacLeod care herself. How could she stay behind and look at Gavin's beautiful, faithless face every day?

Chapter Fourteen: No Tears Left

ANOTHER KNOCK AT the door, and this time, Jenny's heart crashed to her feet. The knock was tentative, with pauses between each, the knock of a person who dreaded whatever was on the other side of the door.

Jenny knew who was knocking. And she didn't want to see him.

Meg tensed, then worked her way out from under Jenny, meaning to answer that knock. Jenny grabbed Meg's skirts in a desperate grip.

"Nay," she whispered in a hoarse voice, "I dinna want to see him."

Meg knelt next to the bed, so her face was level with Jenny's hidden one.

"Ye must talk to the man, eventually. Ye must hear what he has to say for himself. Ewan has most likely spoken to him already and is trying to sort out the mess. Ye must do your part as well."

Then Meg swiveled away before Jenny could grab her again. She yanked the door open to find Gavin sagging against the doorjamb, all the life in his normally bright, boyish face gone.

"She does no' want ye here now," Meg informed him, stating the obvious.

"Please, I just need to see her."

Meg shrugged and stepped to the side, then flicking her gaze to the unmoving Jenny, she exited, securing the door behind her.

Gavin didn't go near the bed, and Jenny didn't fault him for that. To look directly into the face of the person you betrayed the most? 'Twould be gut-wrenching.

"Jenny?"

His voice. Oh, that deep yet sweet voice, the voice that had, until this day, only spoken to her in words dripping with love and fidelity, that voice was presently a knife in her ears, cutting to her heart. New tears formed as she kept her face in her arms on the bed.

If his voice could cause such cloying pain, what would happen when she looked into his boyish, dimpled face, or those eyes like the finest Scots whiskey?

She didn't have the strength to look at him. Jenny kept her face tucked into her arms.

"Go away," her muffled voice demanded. "I canna see ye, Gavin. It pains my heart so, I would think I am dying."

Jenny poured honesty into her betrayed words as she would pour water into a bowl, as her tears poured from her eyes.

"If ye just let me speak, I can explain—"

"Explain what? 'Tis naught ye can do. If she says the bairn is yours, then 'tis yours. 'Tis no way to prove otherwise."

"Other than my words? My vow that I made to ye the day I first kissed ye? The day I wed ye? Ye would trust the words of a lying, conniving grimalkin over mine?"

If her words had dripped with honesty, then so did his. His plea rang of truth that vibrated in her chest. Ellen was a known liar, a known conniver, and a woman who would do anything to sink her claws into Gavin anyway possible.

Aye, his words held so much truth.

But what if those words weren't true? What if, in a moment of weakness, Gavin fell for Ellen's stunningly beautiful wiles? With the Fraser woman's full bosom, enticing hips, and her fondling mannerisms, such a thing might be possible.

And that chance, that slight chance, was too much for Jenny.

"I want to, Gavin," she admitted, keeping her face covered. "I truly do. But if she has that bairn, even if 'tis no' yours, she shall tell everyone that 'tis. She will name ye as the father to any who will listen, lie or no'. And that poor babe will become a schism between us, something always present, even if Ellen is forced to leave after the babe is born. And that babe, that schism it creates, I canna live with a broken love."

She finally lifted her tear-stained face, but her eyes were closed tight, with fresh tears edging out from under her blonde lashes.

"I love ye, Gavin. I will love ye all my life. But I canna live with ye if that love is broken."

Gavin hadn't moved, thankfully. His thick, heavy breathing which blocked the path of his own sobbing filled the room like a fog.

"Then what of us, Jenny?" His low voice cracked on her name, just like her heart. "We are man and wife."

Jenny's chest clenched. That horrible question. 'Twas the same one that echoed over and over in Jenny's head, pounding against her brain as the smith hammers out iron. What of them?

"I dinna know, Gavin. We shall have to figure that out on the morrow. For now, just leave. Dinna speak to me this night again."

Jenny dropped her face back into her arms and her sobbing renewed with fervor. Had she ever cried so hard, so much, in her life? Had she cried like this when her mother died? Was it possible for a woman to cry this much and recover?

Gavin didn't respond. The only sound in the room was of the door closing as Gavin walked out.

***

Jenny laid on the bed, her face squashed against the tear-dampened plaid wool.

Gavin's question weighed her down even more. He was correct — she was choosing to believe a lying woman over the man who probably had never told a lie in his life.

And she hated herself for it.

But the shadow of possibility that Ellen might be telling the truth, no matter how thin that shadow might be, was too much for Jenny.

And his question of what now?

That was the other problem. How could she stay at Lochnora, even if Ellen were ensconced in a croft outside the bailey, and risk seeing her? Watch her belly grow, her belly that might carry Gavin's son?

Ohh, that possibility struck her like lightening. Another woman carrying Gavin's son.

'Twas a good thing she was lying down, otherwise, she would have swooned to the stone floor.

And if, somehow, that brilliant woman, glowing under her pregnancy, sought out Gavin? If Jenny saw that? Even if she separated herself from Gavin, he still held her heart in his tender, rugged hands, and encountering a scene between the two of them would crush her frail heart.

If anything were left of it after tonight, that was.

Lochnora was Gavin's home, as he was raised alongside the laird and his family. Ellen was stuck here at least until her father claimed her, or longer if he demanded Ellen remain and for Gavin to take responsibility for her and the bairn.

Jenny, too, had been raised at Lochnora, but she didn't have any responsibilities or obligations or family here.

That left one person who needed to leave.

Jenny lifted her face from her bedding.

Thunder cracked in the distance. If she were to leave, she must do it soon.

A storm was approaching.

One that sounded unimaginably more tempestuous than the one in the keep.

***

Where she might go or what might become of her, Jenny didn't think on that. Her sole consideration was she needed to leave. *Now*.

The MacLeods had alliances with the MacKenzies and MacNallys, and the stronghold for each was not far south or east, at least as she'd heard mentioned. Having never left the MacLeod lands, or traveled past the shadow of the Lochnora keep, Jenny had little understanding of how far or exactly where those other clan holdings might be.

But she also didn't care. Leaving right now was her primary concern.

A small satchel hung from the water table, and Jenny grabbed it. Her only true valuables were a thistle brooch her mother had given her and the silver wedding ring circling her finger on her left hand. Her mother, however, had taught Jenny to be nothing if not prepared. She tucked the brooch into the satchel, then added the apple that sat next to the water bowl, waiting patiently for a famished wame. That was all she needed — everything else in the chamber was clearly imprinted with Gavin's mark or belonged to the man himself.

Or worse, was like the brooch that had been gifted by Ellen under false pretenses — something she didn't want to see ever again. Better to leave those behind.

She cinched the satchel and fastened it to her waist before lifting her plaid cape from its peg. The weather appeared fair, even if the night air held scents of petrichor. She hoped the rain would hold off until she arrived at her destination. Wherever that might be.

Jenny wrapped herself in her plaid, and peeking out the chamber door to make sure no one was watching, she slipped into the hallways, silent as a church mouse. The hallway was dim and empty.

It seemed to Jenny that everyone in the keep was hiding, trying to avoid the distressing tumult unleashed by Ellen. The sun dropped as a shimmering gold coin, low in the horizon, and if she kept to the shadows, she might pass through the manse unnoticed. Who really noticed the kitchen maids, after all?

At least one thing went right this miserable day — she made it to the kitchens unseen, but now Jenny needed a new plan. Fiona held court in the kitchens, and as time for the evening meal approached, Fiona was assuredly hard at work. Even those who are distraught must eat.

A long-handled basket near the archway to the kitchens caught her attention, and Jenny grabbed it, draping it over her arm. When she walked into the kitchens, Fiona noted both Jenny and her basket.

"Are ye heading to the gardens to gather some greens afore 'tis too dark?" Fiona asked. Jenny's lips pressed into a semblance of a smile, and she hoped it was enough to fool Fiona.

"Aye," she squeaked out. *Church mouse indeed.*

"Ooch, weel ye better hurry before the rains come, and if ye see the marigolds blooming, grab a few heads to add to the greens?"

Keeping her face averted from Fiona, Jenny nodded. "Aye," she mumbled again, and stepped into the gardens. From there, she only had a few steps before she could follow the well-traveled path that led eastward through the shady thicket of trees. East — *the MacKenzies then.*

Jenny set the basket into the dirt near the garden beds. She flicked her eyes left and right, making sure no one saw her as she stepped beyond the gardens, leaving the Lochnora grounds proper.

That was it. Now she was on her own.

Gasping in a deep breath and wiping away the lone remaining tear that fell on her cheek, Jenny followed the worn path into the darkening woods.

She had not planned on the rain. The clouds built quickly as the sun set, obscuring the blossoming stars and turning the woods into a maze of black. With a sudden crack of thunder, the skies opened up in a flood of rain that rendered her immobile. Jenny couldn't see one step in front of her, and her plaid was soaked in minutes.

At first, she tried to trudge on, thinking that if she just made it to the MacKenzies, she might find refuge with a crofter. Surely a few MacKenzies lived to the west of the clan lands? *A croft or hut, a place of refuge must appear soon!* Her thoughts coursed in a dizzying, nonsensical clutter.

After a few steps slogging through the mud, Jenny realized that was not going to work. She couldn't make out the trail that might lead her to the MacKenzies, anyway.

Turning back the way she came, she assessed if she might walk back to Lochnora, but the trail that way was lost in the night and rain as well.

She was stuck.

Stuck?

The thought sent a shiver through her entire body. What was she to do now? Her chest throbbed all the more, panic combining with her inconsolable sadness.

The sound of raindrops hitting the underbrush gave her an idea — if birds could do it, why couldn't she? Mayhap the trees and brush could provide enough shelter for her to wait out the storm.

Feeling around to her right, her hand struck a tree. The rain was only slightly less invasive as she stood next to the trunk, but she found what she was searching for as she traced her hands down the tree.

Large fronds from ferns and other plants that liked the shade sprung forth at the tree roots. The cluster of brush formed a weak covering, but it was a fair sight better than her soaked tartan. Jenny crawled under the leaves, sinking into the squishy ground, and huddled where the rain penetrated the bushes the least.

Jenny pulled her knees to her chest in her meager shelter, rested her cheek on her knees, and wanted to cry.

But no tears came. She had none left.

***

Sitting under the bush, shivering from cold and distress, she tried to rest. Her bones ached, her skin ached — even her hair ached. *If God were truly kind,* she thought, *He would open the ground and swallow me whole.* How did one live with such misery?

Jenny squinted between the leaves into the rain, searching for the sight of anything and assessing her present condition. Was she close to the MacKenzies? Could she see any torchlight in the distance? If the downpour lessened, she might be able to resume her journey. From the barrage above her head, though, Jenny doubted any more travel would happen this night.

She dozed, the lull of the rain like a lullaby, the music of the earth trying to calm her, to bring Jenny a manner of ease. In the peace of the woods, even soaked to the skin as she was, the music of the raindrops soothed the shaking in her chest and the heat in her brain.

The sounds changed — that was what woke her from her light dozing. Not that the rain lessened or worsened, but another sound, something under the rain that she could barely make out.

Yelling. Men's voices calling. Searching for her. Jenny cringed, tucking herself under the brush as far as she could. What care had she for a search party? She didn't want to be found.

Voices echoed amongst the dripping trees — they must have been farther away. Then a sharp voice called her name, and it seemed the owner of the voice was right before the very bush under which she hid. A deep rumbling voice she knew far too well.

How did her luck manage to have Gavin head in her very direction? End up right at the brush hiding her? Jenny clasped her head in her hands.

If she didn't have misfortune, she'd have no fortune at all.

The voice halted, and between the sagging leaves she could make out a pair of tawny legs clad in sopping boots lit by a wavering torch. She held her breath, praying that the rain and the bush hid her from any prying eyes.

Especially Gavin's.

The brush swung away above her head, sending a flood of rainwater cascading over her head and shoulders. Jenny tucked herself under her arms, trying to avoid the water and the desperate, prying eyes of the chiseled man who stood glowering at her. The pounding in her chest sounded much louder to Jenny than the thunder, the rain, or the men yelling. And it ached — a deep, unreachable ache.

Instead of yanking her upward and dragging her back to that dark hell that was Lochnora, Gavin crouched to her level, lifting her arms from her head with his oh-so-gentle grip. Gavin's grip — the one that was as light as a bird's wing as it held power and strength in check.

Jenny waited. Surely, he would reprimand her now. Demand to know why she ran. Curse her for her brash behavior for forcing the Lochnora warriors into the rain to seek her out. Keeping her gaze on her knees, she waited for his harsh, damning words.

Yet none came. Only Gavin's grip and the rain falling on them like tears of a sobbing Heaven.

She chanced a look at his face. No anger. No fury. No irritation.

His whiskey-hued eyes were dark but soft, set in deep purplish circles and pained, just as Jenny was pained. The easy grin of his lips was downturned, carved in sadness, in brokenness, just as Jenny was sad and broken.

They didn't move. The torrent swirled around them, the rain pounding against the earth, yet in this moment, just the two of them existed in the midst of that storm until it fell away. All they saw was each other.

The lines around Gavin's face lengthened, as if the anguish he felt flexed, intensified as it mirrored her pain. 'Twas as if they were cut from one glass, and without the other, they were shattered.

The other voices drifted away as they sat in the rain, sharing that tether of suffering.

Chapter Fifteen: The Tumultuous Side of Love

"JENNY."

His voice was a wisp in the rain, the flutter of a hummingbird's wing, the sound of steam from a pot. And if she breathed, the word would be gone, lost in the thick air and pounded away by the rain.

Rivulets drenched her hair and ran down her face, stinging her eyes and blending with the stain of her tears, yet she didn't move. Neither did Gavin. Only his lips and the breath of a word that was her name.

In that moment, she hated herself. What she wanted was to hate him. To believe that he had betrayed her, broken the promise of their love. She longed to leave him, pack this unabiding pain away, and never look back.

But his eyes … his shattered voice ... that one word, her name on his lips like the most desperate plea.

And Jenny didn't hate him. God save her — it was why she hated herself, because try as she might, her heart was too entrenched. She hated herself for loving this fair, handsome, complicated man.

She tried to harden her heart.

"Nay, Gavin," her voice was nearly lost in the rain. "Dinna say my name."

He dropped his head, his hair, a deep, wet walnut, fell around his face and dripped rain to mix with his tears. In her whole life, she'd never seen him cry. Had anyone, even Ewan, seen him weep? *Nay.*

"What do ye want me to say? Tell me. Anything. Anything I can say to convince your heart, I will say it."

His voice wrecked her heart even more. Jenny unraveled her wrists from his hands.

"I dinna know the words. I just know that I canna live like this. With this woman who will be a breach between us if she has your child."

He lifted his face and blinked rapidly as water coursed into his eyes. His typically bright face with light eyes flashed as dark as the night, a demon flashing as lightening cracked across the sky. Jenny wasn't sure if she jumped because of the lightning strike or because of the shadow on Gavin's face.

"She does not have my child."

His words were a sword, hacking and cutting at the bindings Ellen had wrapped around him.

Jenny scooted back, spilling out from under the bush. 'Twas so dark, Gavin now was naught but a black outline in the night. A devil indeed.

Gavin scrambled after her.

"Why, Jenny?" Oh! Her name on his lips! A chant. A prayer. A breath of life. Her insides quivered at the word. Why did her name on his lips affect her so?

"Why do ye believe the words of a known liar, a woman who so hates the world she would stand by and watch it burn? Who loves no one but herself?"

Gavin yanked her close, and a flash of fear thrust through Jenny. Never had she seen him like this, a forceful vigilante for love, a heathen warrior desperate for her.

"How could ye think so little of me, Jenny? How could ye?"

***

Gavin's voice fractured when he spoke her name.

He didn't want it to. He wanted to change how she was thinking, force fear or fury or desperation on her, anything to rip away her aching emotion of thinking him naught but a rake, a man who would betray the sanctity of his vow, betray the sanctity of his love for her.

He wanted her to see his anger, that he too was entitled to his own fury — that his honorable nature, one he'd cultivated his entire life, his renown as a man of his word, could be so easily discarded by the words of a woman who was naught but a lying trollop and who used people and disposed of them like rubbish.

Jenny was broken almost beyond repair at Ellen's accusation — her anguish was painted on her like a second skin.

And Gavin's fury at that look, that brokenness, ravaged inside him harder than the storm raging around them.

He had every right to be angry, too. Angry at Ellen, aye, but angry that, after all he'd done, all he'd shown Jenny, one stupid, petulant sentence from a lying witch could easily turn Jenny's heart against him.

As he gazed at her face, pasty and sodden from the rain that threatened to drown them where they sat, the fire of his anger extinguished.

Gavin adored Jenny far too much to harbor anger at her.

All he wanted was for Jenny to believe the truth of his words, to believe him still to be the man she fell in love with, the man she wed, the man whose character and integrity were pristine and unblemished.

And he told her thus, nearly shouting to be heard over the rain.

"I have no' changed, Jenny. Never has a lie passed my lips to ye. Never have I broken a vow that I have made, to ye or anyone else. Never. Ye know this. Ye know this!"

Gavin's knees sunk into the cool mud as he grasped her upper arms. She tried to scramble away, but the mud was slick and his grip was like iron. He wasn't about to let her get away. He needed her to hear him. To believe him.

To love him.

"I am the same man I was yesterday." He was weeping now, outright sobbing as his strong arms pulled Jenny close. He wouldn't lose her. Not over a hurtful lie. Not over Ellen. "The same man I was the day ye wed me. The same man that ye pulled from the precipice with your calm nature and your steadfast love. If ye would have believed *that* man, why do ye no' believe me now?"

Jenny's body shook in his hands, her sobs wracking her slender form.

"Hear me, Jenny. Hear me the way I know ye can. I love ye." His voice cracked with his desperate sobs. "Ye said one woman can no' change who I am in your eyes. I vow to ye — I am *that same man.*"

***

Streams of raindrops ran into and over Jenny's face and eyes, and she blinked to focus on the barely visible outline of Gavin

173

in the stormy dark. No tawny hair, no dimples, just his hulking outline in the rain.

His words, like her name on his lips, tore at her conflicting heart. Gavin was right — *he was right!* And she knew that in her head. He was the same man, full of nobility and character and loyalty. The measure of a man to which all others paled in comparison. Her mind knew that, she knew it with every drop of blood in her veins, with every inch of skin on her body.

But her heart . . . Oh, her heart! All her heart heard was that echoing accusation that Gavin had not been the truthful, faithful man she knew him to be. That Laird Ewan knew him to be. That he prided himself on.

"Then why, Gavin? Why make such a maniacal accusation?" Jenny screamed into the void of the wet, black night, clutching her plaid at her neck. Screaming was the only way to make herself heard over the raging storm. And she needed to make her heart understand the same way her brain did. Could she do that? Could she mend her crushed and woeful heart? Was such a thing even possible?

She felt more than saw Gavin move close, the heat of his skin impossible in the cool, torrential rain, yet there it was, pressing against her as steady and steadfast as Gavin the man. His hands still clutched at her upper arms, gripping her hard enough to bruise her. His breath was hot on her face, steamy in the rain.

"I am that same man," Gavin's gruff voice rose above the storm. "I pride myself on my fidelity, my loyalty, my character. I would no' give it up to anyone, no' for ye, no' for Ewan. Never for someone I see as nothing more than an invasive devil in my home. I have cleaved myself to ye, Jenny. And ye alone. There is no one else on this earth for me! Only ye!"

Jenny opened her mouth to try to protest again, but no words formed. She had no argument, nothing to say to counter it, for he spoke a basic human truth about his loyalty.

Gavin had no such hesitation. His lips landed on her open mouth, hard and pressing, an aggressive kiss that claimed her lips, claimed her for his own. If she still disbelieved his devotion, his desire for her, then Gavin would show her the true depths of his love.

The kiss was almost painful as he ground his lips to hers. His teeth knocked against her teeth, and his tongue plunged deep into her mouth, as though he were swallowing her.

Her heart pounded, throbbed at his attack on her mouth, wanting to deny him while at the same time wanting him to claim her, to show her that he was indeed hers and hers alone.

Jenny shoved off her heart's immediate urge to pull away. Gavin was hers, and Ellen must have done something to set him up — God knew the woman was devious enough to do such a thing.

Once Jenny made that decision, her body followed her mind, and her hand reached for his tunic, gripping it to pull him even closer as the rain whipped in cold fury around them.

A low, guttural raging emanated from his chest and vibrated against her mouth, like her response to his ferocious kiss released a wild animal, one over which Gavin had no control.

Jenny didn't want him to have control. She wanted him to claim her, to know that they belonged to each other. And just as they had vowed before the clan, before the priest, before God, they would let nothing tear it asunder.

***

Lightning flashed overhead, illuminating the trees and their bodies in tense moments of blaring brightness. Their skin was shockingly pale against the black of the storm, dark woods, and night sky, but they didn't notice. Rain poured over them in a wash, cascading rivulets, streams, rivers that plastered their hair to their heads like drenched ropes and their clothes clung to their bodies. Yet their lips still crashed and teased and consumed, as if their very lives depended on one kiss to the next.

Gavin ran a hand down her back to the curve of her rain-soaked backside, then lower, and lifted Jenny's leg to wrap around his hips. Her skirts stuck to her thighs, and she yanked at the sodden fabric to move it away. Then Gavin's powerful legs knelt on the soft carpet of wet grass and mud, pressing Jenny backward. His face flashed all his emotions – anger, frustration, and desperation. Though he tried to temper his raging desire, he forced her wrists to the wet earth, pinning her beneath him.

Still their lips never parted, a continuing dance of lips and tongue and passion.

"I need ye, Jenny," he gasped into her mouth, his teeth grinding against hers. "I need ye, and only ye. Now, please."

She couldn't refuse his plea. His words were sound — this man she knew well, this man who was known far and wide for his loyalty. How could she doubt him when his reputation was on the line? And for someone who was a known liar? Jenny didn't doubt him. In her heart of hearts, she didn't.

As rivulets of rainwater splashed onto her face, Jenny closed her eyes and wiggled her hands free to hold his wet hair. She kissed his rain-logged mouth, sucking his tongue between her lips and devouring his panting breath.

With a swift move of his hand, Gavin lifted his kilt to expose his pulsing cock and drove it between Jenny's open, willing thighs. He drove himself home, to the hilt, and they exhaled into each other's mouths, breathing for each other, gasping for breath in the deluge of rain.

They rocked together under dripping leaves of the trees, with the thunder crashing in the distance and vibrating in their ears and the lightning flashing, blinking their faces in and out of darkness. Raindrops dripped down their necks, over their legs, and they splashed in the rainwater puddles as they loved as furiously as the storm raged. And their lips never parted.

When Jenny cried out his name, which was lost in the fury of the storm and crashed like the thunder, Gavin roared into her mouth — all his rage, all his despair, all his love pouring into Jenny over and over.

And still their kisses continued as their raging calmed and the storm moved off until all that remained was a gentle fall of rain washing them clean.

Chapter Sixteen: The Lad is Smitten

FOR DAYS, AMONG the inhabitants of the keep and the Lochnora demesne proper, the irritation of Ellen and the tumult she caused crept about like a ghost. The air at Lochnora was thick with strife, heady and suffocating even when Ellen wasn't present. It was as though that woman haunted the manse, her foulness painting the stone walls in swaths of bruised hearts and black souls. How did one insignificant woman mark every corner, overwhelm the entire stronghold?

And those in the keep tiptoed in their own home, peeking around corners and jumping at every sound. Fiona's round, open face became pulled taut, and even the strapping lad Davey failed to bring the light of joy to her face.

Davey, too, sensed the weight inside the manse, and tried to bring his youthful light inside with wildflowers from the woods and heather from the glen. He tried to do more around the kitchens for Fiona as well — emptying the waste buckets or stoking the fire as needed, but even those minor tasks were completed with an air of tension.

Meg, however, pushed these concerns to the side and catered to Jenny like a mother hen whose large, shadowy wing veiled Jenny in a protective covering. If Gavin hadn't known already of Meg's forceful nature, watching the Laird's diminutive wife guard over Jenny might have been comical. The lady of the keep was a wee slip of a lass, but Gavin didn't want to find himself on her bad side. Especially since that meant getting on Ewan's bad side, and for all that Meg appeared a delicate angel, Ewan could transform into a black devil if his ire was turned.

But Gavin was grateful to see it. He strove to show Jenny that his thoughts were never far from her and sought her out throughout the day — both to reassure her that he wasn't elsewhere and to reassure himself that she was still with him. It had become a precarious dance, one Gavin conducted with forthright attention daily.

Meg, too, kept Jenny busy with the growing Caitir, who had recently started to crawl and seemed to get into everything. If Jenny wasn't assisting Fiona in the kitchens, Gavin would find her in Meg's solar, weaving, sewing, or chasing the baby around the room.

Only today, when Gavin was searching for her, Jenny wasn't there in the solar. Meg had bid him enter at his knock, and opening the door, he saw Meg reclined on an overstuffed chair, her black-haired daughter sleeping peacefully on her chest. The babe, it seemed, was the only one at peace in Lochnora as of late.

Meg lifted a finger to her lips and shook her head, indicating to Gavin that Jenny was not within. He bowed his head politely and shut the door as silently as he could.

The kitchens, then. Jenny must be helping Fiona for a change. With his plaid sweeping around his thighs, Gavin spun and headed back toward the stair.

***

The sun, though little more than a pale dot in the cloudy sky, gave off enough warmth to make tiny beads of sweat form on Jenny's fair brow line. A gray-blue kerchief tied her smooth tresses at her neck, but wispy strands escaped their bindings and stuck to her face.

She didn't notice them, though, as her hands were deep in the rich earth, yanking out rogue weeds and pulling up tender young turnips. The day was perfect for tending the vegetables. Jenny adored the kitchen gardens as it was her real passion — tending the wee plants until her fingertips were green. There was nothing better for one's tortured soul than a day in the garden, dirt beneath her fingers, creating life.

Her mind escaped the confines of the keep, dancing around images of Gavin as he'd appeared the night before, his broad, tawny chest in the firelight, his skillful hands on her skin, knowing right where to touch to bring a smile to her oft-smile-less face. Even now, the mere thought of his naked skin on hers brought a thin curl to her lips, a sensation she had missed as of late. She could almost forget about . . .

The rustle of crunching footsteps in the garden drew Jenny's attention, and she lifted her eyes. Expecting to find Gavin's robust form and boyishly dimpled face kept a smile on her lips.

She spoke too soon. A hard shudder burst through Jenny as her gaze fell on the red demon who had wrought nothing but misery. So much for losing herself in the garden.

Jenny tried not to pay the woman any mind, forcing her eyes to stare at her hands and at the plants beneath her fingers. But she couldn't keep from snatching glances at Ellen from the corner of her eye.

Ellen had sauntered outside and seated her lazy self on a wobbly bench near the edge of the manse, a shining ruby with her red tresses loose about her shoulders and russet gown clinging to her nubile shape. In Jenny's estimation, the woman certainly didn't *look* pregnant. But then neither had Meg until her lady was near her fifth month. Of course, the stunning Ellen would be a beautiful pregnant woman. Jenny stabbed her digging stick into the dirt, and God save her, she imagined it was Ellen's black heart she was stabbing.

Reclined on the bench, once again like a queen surveying her demesne, Ellen rubbed her still-flat belly and eyed Jenny, flaunting her state and continuing with her insinuation that she carried Gavin's bairn. Jenny shook her head slightly at Ellen's crass actions.

Jenny believed Gavin, truly believed him that Ellen must have lain with another man, mayhap even her own husband, and was using that babe to lay claim to Gavin.

To a married man.

To Jenny's very husband.

What a vile thing to do.

Yet, when Ellen behaved as she did, heatedly claiming Gavin's complicity in her pregnant state, Jenny's belief in Gavin faltered.

What had she done in this life to deserve such heartache? What had she done to Ellen to deserve this?

All Jenny had tried to do was befriend the woman and make her feel welcome. And this was her reward.

Stab. Stab. Stab.

There wasn't enough dirt in the garden to cool Jenny's ire.

"Jenny." Ellen's harpy-ish voice sent a shiver down Jenny's spine.

Gavin had cautioned against engaging with Ellen at all, as had Meg and Ewan, and this was the first time since that catastrophic night that Ellen deigned to speak to her.

"Jenny, dear. Dinna feel bad. Most men canna be trusted. And ye were not yet wed when he came to me. So, he didn't truly betray ye, lass."

Her words were like hammers in Jenny's mind, each one pounding on top of the last. Jenny bit her tongue, willing herself silent. Nothing good would come of responding to that foul woman.

"'Tis rude, Jenny. I'm a guest here, after all. And ye, aren't ye supposed to be a lady's maid? Why do ye toil in the gardens if ye are a lady's maid? Mayhap ye are no' what ye think ye are."

Why would Ellen say such a thing? What was wrong with this woman, to pretend to be a friend, take advantage of the MacLeod hospitality, lay a false claim to Gavin, and then to speak to Jenny so shabbily? Her breathing quickened, panicking, and her heart thudded in her chest.

Dinna speak, dinna speak, she commanded herself.

"Yet here ye are, covered in dirt and sweat. Unlike me, clean, refreshed. Why would Gavin want a dirty, sweaty lass? Why would Meg want a woman like that around her wee bairn?"

"Lady Meg," Jenny said under her breath.

She couldn't stop herself. What woman spoke so disrespectfully of the lady of the keep?

"Pardon? Truly Jenny, your meek voice can be tiresome. What did ye say to me?"

Jenny thrust the digging stick into the ground with all her might then rose and swung her dirt-stained skirts toward Ellen. That mocking half smile sickened Jenny, and her stomach roiled.

"*Lady* Meg, to ye. Ye might lack respect for everyone here at this keep, but ye are wed to a Sheriff, whilst Meg is married to the chieftain of the MacLeods, and ye will speak of her with the respect she deserves."

"Really?" Ellen's deep red eyebrow rose with derisive interest. "Respect? I've heard the lass was naught but a poor crofter's daughter, the daughter of a treasonous father, truth be told. I dinna think a woman such as that is deserving of the respect of the title *lady*. And ye are a great fool if ye abide by that."

Then Ellen lifted her breasts to sit tall and lean forward toward Jenny, as if the woman were trying to show off her cleavage. Jenny shifted back a step. What was wrong with Ellen to make her behave in such vulgar ways?

"And ye are even a greater fool if ye believe a word Gavin tells ye." Ellen laughed, her buxom breasts jiggling as she patted her near-perfectly coiffed hair.

This time when Jenny's wame revolted, she couldn't swallow it back down. She bent at the waist and vomited near Ellen's soft leather shoes. The red devil screeched at Jenny, jerking her feet off the ground.

And Gavin walked out to the gardens just as Jenny was wiping her face.

***

"Jenny! What ails ye?" Gavin flicked an angry glare at Ellen who reclined on the bench, then turned his attention on his wife. He had a good idea what ailed Jenny.

"Perchance 'tis the heat, or the sun. I suddenly felt sick as I tried to go inside." Her voice was weak and hesitant as she held her arm across her waist.

She's lying, Gavin thought. Yet, he wrapped his arm around her back and escorted her to the kitchens, where a frantic Fiona came to her aid. Gavin gestured to the water pitcher.

"Usually, the gardens are a reprieve for ye. Tell me, did Ellen say something to ye to make ye feel sick? Is she to blame?"

Fiona handed a metal cup to Jenny, who sipped and spit the sour taste from her mouth. She shook her head. Gavin still didn't believe her — too much misery as of late could readily be laid at Ellen's feet.

Jenny held up her hand at Gavin as she took another sip. This time she swallowed, then brushed her hand against her brow.

183

"Nay, Gavin. Nothing serious. I think between the heat, the sun, and the trouble Ellen has caused in general, I couldn't take seeing her today. 'Tis all."

"Weel, the turnips in the garden will hold until Mairi can tend to them," Fiona told her. "For now, methinks Gavin should escort ye to bed. Rest a bit. Ye are a tiny lass, for all the fire in your belly, and ye do too much here in the keep. Take a short break. I will send someone to retrieve ye for supper."

Gavin nodded his thanks at Fiona. Then he walked with Jenny up the steps to their chambers. Her face was still a pasty white, and Gavin had the sense Jenny wasn't telling the whole truth, that she was trying to protect him from any boorish statements Ellen may have espoused.

As he settled Jenny into bed and kissed her balmy forehead, anger filled his chest. Jenny didn't have to protect him from anything. 'Twas *his* job to protect her.

"She shouldn't have come to the gardens, Jenny," Gavin's rugged voice was barely above a whisper. "I didn't want ye to have to engage with her at all. I will report this to Ewan and have her ejected back to her hut. Her presence is a poison, and 'tis likely she poisoned ye today."

Jenny's hand reached to Gavin's face, tracing the sharp line of his jaw. He had shaved his whiskers, so his was skin soft and eager for her touch. She pressed her thumb in the curve of his dimple.

"How much longer will she be here?" Jenny asked in a tight voice. Her other hand clutched at her belly. "Wasn't her father supposed to retrieve her by now?"

Gavin shook his head. He had been wondering the same thing with Ewan.

"I dinna know, *mo ghràdh*. But Ewan has tired of waiting for a response. His brother rode out with a small contingent of MacLeod warriors to bring the man here. We can hope 'twill happen soon."

Jenny dropped her hand to her chest and closed her eyes.

"Aye. Soon."

***

With consternation, Ewan found Hamish in the stables with the other stable lads, in the disagreeable task of mucking out the stalls. *Good lads,* Ewan thought. They weren't griping about it as Ewan entered, and instead were teasing each other and gossiping about the lassies in the clan. Just as young lads should.

"Hamish," Ewan called from the far end of the barn.

Hamish glanced up, his face nearly hidden by his raven locks that hung loosely about his neck. He leaned the shovel against the stall and joined Ewan without hesitation. *Good lad,* Ewan thought again.

"Aye, Ewan. Do ye have another chore for me? Please say aye. Get me out of mucking the stalls."

Even under the layer of grime, Hamish appeared so grown, a man in full, but to Ewan, he was still that little boy who wanted to follow Ewan everywhere he went. The laddie who resembled a mother he barely remembered. Ewan softened at the lad, then pulled back his shoulder to flaunt his full height and establish his presence.

"I'm no' here as your brother, Hamish. I'm here as your laird. I've heard some inklings about ye and my wife's sister, Mairi. And there was that fight a few weeks ago, but I've seen no violence since. The inklings, however, have grown louder. What are your intentions with the Lachlan lass?"

Hamish would have appeared less surprised if Ewan had struck him in the head rather than ask him about wee Mairi. Biting back a chuckle at his brother's reaction, Ewan tried his best to appear stoic about this conversation.

"Mairi?" Hamish squeaked, and that was all it took. A bright smile exploded onto Ewan's face and he clapped his brother on the back hard enough to make the lad flounder.

"Ooch, Hamish. Ye canna believe ye were keeping it a secret, do ye? 'Tis difficult to keep much hidden in this clan, laddie."

Hamish's cheeks burned a rosy pink through the stubbly growth of his beard. A young man's beard. Ewan's smile widened.

"I know the passion of young men burns hard, Hamish," Ewan told him, then lowered his tone. "But 'tis no' just any lass, that ye know. 'Tis Meg's sister, my wife's sister, the lady's sister, and that causes ye a bit of strife. She's no' a lass to dally with."

Hamish's deep blue eyes went round at Ewan's comment.

"Ewan! Nay! How can ye think such a thing of me? I dinna want to dally with the lass! She is everything I could want in a woman. No' just her looks, but how she looks at me, and when she laughs! Ewan, have ye heard her laugh?"

Ewan's mouth worked hard not to chuckle at his brother's declarations. *Oh, the lad was smitten!* And in truth, he was not much younger than Ewan had been when he wed Meg. More than that, Hamish was not like Ewan and Duncan, who had been rakish in their youths, ready to rut with any woman who might open her legs.

Hamish was a quieter sort, a man who watched and only acted when demanded of him. A more tender man, he didn't banter with the lasses. He didn't chase skirts. He didn't make trouble at all. Until Mairi. That realization struck Ewan like a bucket of cold water to the face.

Nay, Hamish didn't dally with the maids. Mairi must have cleaved to Hamish's heart completely. Ewan rested a bear-like hand on his brother's soft, black shock of hair. A tender heart Ewan would protect, and he would grant Hamish's every desire if he could.

"Would ye like me to speak to Meg, to Elspeth, and to the lass? If she is amenable, ye two could be betrothed in a sennight."

Hamish's eyes alighted like joyful blue stars, and Ewan lost his chieftain's bearing. Cupping Hamish's head, he yanked the lad (*the young man,* Ewan corrected himself) into a fierce, brotherly embrace.

186

Now to convince Mairi and her family.

Chapter Seventeen: When We Look Doom in the Eye

DUST KICKED UP in a storm, creating a dirt devil far down the road.

Riders from the east.

Gavin froze momentarily, then spun away from Hamish's pathetic attempt at an overhand attack, almost in a dance, sheathing his broadsword as he moved. Ewan was in the barn, looking over a lame mare with one of the stable lads, and Gavin raced for him there.

Ewan barely glanced up at Gavin's appearance.

"What now, Gavin?" Ewan dropped his eyes to the horse's foreleg.

His tone told Gavin that if the archangel Gabriel landed in the bailey and handed out oatcakes to the clansmen, Ewan still wouldn't be surprised.

Not that Gavin blamed him. In truth, Gavin's mind had repeated a litany of *what now?* for the past several months, it seemed. Ewan felt the same.

"Riders," was all he said.

Ewan's head snapped up, that deep blue gaze becoming an intense fire, blazing into Gavin's soul.

"Riders," he deadpanned, waiting for the rest of Gavin's statement.

"Aye. From the east."

A pitch-black eyebrow rose on Ewan's forehead.

"Fraser? Is Duncan with him?"

"I dinna know. They're too far away."

"Where is Ellen? If 'tis her father, and who else might it be, she should be here to meet the man, aye?"

Gavin nodded once. "Aye, but I dinna know where she is. Shall I send Hamish to search for the woman?"

The underlying implication of Gavin's words wasn't lost on Ewan. Gavin certainly didn't want to go searching for her. Ewan dipped his head.

"Aye. Send Hamish. We should go greet the man, then."

Gavin waited for Ewan to finish with the stable lad, giving him directions on keeping the mare from using the leg, and then stretched to his full, astonishing height. Ewan stormed from the stables in the bright afternoon sunlight, his kilt sweeping about his legs, and Gavin followed.

Though Gavin was eager to have Fraser here at Lochnora to deal with his errant daughter *finally*, a wave of nervousness surged over him. A strange sensation indeed. Even when he had faced fearsome opponents, English enemies wielding their giant swords and threatening to separate Gavin's blood from his body, he didn't feel the expressed sense of anxiety as he did now. Who knew how Fraser would react, especially if he believed his sole, beloved daughter had been maligned? Would he send a request to the church and force an annulment between Jenny and himself? And would the church do such a thing with only the word of a known liar as evidence? Perchance. Church leaders had done more with less.

But they couldn't force him to wed Ellen, could they? Other than royalty or high nobility, he'd not heard of such a thing happening. No one could force a man to make a vow before God he didn't intend to keep.

Could they?

Another shudder rang through Gavin at the prospect of being tied to that woman. No amount of silver in all of Callum Fraser's mines was worth it.

***

Gavin wasn't the only one who noticed the incoming riders, and by the time he reached the bailey with Ewan, a small crowd had gathered. He didn't see Jenny among them, and for that, Gavin was grateful.

Duncan led the lean Callum Fraser into the yard, the older man's face a mask of patriarchal anger. His dark russet hair, showing streaks of steel gray, stood on end, and his richly colored tunic made even Ewan's finely woven clothing appear shabby. No wonder Ellen exuded a sense of wealth and entitlement — she had inherited it from her father.

But it wasn't just the two of them. Fraser brought reinforcements with him. To Gavin's eye, they didn't appear to be Frasers, not men he knew from his distant Fraser kin lest-aways. Men from Beauly? Andrew Fraser's men? A sharp tingle pricked at Gavin's neck. Suddenly, Gavin had the idea that the Sheriff of Beauly's death may have been more than a coup by his own soldiers. Perchance the men had been financed.

Swinging down in a smooth leap, so much like his older brother, Duncan grabbed Ewan's upper arm with an air of zealotry.

"The man is irate beyond measure." Gavin heard Duncan say in a low voice to the laird. Ewan's stony expression never shifted. "He's been silently steaming for the entire ride. When he did speak, 'twas a biting word. He will want reparations at best. I had to tell him about Ellen. He did no' want to come otherwise."

Ewan pounded his bear-like hand on Duncan's back, letting him know he understood the young man's predicament. Then he flicked a glance at Gavin, whose severe features matched Ewan's. The two men strode to Fraser, who had dismounted and stood next to his steed, a picture of paternal fury.

"MacLeod. Your man has told me a very demoralizing tale that I can only pray is no' true. Otherwise, we will have discord between us. And I dinna think ye want to have that. No' with me."

Fraser was known to throw his influence around in the same way he threw his money, his silver, and he was rumored to pay well for hired soldiers to fight on his behalf. The man alone lacked the power to affect his words. The hired hands with Fraser, however, were more than ready to do battle for the man's coin. Gavin had noted their leather armor and broadswords at their sides. Oddly heavy weaponry for visiting a man's daughter.

Ignoring Fraser's sell-swords, Ewan looked down his nose at the sad excuse for a man.

"Fraser. We will no' discuss this here. Ellen has only recently informed us of her supposed condition. As of yet, she has provided no evidence. Please come to the hall—"

"No evidence! Her word is evidence!"

Ewan's jaw twitched at the man's words, and Gavin had to clench his lips tight to suppress a grin. If the old man didn't watch out, he'd find himself at the wrong end of Ewan's fists. Gavin had been there before, and it was a painful place to be.

"I said, let us collect ourselves in the hall. My lad will take your horses to the stables."

Gavin nodded to Aren, who scrambled to the horses and led them to the stables. Fraser and his men followed Ewan and Gavin to the hall, grumbling under his breath the entire way. As they walked, Ewan asked Fraser about the Sheriff.

"Aye, the man is dead. He thought himself greater than his position, and his men feared he'd overstep more than he already had. When he fought them to retain his power, one of his men slayed him in a challenge. Rumors make it seem that 'twas a coup, but 'twas nothing of the sort. Just a man who thought he was untouchable."

Ewan shared a knowing look with Gavin. "Rumors aren't the only ones making the attack on the Sheriff seem a coup. There is no animosity betwixt ye and the men of Beauly?"

Callum Fraser shook his gaunt head. "Nay. In fact, 'tis why his men are here, trying to re-establish control and security to the sheriffdom. The Bruce does no' need infighting right now."

Gavin cleared his throat. That much was true, and Fraser's devotion to the Bruce was well known throughout Scotland.

"Nay, he does no' need infighting," Gavin petulantly agreed.

They entered the keep, and in the time it took for Gavin's eyes to adjust to the dim interior of the hall, his heart fell to his feet. Ellen stood near the hearth, almost hiding, her eyes wide with fear at the appearance of her father. Jenny and Meg hovered with Fiona at the entryway to the kitchens. The convergence was uncanny, as everyone sought to witness the drama unfolding in the hall before them.

Gavin gave a wavering sigh and strode to Jenny in a paltry effort to protect her from, what? He wasn't certain — from Ellen? Her father? These strangers from Beauly? From any information that might arise from this less-than-serendipitous meeting?

It didn't matter. Gavin would shield her from everything.

***

Relief washed over Jenny when Gavin approached her, like a golden god of yore back lit against the summer light pouring in the main doors. His face gave her pause — he didn't appear pleased to see her. Instead, his muscles clenched rigidly, and his broad chest blocked her view of those in the hall.

"Gavin! What's amiss?"

"Just stay near me. Fraser is here, and we dinna know what the man will want."

His voice was firm. He grasped her hand in his warm grip and squeezed it reassuringly. If only it were as reassuring as he desired it to be. Keeping the bulk of Gavin in front of her, she peeked over his shoulder to the intriguing events in the hall, which was bleak with an air of turmoil, a horrible dream.

"Here I am, MacLeod. Bring my daughter. From what your man here says, it seems your clan owes my kin and daughter recompense for Ellen's condition."

Ewan's outward expression was calm, but to those who knew him, the anger at Fraser's presumptuous nature boiled under Ewan's skin. Jenny marveled that the laird reined in his temper. Ewan, like Gavin, was renowned for his hot-headed nature, and she gaped at the present state of control in both men.

"First, we dinna know if Ellen is in any condition or not. Further, she might claim —"

"Claim? Might?" Unlike Ewan, Fraser's fury spewed from every part of his body. *Did the man have any guile when it came to his daughter?* Jenny wondered. "I take my daughter at her word."

"I wouldn't," Gavin chimed in.

Fraser spun his sputtering anger to Gavin. "Are ye calling my daughter a liar?"

Gavin held his ground, his jaw setting into a hard line to conceal the fury he tempered.

"'Tis the least I would call Ellen."

Fraser launched at Gavin but was yanked back by one of the Beauly men.

"Who do ye think ye are?"

"He's the father of my babe, Father." Ellen's high-pitched voice echoed in the hall, and both Ewan and Gavin visibly grimaced.

"Ellen! My lass! What has this vile clan done to ye?"

Fraser rushed to the hearth to take his daughter's hand. Jenny had to bite her inner lip to keep from groaning audibly at Fraser's fawning over Ellen. The sight of it made her physically ill, and she had to swallow several times to calm her churning stomach.

Ellen, on the other hand, smiled brightly.

"Ooch, Father. Ye know Gavin. 'Tis he who is the father, no' the clan. Please have some respect for the man."

"Are ye certain 'tis no' the child of Andrew Beauly? Your husband?"

"Ye mean my dead husband?" Ellen spat out. She glared at her father and the men who accompanied him. "Nay. A woman knows. That man is the babe's father." Once again, she pointed that insidious, accusing finger.

Fraser turned his vitriol onto Gavin, and his men closed in to join him. Jenny wanted to stand up for her husband, deny Ellen's accusations, and point a finger back, but fear overwhelmed her, and she cowered behind Gavin. Her husband, to his credit, stood like a stone monolith shielding her from both the accusation and Fraser himself, and pride blossomed in Jenny's chest at him for it.

"Ye must provide satisfaction for my daughter. If ye dinna have a child yet with this woman, your marriage should be annulled and ye must wed my daughter."

Gavin exploded into a bitter laugh, surprising Jenny that she flinched backward. *Why was Gavin laughing?* Their lives hung in the balance, and he openly mocked Ellen and her father? The crowd in the hall had increased, Meg, Gavin's men, and the kitchen maids, all with mouths hanging agape at Gavin's unseemly reaction.

"Ye must be a complete fool if ye expect me to set aside my wife, *my wife*, for your lying trollop of a daughter. She would spread her legs for anyone if it served her purposes."

Jenny's hand flew to her mouth as Fraser leaped at Gavin, who drew his sword in a smoothing, ringing move. He held Callum Fraser at the sword tip and wore an irritated expression on his face. Gavin had reached the end of his patience with Ellen and her kin.

"Gavin!" Ewan called out, trying to maintain a manner of civility in his hall.

"Ye shall provide for my daughter and your babe, then. Unless, another solution can be found," Fraser spat out, and he flicked his eyes to the Beauly man standing near Gavin.

Before Jenny could blink, the hired soldier unsheathed his sword and held it at Jenny's neck. She froze. The world seemed to fall away, leaving only the sensation of cold steel against her tender skin and the sight of Gavin's horrified look on his boyish face. She'd never seen him afraid before — the man lived like he had nothing to lose. But now he did, and that fear ate at him like a beast.

Jenny whimpered, the sound breaking the shock of those in the hall. She watched as the expression on Gavin's face transformed from one of absolute fear to one she *had* seen before — an angel of death. In a movement so quick, so practiced she almost didn't see it, Gavin twisted his blade under his arm to the Beauly man holding his wife at sword point, spinning as he thrust the tip under the man's ribs. The broadsword dropped from Jenny's neck as the man fell in a pool of his own crimson blood.

Gavin didn't pause, confident his blade struck home, and continued his spin until he was once again holding Fraser at the tip of his steel. The ringing of other swords unsheathing echoed, but no one else moved. Fraser's look of anger had turn into surprise. Jenny rubbed at her neck, shocked that it was not separated from her body, and in awe at Gavin's precise, masterful movements. His practice in the yard and efforts in combating MacLeods' enemies had led him to this moment where his skill was genuinely necessary. He was a true Highland warrior in every sense of the title.

And he had the attention of everyone in the hall.

"As I said, I will never set aside my wife. She knows, as do I and the rest of those present here, that I never laid with your daughter. Not since she departed to wed her Sheriff. She has been naught but rubbish to me since."

"If my daughter says ye are the father of her babe, then ye are the father. Ye have no recourse for that."

Gavin's head hung slightly at those words. What Fraser said had validity. A man had no way of knowing the parentage of a bairn. Ellen's accusations might as well be the truth.

"I warned ye of this, Ewan," Fraser said, raising his voice toward the Laird.

Ewan's gaze jumped from Fraser to Gavin, whose brow furrowed at Fraser's statement.

"What warning? Ye warned me of naught. I was unable to read your response to my letter, and I had to send my own kin to retrieve ye to deal with this . . . situation." Ewan flapped his hand at Ellen.

What else could they call Ellen but a *situation*?

"What? I sent ye a response, telling ye to send the lass home. That I would protect her from any attempt from those in the Beauly coup." Now Fraser appeared confused, his face twisted, and Gavin and Ewan shared a grim glance. That was the letter Ellen had intercepted. "I responded, but ye didn't return the lass. Next thing I know, your man here is telling me a loathsome tale of my daughter and her current state."

"I was unable to retrieve your letter." Ewan's voice was hard. The man was proving his daughter was a problem, and he wasn't even aware of it.

"Aye, my laird's correct," Duncan commented. All attention shifted to Ewan's younger brother.

Ewan remained quiet, as his aspect was fearsome enough to make any man cringe, and Duncan was no' different.

"Master Fraser, I brought the letter back a few weeks ago. Right when I returned."

"What did ye do with it? *I* never saw any missive from Master Fraser." Ewan was egging him on. Duncan saw that readily enough, and he was using this information to show Callum how misguided his daughter truly was.

Duncan leaned to peer around Ewan. The laird followed his gaze to where Duncan was staring, and an expression of ill-suppressed ire crossed his face. Duncan's accusatory eyes stared at Ellen.

"I gave it to Ellen. 'Twas from her father, after all, and she said she was going to your study to speak to ye. I handed it to her."

Duncan kept his head bowed as he spoke. He had made a gigantic mistake, and though he had rectified it by bringing Fraser to Lochnora, his failure was now made public.

But Ewan's eyes weren't on his misguided younger brother. They were throwing daggers at the woman who caused strife in his clan.

"Ye mean to tell me, ye could have been back in the graces of your father before ye wreaked such havoc on my clan? On my beloved friend and man-at-arms? What is wrong with ye? What did ye do with the letter?" Ewan demanded.

The incriminating tone of his voice echoed in the hall. Callum Fraser's guileless face was unable to hide the shock of Duncan's words or his daughter's actions. Ellen didn't hesitate. She turned her pretentious face to Gavin.

"Your brother failed in his duty, Ewan. Dinna place that sin upon me if ye did no' receive the letter. I placed it on the edge of your desk. If ye lost it, then that sin is upon ye. Regardless, we still must come up with a plan for how Gavin will support me and his babe."

A harsh smile crossed her lips as she caressed her belly. Her still flat belly.

Then a new voice, a sweet, crystalline-like voice broke the thick air of the hall.

"Wait, ye think Ellen is with child?"

Chapter Eighteen: Timely Revelations

JENNY'S GAZE, ALONG with everyone else's, slowly turned to the delicate Mairi, who had entered late and stood between Meg and her devoted admirer, Hamish. Meg's brow crinkled at her sister.

"Mairi, what do ye mean, *we think*?"

Jenny hated to admit it, but the bubble of hope that swelled within her made her light-headed and dizzy. Was it possible? Did someone, somehow, have evidence that Ellen's babe was not Gavin's? What did Mairi know? Tears burned behind her eyelids, and Jenny blinked rapidly to push them away.

Such evidence could not possibly exist. Could it? Why might the unassuming Mairi speak otherwise?

Mairi leaned into Meg, whispering in her ear. Meg's hand flew to her mouth.

"Show me," she commanded. Ewan joined Meg.

"And me," he added.

Mairi blushed a deep rose from her hairline to the rounded neckline of her bright kirtle. She appeared traumatized at the prospect of showing Ewan whatever she wanted to reveal to Meg.

Meg, however, lifted her hand to Ewan.

"Nay, Ewan. 'Tis no' the purview of men. I'll accompany Mairi. Ye keep everyone here. We shall return shortly."

Ewan, ever contrite when it came to Meg, deferred to his wife's request and bowed as they swept to the stairs.

The silence in the hall was staggering, and Jenny shook to her bones. First the shock of having a sword at her neck, the dead man still lying near her feet, and now the prospect of learning if Ellen was lying or not? Who wouldn't shake over all that had transpired in so short a time?

Her eyes fell on Gavin. He didn't shake. He remained hardy and resolute in front of Jenny, his body guarding against the harrowing events of the hall. Then realization dawned on her like the warm summer sun. Of course, he wasn't shaking — because he *knew*. He was standing tall and proud in vindication. Because he was a faithful, loyal man, a man of integrity, and now the long-sought evidence of his innocence was within his grasp.

Jenny didn't need to see any proof — no matter what it was. Gavin's stature was enough to convince her that his pleas to believe him, to know him as the stalwart Highlander he'd been the day she met him was the same man who stood before her today, weren't in vain.

Jenny was convinced.

She lifted her hand and rested it on the thick, bunching muscles of his shoulders. No words came to her lips — what might she say in this dire moment? But the feel of her light touch on him was enough for Gavin to step back to her, pressing against her body, reinforcing that tether that united them.

Jenny dropped her forehead against his powerful backside and exhaled a long breath. 'Twas as though she'd been holding that breath since Ellen had first arrived, and now, understanding what she did, she could breathe again.

Her stomach began to calm as well. Jenny's other hand slid to the front of Gavin's tunic, and he placed his hand over hers, clasping her palm against his heart in a silent sentiment.

After all her doubts and his frustrations, she yet held his heart.

***

Meg and Mairi returned to a subdued room. Meg carried a leather satchel and patted Mairi's arm as they approached Ewan. Though she tried to suppress the triumphant smile on her face, she was not as accomplished as Ewan at masking her emotions.

"Ellen is lying."

Meg's attempt at a whisper fell flat — the phrase echoed on the stones, as though the keep breathed her statement. Everyone in the room, the very hall itself, hung on every word she spoke. Even Ellen's confident, pretentious expression cracked as she set her jaw.

Ewan didn't flinch. Under Jenny's hand Gavin's heartbeat sped up, thumping in an irate staccato against her palm.

"How can ye know this for certain? No' with Gavin's child? Or no' with child at all?" Ewan pressed.

The intensity of Meg's gaze bore into Jenny, sending a silent message of delight.

"No' at all."

In slow, drunken-like movements, they shifted to Ellen, who responded by tossing her mass of russet waves over her shoulder. The words Meg spoke had no impact on her.

"How can ye know this?" Ewan asked.

Meg opened the satchel, and Mairi withdrew a clay pot and a set of old cloths. Ewan's and Gavin's twisted expressions mirrored those of the men in the hall. For women like Meg and Jenny, the evidence was obvious. Jenny glanced at Ellen before returning her attention to the pot Mairi cupped in her hand. Ellen ground her teeth and glared at the laird's wife, and Jenny didn't doubt the woman would have killed Meg where she stood if she had the chance.

"What is this, Meg? A pot and old fabric? How does this prove anything?" Ewan sniffed at the pot and crinkled his nose at the lingering sour scent.

Meg rolled her eyes heavenward. And Jenny had to choke back a surprising burst of giggles that threatened to explode in this completely inappropriate moment.

"Of course, ye wouldn't know what these are, Ewan. These are the purview of women. The pot contains an oil that, when soaked in a bit of fabric and inserted, might prevent a woman from conceiving a bairn."

All the color drained from Ewan's face, and Jenny's chest vibrated with those withheld giggles. She pressed her face into Gavin's tunic. *Do no' laugh! Do no' laugh!* she told herself fruitlessly. How could she laugh at such a trying time? Gavin's confused face spun around to Jenny. Poor man. Poor men, unknowing about the ways of women.

"Ye said *might* prevent. Then ye dinna know with a measure of certainty that Ellen is no' full with child." Ewan intoned.

Meg sighed, and Mairi flicked her pale green eyes to her sister and then looked back at the items in her hands. She, too, was trying desperately not to laugh at the absurdity of the situation. Meg pointed to the cloths Mairi held.

"These are cloths for a woman's time, Ewan. Mairi found them in Ellen's bed space before she left for her own hut and said that Ellen left one behind last time she was here in the keep."

Ewan's mouth opened and closed like a fish out of water.

"I dinna understand. She was just at the keep yesterday, right? Why would she have cloths? Do women need cloths when they are full with a bairn?"

If Ellen had lied about the babe, then 'twas proof she lied about everything, including her supposed interludes with Gavin. At this, Jenny could contain herself no longer. Her giggling was clipped, snickering, and she clasped her hand to her mouth. Meg's humor spread across her face at her husband's discomfort and was a match to the grin that danced across Mairi's mouth.

The only woman in the room who didn't find humor in the situation was Ellen. Her hands clenched into fists as tight as her jaw. Her subterfuge was uncovered, and she had no recourse.

"Ewan, *mo ghràdh*." Meg placed her hand on his cheek. "If she needed the cloths as of yesterday, then 'tis completely impossible for the lass to be with child. Women dinna need the cloths if they are carrying a bairn. If ye need to confirm that, I can bring my mother here."

Ewan shook his confused head and waved his hand to his wife. "Nay. 'Tis no' necessary. I trust ye understand the workings of women." He whirled to Callum, ignoring the fury that steamed from Ellen.

"Callum, there shall be no recompense. Gavin will no' set his beloved wife aside, nor will he support any issue from that woman's loins."

This time, the accusing finger pointed to Ellen, who should have looked wide-eyed and stricken. Instead, her eyes narrowed, hatred flowing from her like blood from a wound. Callum Fraser bowed his head and flapped his hand at his daughter.

"Take her," he directed his hired soldiers. "'Tis long past time since Ellen should come home. She can explain her reasoning for her actions on the ride back. My apologies, Laird MacLeod." Then he shifted, and any pretension he'd brought with him was gone, replaced with a solemn sense of remorse.

"And to ye and your wife, Master Gavin, I apologize for my actions, the actions of my men, and for the twisted antics of my daughter. We shall leave ye in peace."

Several of Fraser's men lifted their fallen brethren from his spot on the floor to carry him home. Jenny's stomach roiled at the sight, and she didn't envy whoever had the chore of scrubbing the stones.

Another Beauly soldier grappled with Ellen, scuffling with her and dragging her toward the main doors. In a moment of mettle, Jenny stepped around Gavin and placed herself directly before Ellen.

"Why, Ellen?" Jenny asked, her voice choked with trepidation. "Ye have such a future ahead of ye, a wealthy father, striking beauty. Why would ye fight so hard for a man who didn't want ye when there are so many who do?"

Again, those gathered in the hall held their collective breaths, waiting for Ellen's answer. But what answer could she give that would make any sense?

Jenny wasn't ready for the spray of spittle that struck her face. She flinched at the vile attack and wiped her cheek with her sleeve.

"Ye will never understand. Ye weren't sold for your position. Ye've always had a measure of freedom here. Me? A child with Gavin would guarantee I'd live my life for my own, no' under the domineering roof of my overbearing father or be sold to a man who thinks he can control me, dictate my life. I could have everything on my terms."

She cut her deathly gaze to her father. "Ye might bring me home, Father, but ye will no' keep me there. I'll be yoked by no man."

Gavin remained stiff and tense under Jenny's hand but gave a curt bow of his head to Fraser before shifting his intense amber eyes on Ellen.

"If a man does love ye, he will no' dictate your life. I have heard a powerful statement as of late, Ellen. One ye might take to heart. While I dinna fully understand what ye hoped to achieve here, I can tell ye that ye can no' force someone to love ye. No matter what ye say or what ye do, if they dinna love ye, then ye must move on. Ye can no' accomplish anything trying to lie or deceive."

Ellen lifted her prideful chin and looked past those in the hall to the pale horizon outside. She was done with her sermonizing. Jenny stepped to the side and let her gaze linger on the bright red woman who had nothing in this world but a fatalistic view of her future. Even though Ellen was nothing but a destructive force, Jenny found it difficult not to feel some measure of pity for this sad woman. A hint of sympathy welled in Jenny's chest, tight and clenching, momentarily displacing the loathing she felt. Then all the misery Ellen had put her and Gavin through crashed in her mind, the pity was gone, and she resisted the urge to place a reassuring hand on Ellen's arm as the woman marched past.

Ellen probably would have just bitten a finger off, anyway.

***

The shared release of breath in the hall would have provided levity if the whole situation and Ellen's departure hadn't left them haggard. Mairi handed the pot and cloths to Meg and took Hamish's arm, letting him escort her from the hall. She'd done great work, solved the Ellen problem in one swift presentation, but it wasn't the type of attention Mairi craved. Her desire to leave and find peace after the chaos in the hall was more than evident to everyone in the keep. Most of them felt the same.

The rest of the stunned crowd returned to their chores now that the captivating drama in the hall had ended. Finding themselves in a now empty main hall, Gavin swiveled around in Jenny's arm and grasped her waist in a powerful, almost desperate grip. And he was desperate — Ellen was gone, gone, *finally*, and he could focus on Jenny with no further interruptions. They had encountered enough interruptions, enough to last a lifetime. A boring life with Jenny by his side held significantly more appeal.

And Gavin still wasn't sure what happened with the pot and the cloths. The women in the hall evidently did — covering their giggles with their hands or stiff lips yet failing miserably. After all they had been through, how could the women be laughing?

Even Jenny wore a smile like the sky wore the sun, bright with a fullness of life unencumbered. Hers was an expression Gavin hadn't seen in months, and he craved it, adored it, and vowed to help her keep it so he might see it every day.

That smile changed her whole visage — instead of tight and fretful, her skin was as smooth as milk, English roses in her cheeks, and her blue eyes sparkling to rival any loch at daybreak. Even her body seemed fuller, more ripe, ready for the picking. Blood pounded in his head and chest, and lower, causing his groin to twitch. Gavin pulled her to him, clutching her as close as their clothing would allow.

"Ye are fairly glowing," he told her. She flushed an even deeper rose.

"And the relief in your face is obvious, *céile fir,* my husband." Jenny rubbed her face against his cheek, nuzzling the stubble of his jaw.

"'Twas like we had a yoke about our shoulders. And now that weight is lifted. Oh Jenny, I am so verra sorry —"

She lifted a finger to his lips, quieting him.

"Ye have naught to apologize for. None of us could have predicted a tempest like Ellen invading our lives, causing such strife. But she is gone now . . ." Jenny's voice drifted off.

"What is it?" Gavin asked, suddenly concerned. Had Ellen left something behind? God save them, that was the last thing they needed.

"Nay, nothing of grave concern. I just wonder what will happen to her now? Her unhappiness, her anger, to live again with her father? 'Tis a disaster in the making."

Gavin kissed her fingertips, relishing in her heady scent of heather. Oh, how he had missed being able to focus on her scent!

"Dinna fret, *mo bhean.* Ellen is a survivor. And if she doesn't find a husband to meet her needs soon, she will undoubtedly leave her father, strike out on her own. Any strife she encounters is on her."

Jenny's hand flew to her neck. "Run away? Surely 'tis too dangerous for a woman to do that!"

A grumbling laughter burst from Gavin's boyish face. "Ooch, didn't she do just that to arrive here? Methinks Ellen can take care of any strife or danger she encounters. Ellen will find her way, of that I have no doubt."

Gavin swung her around, pressing her back against the cool stone wall. His lips found the curve of her neck, and he nibbled at her savory skin, licking like she was the sweetest honey on his tongue.

"But 'tis time to forget about the havoc of Ellen and the Frasers and attend to us, to ye. I rather believe we have been lacking in that endeavor."

"Nay, ye haven't," Meg's voice called to them from the passageway to the kitchens.

Gavin jumped back from Jenny to find Ewan and Fiona standing with Meg, their glee filling the room. *What audience was this?* Gavin tugged at his tunic and regained his composure.

"I dinna think ye are one to judge, Lady Meg," Gavin teased, tearing his face from the succulent Jenny to address Meg.

Something about the three of them staring at Gavin and Jenny appeared peculiar to Gavin. *Why were they smiling like fools?*

"Ooch, I rather believe I am, especially after Mairi shared a wee bit 'o information with me."

Jenny's face scrunched up at Meg's enigmatic words. Ewan and Fiona, however, beamed.

"What information?" Jenny asked.

"Jenny, I know that we've been distracted, but no' so distracted that surely ye haven't noticed. Ye have been feeling ill as of late, aye?"

Jenny nodded. "Aye. All the fretting over —"

"And ye haven't noticed that ye haven't needed any cloths this month? Mairi shared that news with me."

"What? I don't understand —"

Ewan trembled with anticipation, unable to contain himself. "'Twasn't Ellen who was with child! Good job, Gavin! Ye took care of that straight away!"

Gavin froze where he stood, one arm looped around Jenny's waist. His Jenny, whose clear skin had seemed a bit drawn just as her breasts and hips were fuller. His Jenny who'd complained of illness and fatigue over the past few days. His Jenny, who'd been sick in the garden and attributed it to Ellen's presence. Gavin had assumed 'twas Ellen, the heat of summer, and overwork, not . . .

He shifted stiffly, his furrowed gaze locked onto Jenny. "What? Are ye . . .? A bairn?" His whisper barely broke through the excitement in the hall.

The possibility of a babe, one with Jenny, had not entered his mind, as preoccupied as they had been with Ellen and her miserable antics. And so soon? Was it possible?

Jenny dropped her hand to her belly. "So soon?" She echoed Gavin's thoughts.

Their answer was Fiona screeching with joy and clapping her hands. She rushed them, wrapping Jenny and Gavin in a full-armed embrace.

"Ooch! More bairns! Blessed ye are! Blessed are the MacLeods!" She cheered before racing to the kitchens to share the news with the other kitchen maids.

Meg and Ewan followed, with Meg promising to send her mother to visit Jenny in the morn, and Ewan clapping a shocked Gavin on the back, rocking him on his toes.

"Well done, man!" he cheered again before escorting Meg from the main hall.

Just the two of them remained in a stunned silence, staring at each other.

Gavin's brain was hot, fevered, struggling to form a single word. This day had wrenched the soul from Gavin before shoving it back, and now this news on top of what they had been through — he marveled that Jenny was still on her feet. Gavin barely held his own.

"Gavin?" Jenny's soft voice rang in his ears, drawing his attention. He blinked hard, trying to regain command of his thoughts.

"Aye, I'm here, lass." He threaded his arms around her waist again, this time more for support than unbridled lust.

"What do we do now? This seems so soon. We've been wed just under two months, and with everything regarding Ellen . . ."

Her distress weighed on Gavin, and he would do anything to relieve her of that weight. He was strong enough to carry it for her. He brushed filmy tendrils of hair from her face.

"I presume we will have confirmation on the morrow. For now, I am going to fulfill the promise I made to ye earlier and take ye up to my bed and worship your body and love ye until I can no' any longer. If ye are well enough for it that is."

Jenny nodded once. Then his lips found hers, claiming her mouth in an eager kiss of new opportunities, of starting fresh, and of all the hope their anchored future now held.

They didn't make it back to supper that night.

Chapter Nineteen: Bearing Good News

THE SCENT OF RAIN hung in the air, signaling wet weather approaching after another span of warm, dry days. The MacLeods scrambled about to finish their outdoor chores, lest they be caught in a drizzle, or worse.

Mairi pulled clothes from the drying rack at the garden's edge, an area well away from any dank shadows of the keep where mold might grow. She patted and gripped the different clothes, grateful they had dried, then threw them in the basket that dangled from her arm.

The rain would be welcomed by many, including Mairi, who wished to wash away the rank odor of the past several weeks and any lingering reminder of the red Fraser woman. The woman had left several days earlier, and Mairi still felt like the stench of the whole affair clung to her skin.

Separately, Jenny, Gavin, Meg, and Ewan had come to her, thanking her for her role in absolving Gavin of any guilt regarding Ellen Fraser, and ensuring the red tempest returned home. Mairi didn't see it that way. The attention made her rigid with discomfort. In her mind, she had been merely correcting wrong information.

Her celebrity as the woman who saved the day made her uncomfortable, and keeping herself busy with simple, necessary chores was a sound way for her to forget the whole affair entirely. A peal of thunder rolled in the distance.

"Mairi? Might I assist ye before the rains come?"

Hamish's soft, deep voice resonated in her ear, closer than she expected, and she spun. He stood so near that she would have crashed into him if she hadn't been holding her basket. Instead, the basket slammed into his stomach. Hamish emitted a surprised "oof" sound and blushed to the roots of his hair.

"Och, Hamish! I'm so sorry! I did no' see ye there!"

Hamish bowed from his waist like a proper gentleman and slipped the offending basket from Mairi's slender arm.

"Aye, that I noticed." He covered his blush with an endearing smile. "Do ye have any more clothes to collect?"

His flashing blue eyes flicked from the clothes in the basket to Mairi, and a flare of excitement stirred in her chest. Those eyes, his barely-there scruff of black beard that ran along the edge of his jaw, his broad shoulders . . . These features were handsome, but something else about him — the way he gazed at her as though no one else in the world existed. Mairi had never encountered such a look, and her heart fluttered again under her breast.

She was powerless in her body's response to Hamish, she had finally admitted to herself. And with the attentiveness he paid to her, could he feel the same? Mairi shook her head at the thought. But they were young, their relationship so new . . .

Could one find love so early in life?

"Nay. I believe 'tis all. But we should head inside before the rain catches us," she answered.

Hamish cast his eyes heavenward, searching the skies.

"Nay. The clouds are collecting to the west, but still break for the light of the sun. We have hours afore we have to fear getting caught in the rain."

Mairi's brow knotted, and she copied Hamish's movement, searching the clouds. "Really, ye can tell all that by where the clouds are?"

When she dropped her gaze back to Hamish, he was no longer studying the skies. He was studying her.

"Aye."

They fell silent, and Mairi dug into the dry dirt with the toe of her shoe.

"Did ye have something else ye needed, Hamish? Otherwise . . ."

Mairi lifted her hand to gesture towards the open kitchen door, and Hamish caught it in his own large hand. Her breath caught in her chest, and when Hamish brought her fingertips to his lips to kiss them, she fairly swooned. Then he threaded his fingers with hers.

"Aye, I do have something else I need," he said, his voice so low it shook her to her bones. Mairi shivered.

"What is it ye need, Hamish?" She was shocked at how muted her voice was.

Hamish shifted the basket to his side and stepped so he was separated from Mairi by a breath. He was nearly as tall as his brother, and she had to lift her chin high to gaze onto his face.

"Ye canna guess?" he breathed more than asked. Mairi shivered again.

"My sister had said that I should no' tempt ye, no' unless we are to be betrothed. Are ye ready for such a large step?"

Hamish's jaw tightened at her question.

"My brother told me the same, to keep my distance unless I am ready to ask ye to wed."

"And?"

"Where am I standing, lass?"

Mairi dropped her eyes to Hamish's tunic-covered chest that was close enough to kiss, if she desired. And she desired. She quickly flicked her eyes back to his.

"Oh." She exhaled shakily. "But we're only newly met, Hamish. Ye are so young. Aren't men supposed to wait to wed? Make certain of who they want to wed?"

"Most men wait because they have to search for that person who makes them whole. I knew ye made me whole the day I met ye, Mairi. Ye were standing next to Fiona in the dappled spring sunlight, your hair a halo of gold and sunset, and ye stole my heart that very moment."

Mairi inhaled her surprise at his impassioned words. "Why did ye no' tell me, Hamish? Here I was, playing with your emotions, baiting ye with Aren . . ."

"I know Aren, and I knew ye would no' care for him once ye grew to know him well. And if he stood in my way? Weel, I would fight the entire English army with naught but a dirk if it meant winning your heart. And as ye said, we are young. I did no' want ye to feel rushed."

Hamish's sweet words took her mind by storm, and she couldn't focus on the man before her, let alone what he was saying. She had to find a quiet moment to hear her heart.

Even though she already knew what her heart wanted. Hamish waited with marvelous, stoic patience.

"Ye dinna think 'tis too soon to be betrothed, especially after everything that happened here?"

Hamish held out his other hand. "I think being with ye is the chance of a lifetime, and I am willing to take that chance if ye are."

Mairi stared at his intense eyes for several heartbeats, then dropped her gaze to his open palm.

And grasped it.

***

A rider trotted into the Lochnora bailey in a flurry, kicking up mud like heavy, mucky snowflakes. The storm might have departed but the mists and mud still clung to the earth. Ewan and Gavin's heads peered around the side of the smith's stall, like lowland voles, their eyes narrowing at the man atop the steed. He bore the red and black dragon banner of King Robert the Bruce, and they caught each other's eyes as they abandoned their work to meet the rider.

Unannounced messengers from the king rarely bore good news.

Gavin knew something about this rider that few knew — that he was here to gather the MacLeod men and lead them to the Bruce. At least, that was what the missive Ewan had received intimated. Gavin had warned Jenny this was expected, but it seemed too soon. Jenny and Gavin had only had a few days of marital bliss after Ellen's departure.

Too soon indeed. But would any time *not* be too soon? Nay. 'Twasn't enough time in the world to spend with Jenny, in Gavin's estimation.

A sinking sensation filled Gavin's chest. He glanced pointedly at Ewan, who had inhaled into his full, commanding height. They shared an unfortunate look.

Gavin and Ewan knew why the rider was here at Lochnora, why any warrior under the Bruce's banner would ride this deep into the Highlands. Some MacLeod men had set out and joined the king's army earlier in the year, shortly after the Bruce arrived back in Scotland. Yet the Laird, Ewan's brothers, and Ewan's man-at-arms remained on the clan lands.

Given the close relationship between the Bruce and Laird MacLeod, Ewan's absence had to be a thorn in the Bruce's side, and Ewan had already decided to rectify that. Meg's health, Gavin's marriage, these things had kept the men away, and now 'twas time for the rest of the MacLeods to take up their swords, mount their steeds, and ride south under the Bruce's banner.

Though his gaze fixated on the warrior leaping from the destrier, Gavin's mind was elsewhere, dreading how he might explain to his pregnant wife that he had to leave her side. After all Jenny had been through, and now carrying a babe, Gavin knew that she was not going to receive that news well. He sighed audibly as the young, black haired man approached.

"Laird MacLeod?" he asked, his rich brown eyes shifting from one man to the other. Ewan stepped forward.

"Aye. I'm the MacLeod. What can I do for the king this fine day? I assume ye are here under the king's command that we ride south to his army?"

The lad shook his head and tugged at his damp plaid.

"'Tis what I need to discuss with ye. The king's command for ye is a wee bit different. Might we speak inside?"

Ewan gestured to the hall, and Gavin fell into step right next to his Laird. The mysterious message from the youthful emissary piqued his interest.

"Gavin, can ye ask Fiona or Mairi to bring the man some water. Or ale?" Ewan raised an eyebrow. The lad bowed his head.

"Water. I'm fair parched."

Gavin delivered the request to Fiona and rushed back to Ewan. He joined the men where they sat in conversation at the main table of the hall. The lad had just introduced himself as Ian Douglas, a close cousin to the fabled Black Douglas, before Fiona sauntered in with a tankard of water.

Ian gulped at the water, splashing droplets onto his thinly bearded cheeks. Once the tankard was empty, he slammed it onto the table and wiped his face with the back of his hand.

"I understand ye expect to join the Bruce. He had been successful in the Great Glen, south of Ben Nevis, and is presently working to retake Inverlochy Castle. He has men aplenty for that. I've been sent here to coordinate something else with ye."

Ewan leaned forward, his brows high on his forehead. Gavin reclined against the cool stone wall and crossed his arms over his brawny chest. *Something else* wasn't exactly good news.

"What does the Bruce want from us?" Ewan asked.

"Your hidden port. That small inlet?" Ian probed.

The hidden inlet, where a narrow strip of MacLeod land dropped in a sheer rockface that touched the water, was under-used and not well known. Ewan and Gavin shared a wide-eyed glance at Ian's knowledge of it.

"The king wants to make use of it. And ye. We can use the inlet as necessary to move weapons, men, whatever we need, right under the noses of the English. 'Twill be a sight quicker than moving those supplies overland as well. The Bruce does no' want to risk encountering the English, risk them acquiring our own weapons to use against us. The English think us foolish, lacking strategy. Using boats, keeping close to the coast, hiding the port, these things the English will no' expect."

Gavin remained still as he studied his laird. That shoreline was such a small strip of land for the MacLeods, they rarely broached it, which was why the English had tried to use it against the MacLeods the year before. But the MacLeods had slayed those foul brigands, so word of that narrow patch of beach may not have returned to the English. 'Twasn't a sound place for a formal port, as the sheer rock wall made maneuvering the landscape to reach the shoreline difficult.

All of which made the Bruce's plan a brilliant one. Gavin's cheek pulled a grin across his lips at the part Ewan and the remaining men at Lochnora would play in the Bruce's quest for a free Scotland. The subversiveness of the plan touched on Gavin's sly nature.

Laird Ewan, Gavin knew, would jump at this chance. Pride in using his very land to aid the Bruce. By God, what man wouldn't relish that idea?

Ewan's brows lowered, and the lines around his eyes smoothed. Gavin was right — the laird did love the idea.

"The Bruce is certain, he'd rather have us use our port than use my sword?"

Ian nodded. "The MacKenzies will help coordinate the supply runs, and the MacDonalds from the isles are bringing boats, running the coastline. Ye will have to ensure the two meet at the proper times, store supplies as necessary, and keep the inlet hidden. If any English come sniffing around like mangy dogs . . ."

He didn't have to finish his statement. Ewan and Gavin dipped their heads in unison, accepting the king's decree.

And the tightness plaguing Gavin's chest eased. Staying here with Jenny? Watching the birth of his first babe?

Few men had such an opportunity, especially in these uncertain times, and Gavin was not about to take it for granted. They escorted the man to the kitchens for food while Ewan called for his brothers to find a sleeping pallet for Ian. He would leave on the morn to return to the Bruce with Ewan's acceptance of the king's command.

Gavin, having received a sharp slap of rejoice on his back from Ewan, raced up the stairs to Jenny who rested in their chambers. She would be ecstatic at the news.

Too often, men search for what they want in the wrong places. Gavin had committed that same mistake when he first fell for Ellen many years ago. It seemed like a lifetime ago. Yet, that misguided journey put Gavin on the path that led to the very place his heart desired. A place that rivaled the treasures of heaven.

His home, a family, a friend like Ewan who put his people first in all ways. His wife and soon-to-be bairn.

Gavin took the steps two at a time. He was a fortunate man indeed.

The End

If you love this book, be sure to leave a review! Reviews are life blood for authors, and I appreciate every review I receive!

Want more from Michelle? Click below to receive Gavin, the free Glen Highland Romance short ebook, free books, updates, and more in your inbox

Get your free copy by signing up here!

An Excerpt From The Blackguard of the Glen

JAMES DUCKED BEHIND the brush hidden in the trees to the east of Douglas stronghold in Selkirk Wood. Douglas Castle. *His castle,* the one robbed from him by the vile King Edward Longshanks and granted to the loathsome Baron Robert Clifford, who rose to power by slaughtering fine Scots warriors, including the beloved Guardian of Scotland William Wallace. James's heart burned black at the mere thought of this man, nay, not a man, this devil that drew Scotland through hell.

Everything inside James was empty, carved out and burned to black ash by the English who had stolen everything from him — his mother and father, his lands, his castles. Even his very youth wasn't spent in his family lands, as his father sent him to France when their castle and the surrounding lands were seized. Hiding him from the King of England. *Hiding him!* The towering, powerful James Douglas?

Robert the Bruce, who had taken up the banner for Scotland after the death of Wallace, would assuredly welcome James with open arms. James hadn't been there at the failure of Methven, but he'd heard about it, and vowed to have his moment where he might swear his alliance, his sword, and his friendship to the bumbling lord-turned-King. When Robert escaped, with the Douglas clan's help, James realized 'twas time leave his refuge and come home.

The first thing James had tried when he'd arrived in England was to petition for the return of his ancestral lands. He'd begun by requesting a meeting with King Edward Longshanks of England to see about taking his clan lands back. Lord Robert Clifford had been installed at Castle Douglas after the English had razed the Douglas lands. Since James had been absent for all of that, the king might not think him to have allegiance to the Scots. Clinging to that one, unlikely hope, James had traveled to England with his companions.

And Longshanks, hearing the mere mention of his name, rejected him, kicked him and his men out of the castle and out of England.

And the rock-hard, burning ball of fury in his gut only increased.

James would have his lands back.

Once he'd returned to Scotland, 'twas easy to hear of the Bruce's acceptance by the clans, and how he was building his army.

James informed his men they, too, would be joining the Bruce. But they had something that needed to be done, first.

Douglasdale, Scotland March 1307

Only a handful of men were brave enough to join James on this senseless scheme. But if he played his strategy right, he would only need a handful.

James studied the stout tower, drop and gray against the cloudy sky. The seat of his clan, his birthright as dark and subdued as he felt. As dark as his life had been for the past several years.

He wasn't focused on the stones of the tower that called him home like a siren called sailors to their doom. Instead, his gray eyes, harder than the stone of the tower and as gray as the skies that hid the bright sun from those undeserving, studied the men, those pathetic English soldiers who couldn't fight their way out of a burlap sack. Lazy, skinny, encased in overly large metal plates that prevented them from running or fighting like true warriors.

Hell, half couldn't even raise a sword over their heads if needed.

Fools.

Two men, James couldn't bring himself to call the soldiers, stepped inside the gate, leaving it open, exposed.

Were these English so assured of their presence, of their prowess, that they just left the open gate defenseless?

Of course they were. James had watched them do it time and again over the past several days. The English were nothing if not predictable.

Two of James's own men joined him at the edge of the brush line of Selkirk forest, just east of Douglasdale — his old friend and tenant farmer, Thomas Dickson, with hair as black as his own, and his loyal confidant and paladin from France, the dark-skinned Moor, Shabib.

"What are ye thinking, James?" Thomas asked in a whisper as he crouched behind a bush. The man was devoutly loyal, having joined with James Douglas shortly after he watched helplessly as the English burned his crops, barn, and home to the ground. He'd taken his wife and son live with her kin, and sought out the Douglas.

Shabib squatted on James's other side, his rich blue robes pooling on the ground as he peered through the bushes.

"You have mentioned that your people have a holiday soon. Is there a dictum that prevents you from military action on that date? If these English celebrate it, then their guard might be even more lax."

James nodded. "Aye. The Lenten season ends with Easter and 'tis Palm Sunday in two days. Clifford is gone from the tower already for the season. and only a shell guard remains. Shabib's idea has merit. They will no' expect an attack on one of the Lord's most holy days."

"James," Thomas's low voice dropped lower. "Ye canna do such a thing on the Lord's day. 'Tis sin upon sin. Some things must remain sacred even in times of war."

James's gray eyes hardened to slate, cutting Ian in a murderous glare.

"Thomas, I love ye like a brother, but ye must understand. These English have stolen and desecrated my birthright, slaughtered my kin and clan, your kin and clan, and are using it as an English stronghold against the Scots. And when I forfeited my pride, shamed myself to crawl like a lowly dog and beg the English king to return my lands, he had me removed from his grounds and threatened my life if I ever dared return. I tell ye, Thoma, if I canna be personally responsible for Edward Longshanks's death, then by God himself, I will slaughter every last English soldier I can get my hands on. Including those whose horrendous English asses sit in my keep!"

Shamed, Thomas bowed his head. As a tenant farmer with distant kin, he'd never had a strong connection to the seat of the Douglas lands. He couldn't judge James for the actions he was compelled to take, but that didn't make an invasion on the day the Lord entered Jerusalem any more palatable. 'Twas an abuse of a sacrament, in Thomas's lowly opinion.

"Aye, James," he whispered.

"Your friend has a solid argument, James. Naught good is to be had when one offends his God."

James swiveled on his toes to face Shabib. Beads of dew had formed on his tightly curled hair and the shoulders of his robe, creating a shimmering hood on the man.

221

"These words may be sharp on your ears, Shabib, and I mean no offense to your relationship to your God, but my God, he has abandoned the Douglases, and probably all of Scotland. There's no one left to offend."

Shabib's face never shifted, not even a twitch of his cheek — 'twas one of the reasons James found the man so agreeable. He wore no emotion, keeping those useless feelings in check. Feelings, emotions, those were as useless as a one-winged bee, and Shabib never bothered James with such petty inconveniences.

Thomas, on the other hand . . .

"If you believe that, James, then we must accept it. Even Allah permits fighting during sacred months in response to acts of aggression. And what these English have done, aggression is too ligth a word. So if you have no qualms about an invasion, then nor do I."

"Shabib," Thomas pleaded, "I would hope ye might talk some sense into this man. His compulsion knows no bounds."

"We all have a calling, Thomas. If this is James's, then I will assist him as he needs." Shabib shifted his doleful brown eyes to James. "That does not mean I will not pray for your soul, James. Allah knows, someone must."

Coming in Spring 2021!

A Note on History —

For this story, we return to book 1 — *To Dance in the Glen* — which was a wonderful trip down memory lane, both in the reading and the writing. So many had asked for Gavin's story, but I didn't have it yet. Some ideas started to from when I wrote the ebook, *The Heartbreak of the Glen,* which you can get if you sign up for my newsletter above. It gave Gavin a backstory, and someone to serve as his antagonist.

And I love my female villains.

As usual, though I try to retain historical elements as much as possible, such as Robert the Bruce's army advancing and the clansmen flocking to his banner when they could. Though this is set in the middle ages, there is still brief mention of kilts (to help setting and just because I love the idea of all Highlanders in kilts!). This book does have less reference to military movements as compared to my previous books, given the story line. However, I might have changed or modified historical elements to fit the tone and mood of the story. It is still fiction at the end of the day!

I do hope the history seems as real for you as it does for me, regardless of any of that. And if there are any mistakes in the history, or from the first book to this one, those are completely mine — reconstructed for creative licensing, of course!

Then look for *The Blackguard of the Glen,* book 8, coming soon!

A Thank You–

Once again, Thank you to all my readers who keep coming back, digging into my stories, and asking for more!

I would like to thank those who helped this book come to life – the great people at Period Images for the cover art; to my editors/beta reader Sarah and Kaya; and to all my ARC readers who are kind enough to leave reviews – some of which are so amazing I could just cry!

I also want to thank the great community of writers I have found on social media who provide unending encouragement when it is needed most.

And a final thanks to my family – my kids and hubby – who are ever so forgiving to mommy when she has writing on deck and needs to lock herself away!

About the Author

Michelle Deerwester-Dalrymple is a professor of writing and an author. She started reading when she was three years old, writing when she was four and published her first poem at age sixteen. She has written articles and essays on a variety of topics, including several texts on writing for middle and high school students. She is also working on a novel inspired by actual events. She lives in California with her family of seven.

You can visit her web page, sign up for her newsletter, and follow all her socials at:

https://linktr.ee/mddalrympleauthor

Also by the Author:

Glen Highland Romance

The Courtship of the Glen –Prequel Short Novella
To Dance in the Glen – Book 1
The Lady of the Glen – Book 2
The Exile of the Glen – Book 3
The Jewel of the Glen – Book 4
The Seduction of the Glen – Book 5
The Warrior of the Glen – Book 6
An Echo in the Glen – Book 7
The Blackguard of the Glen – Book 8 coming soon!

The Celtic Highland Maidens

The Maiden of the Storm
The Maiden of the Grove
The Maiden of the Celts – coming soon

Historical Fevered Series – short and steamy romance!

The Highlander's Scarred Heart
The Highlander's Legacy
The Highlander's Return
Her Knight's Second Chance
Her Knight's Christmas Gift
The Highlander's Vow
Her Outlaw Highlander

As M. D. Dalrymple: Men in Uniform Series

An Echo in the Glen

Night Shift – Book 1
Day Shift – Book 2
Overtime – Book 3
Holiday Pay – Book 4
School Resource Officer -- Book 5
Holdover – Book 6 coming soon

Look for the Campus Heat series by M.D Dalrymple, coming in
_2021_

Made in the USA
Monee, IL
14 September 2021